Chaotic Books

©Trevor Womack 2021, 2024 - all rights reserved

GB 8

ISBN: 9798478292294

This book is sold subject to the condition that it will not be printed, lent, hired out, copied to third parties, sold, circulated or distributed without the publisher's prior permission.

Gang Boss is a work of fiction. Any resemblance to any person or persons living or dead or to any event or to any organisation of whatever constitution or legal standing is entirely coincidental and unintentional.

Consulting Editor - Patricia Womack

1

Something was missing. Something important. Hard to put his finger on precisely what when most of everything else was missing, too. It was almost as if he saw the gaps in his memory. The shapes they had. And he sensed the firm edges of feelings he could no longer identify. No focus. Weird. Like waking from a powerful dream that, try as he might, he could not recall.

Little pieces drifted back. He remembered that he used to use the old Georgian-style pub near the station. The strange shade of off-white covering the brickwork and the starkness of the lettering spelling out the name. Railway Hotel. He was sure he'd eaten a meal there on more than one occasion.

And he knew he'd been involved in some kind of traffic accident. They'd said so at the hospital.

And he knew that Detective Inspector, Slaughter, had come nosing around, asking questions about how he'd managed to drive his ancient hatchback into an innocent farm tractor leaving a field. The man had been fishing, that was all. Looking for reasons to blame him for the pileup. A waste of time. As he'd told Slaughter, he remembered nothing about it.

Would he have been able to find his house again if they hadn't brought him home in the ambulance? It was hard to tell. They must have traced his address from the contents of his wallet. In any case, his key fitted the front door lock, and the place seemed familiar enough.

Things around the house were where one might have expected them to be, but there was still an overarching sense of a vital something not being in place. When the feeling evolved slightly and became a little more precise, he could see that it was a someone rather than scribbled on the back. At first glance, the notes would not have meant much to anyone, but he knew now that he'd hidden his passwords amongst them. One for his laptop and a longer one for his password manager.

Thank Christ for the password manager.

His phone was missing, though, and that was a significant disadvantage. That guy Slaughter, the cop, had told him they'd searched all around the crash site and failed to find it. And if his guys hadn't found it, he took care to assure him, watching his expression closely, then it wasn't there.

"Why?" he had asked. "Why were you out and about without your phone? Nobody goes out without their phone."

He had shrugged and said, "Well, it could be I forgot it. Left it behind. Don't people do that sometimes?"

"So, is it here then? In your house? I could help you search for it if you aren't sure."

Persistent bastard, he'd thought. Why is he so on my case?

"It isn't here. I've looked all over. No sign of it. Maybe I left it somewhere else."

Slaughter had sucked his teeth at that and given him a peculiar, sideways sort of look.

It was getting on, and the late summer sun was lengthening the shadows around the garden. The soft rain had stopped an hour ago, and it was beginning to make a fine evening. He went out through the patio doors and stood on the paving, drinking in the air.

"Hello there. You okay?"

It was that old guy next door again, Tooth, peering over the fence. Did he live out here or what?

"Remembering much?"

"Enough," he grunted. "Bits and pieces. You?"

"Too much, thanks. Nice evening."

Tooth had been hanging around out the back when

he'd got home from the hospital two days ago, and Jack had had to ask his name. He'd known that he knew the guy, though. That was something.

The nurse who had seen him safely into the ambulance had said it would be good for him to try to interact socially. It could help speed up his recovery.

That advice had gone against the grain somehow. A tendency to interact socially didn't seem to be in his nature. But no harm in giving it a shot. The weather, then.

"Almost like being back in Lanzarote," he found himself saying.

Lanzarote?

Tooth went off to water his greenhouse tomato plants and left him to stand in silence for a few minutes more, watching the shadows beneath the tall hawthorns by the lawn turn to velvet. It was enough. He'd been outside. He'd conversed with a fellow human.

He went back inside, into the lounge. The blinds were drawn, and it was dark now. As he reached out to flick the light switch, he heard the creak of a floorboard behind him. He'd been half-expecting something like this. God knew why. He didn't.

He raised his elbow and got ready to pivot so that he could drive it into the throat of whoever was closing on him. Too late. There was an arm around his neck already, pulling him sharply backwards and causing him to choke as he struggled to keep his footing. Suddenly, his attacker released him and pushed hard at his back, sending him crashing into the wall. It was too much. The impact knocked the breath out of him, and he saw stars as his face made contact with the plasterwork.

Another sodding head injury.

He hit the floor in a sudden heap and gasped as his

assailant's heavily-shod foot drove into his abdomen.

"Enough," he croaked. "You win."

He was gasping for breath. "Just tell me what the fuck it is you want."

"Get up!"

He staggered to his feet, coughing.

"You can sit."

He collapsed into an armchair and tried to focus on the figure, sitting now, on the sofa across from him. It was too dark to see clearly, but his assailant was a big man and well-built. From the look of him, there was no way he would have felt the need of any help in dealing with the likes of Jack Charnley. Most likely, he'd come alone.

"Please forgive intrusion, but kitchen door is unlocked. Should take more care."

Foreign accent. Eastern European, for sure. Russian?

"And that would have kept you out?"

"Couple of minutes. Tops."

The Russian, for lack of any evidence either way he had settled on his intruder being a Russian, seemed to be relaxed. This wasn't some sneak thief taking a chance. There must be more to it.

"So, what is it you want?"

"Can't guess?"

"I doubt it."

The intruder sighed and shook his head.

"Is not good to make this harder. Very hard for you already, Jack Charnley. Craig send me. Clear now?"

"Craig?"

The man shook his head again and got to his feet. In three strides, he was standing next to him and pushing him back down as he struggled to rise. He grabbed Jack's windpipe and squeezed. Jack clutched at his assailant's arm and tried to free himself, but he was totally outmatched. He knew his situation was hopeless. The Russian was younger, and he was fitter, bigger and stronger than Jack had ever been. And just now, he was far from being at his best.

"Listen to me, Jack Charnley. I warn you. Watch your step. Your partner also."

He released his hold on his windpipe and left him gasping again for breath.

"I go easy because you are not well. When I find your partner, I explain him also. Harder for him. He hides now, but I find him. Soon."

Craig? Partner? What the? He's leaving. Thank Christ!

He heard the kitchen door slam shut as he groped his way across to the sideboard, sucking in desperate lungfuls of air as he went. His legs struggled to support him, and his hands shook as he uncorked the whisky and poured himself a big one.

So, he thought, downing a couple of gulps and coughing, this stuff has its uses.

The following morning, he was up early. The face staring back at him from the bathroom mirror displayed the promise of a sizeable bruise gathering on the forehead and a cluster of smaller ones on the front of the neck. Perhaps taking his time to relax and rest wasn't going to be an option after all. It was clear that he had enemies who were targeting him. And somewhere out there, he must have a life. He should take steps to regain it.

He found his paperwork in a box on the old desk he kept in the corner of his bedroom. He took it downstairs and put it on the kitchen table next to the pile of unopened mail. Over a plateful of scrambled eggs with toast and coffee, he sorted through it all and read anything that might give him some kind of clue about how his life had worked.

Money didn't seem to be a problem. There were

sizeable amounts arriving regularly into his current account from some unidentifiable source. His debts had all been paid off months ago, just after the payments into his bank had begun. The newish-looking gunmetal Qashqai standing out on the drive was his, according to the paperwork. He hunted around and discovered the keys sitting in a tin on the kitchen shelf. The Qashqai started up first time when he tried it. Not bad, considering it must have been waiting out there for weeks.

He used the password manager to get into some of his accounts and found a few more clues online. He'd taken flights out to the Canary Islands in the months leading up to the accident. Fuerteventura and Lanzarote. And there were items on his card account covering payments for purchases in bars and cafes in Amsterdam, Paris, Naples, and Madrid.

It was strange. This international lifestyle wasn't what he had been expecting to find. Stoical endurance, wasn't that more his kind of thing? A middle-aged drinker with an image problem?

He checked through his emails. Mostly junk. Nothing suggesting much in the way of a social life, but twenty minutes got him a list of individuals who appeared to have loomed large on his horizon. Hamish, Freddy and Stella seemed to be the main ones. Other words claimed a place on his list: Warehouse, Project, Villa, Rosario. It was enough for now.

Maybe he should email some of the contacts and see where it led? But then he remembered the Russian and decided to play safe. Give it space.

Most of the interesting emails had stopped coming in around the time of his accident. There had been one, though, from the person listed as Stella, suggesting he should come to stay with her at the place given as the Warehouse as soon as he was ready to leave hospital.

He remembered Stella now. She had come to sit by his bed as he had lain there, covered in bandages and surgical dressings. He had seen her through a haze of pain-relieving drugs. She had talked to him, sometimes at length, but he had understood nothing of what she said. And then, suddenly, the visits had ceased.

Looking again through the contents of his wallet, he found a dog-eared business card he had overlooked. The card had his name on it and claimed he was a private investigator. And he had a webpage that told him, when he searched it out, that he was available for hire at reasonable rates to investigate a long list of potentially tricky situations.

He wandered into the lounge and sat down in an armchair to think, his brow furrowed. He needed to concentrate. He fell asleep.

When he woke a couple of hours later, he realised that reconstructing his life from the scraps of information he had to hand might take a while. There was a lot to assimilate.

He remembered the scrambled eggs he'd eaten for breakfast and felt hungry again, so he ambled back to the kitchen to see what supplies were left in Tooth's welcome-home bag of groceries. He was sure he'd seen a tin of mackerel in there yesterday. And there was bread in the freezer.

Just as he found the mackerel, he looked up to find Tooth grinning at him through the window. The man was holding up two kittens for him to see. Fearing the worst, he opened the door, allowing Tooth to march in.

He's going to leave me looking after two baby cats? Is he nuts?

"Kittens, Alan? For me? I mean, really?"

"We've discussed it, me and the wife, and we think they'll be good for you. Company. Something to be responsible for and take care of. They can be very affectionate, and they'll give you focus.

"Is that a new bruise on your forehead?"

"It's nothing. I walked into the bedroom door in the dark. Clumsy."

Tooth didn't come right out and ask if he'd been drinking again. Their relationship wasn't as close as all that, but his look was enough.

What he said instead was, "You'll need to be careful with these two around."

"Well, you know, Alan, I'm not really sure..."

Tooth put the kittens down on the kitchen table and grunted.

"Madge and Nancy. After the wife's sisters. Both dead now. I think the one with the blob of orange on her forehead is Madge."

He took a large plastic bag from under his arm and placed it next to the kittens. Then he left. Jack looked down at his new house guests, now parading about on the tabletop.

He opened one of the cans and put a saucer of cat meat on the floor. Then he added a breakfast bowl of water. Picking up the kittens, which were mewing loudly, he took them through to the lounge and placed them on the sofa.

"Just play there nicely. You know where your stuff is. I'm busy."

He went back to the kitchen and looked inside the bag Tooth had left, hoping for more food. Instead, he found cat litter and a tray. He sighed and checked his laptop for emails. There was a new one.

```
Railway Lunchtime Hamie
```

2

"Been in a fight?" asked the guy behind the bar. From his tone and from the way he was getting preferential service through the busy lunchtime scrum, he guessed that the barman knew him pretty well.

The barman was wearing a label that told anyone interested enough to look that his name was Phil.

"It's nothing. Walked into the bedroom door in the dark."

"That'd be the whisky, I imagine. Usual?"

"I was thinking I might try the pie and chips. Is it good?"

"It's all fairly average. And I've never known you have anything other than steak and chips in all the years you've been coming here."

"Not pie?"

"Never."

"I'll try the pie then, Phil. If that's okay."

"Your funeral."

"And a pint of whatever I usually have."

He paid with the card he'd found in his wallet and got himself a table in a quiet corner. From the overhead speaker came the soothing sound of John Denver, who was leaving once more - on a jet plane. It was only lunchtime, but the subdued lighting was making him sleepy. It was an effort to stay awake.

He was on the point of dropping off when someone arrived with his meal and his drink.

"Thanks."

He didn't look up.

"You're welcome," said the someone as he took the seat across from Jack.

"You're staying to watch me eat?"

"I'm here to talk. You do know me, Jack. Don't you?"

He picked up his fork and studied the face across from him. Young, long hair, beard, heavy tan, nice suit. He did know him. He could feel it. This one wasn't a threat.

"Remind me."

"Stella told me your memory was shot. No worries, we'll get there. I'm Hamish. Your partner? I sent you an email."

"You work here?"

"No, I don't fucking work here. I'm in here to speak to you. I took the chance you'd at least remember where we got lunch."

"I think I do know you. It's kind of vague. Fuzzy."

He sipped from his glass and studied the features of the young man sitting opposite.

"I had an accident. Car crash."

"I'm well aware of that, buddy. I was there. I was luckier than you. Saved by my seat belt and a few airbags. Got away with a couple of cracked ribs and a lot of bruises. Even better, I'd gone before anyone could place me at the scene."

"Oh."

"All better now, more or less. But you look as though you've had another one since."

"A visitor. Last night."

"Pity. I was hoping I could get to you first, but I couldn't risk going to the house. I don't suppose you recognised him? This visitor? What did he want?"

"It didn't feel like I'd ever seen the bastard before. A bit older than you, I think. Big guy. Could be Russian or similar. He came to warn me and my partner, your good self presumably, to stop doing whatever it was we were doing that was annoying someone called Craig.

"It was you sent the email?"

"It was. I just told you that."

"So, you can tell me what's going on?"

"Happy to. You eat. I'll talk."

As he worked his way steadily through his meal, he listened to Hamish telling him all about how his life had been. Part of it, anyway. Hamish's take on it.

Speaking in a cautious undertone, he explained that they had a joint interest in an antique furniture salesroom in Liverpool's Baltic Quarter, where the stock they imported provided a front for their highly lucrative drug smuggling operation.

"We refer to all this as the 'Project'. Okay?"

The Project, he continued, was distinct from the interest they had in the money-laundering enterprise, which they ran in association with the remnants of a Liverpool family called Davidson. Junior Davidson, who had a limo hire business in the Baltic and his grandfather, Freddy, who lived on the slopes of an extinct volcano on Fuerteventura.

He listened and ate and sensed things beginning to fall into place as Hamish filled in the details. Everything Hamish was telling him, incredible as it seemed at first, felt right.

"Is this all making sense to you?"

"I think so," he said, pushing away his plate and reaching for his pint. "So far, maybe."

"That's good. And it's a relief. Because I need you to get back on the job just as soon as you can."

"Doing what, exactly?"

"Nothing onerous. We've already done all the heavy lifting. For now, at least. We have a couple of guys running things down there at Baltic Antiques, Fat George and the youngster, Leggy. And there's a guy we have on call, name of John. Known as John D on account of there being so many Johns around. You'll know him."

"So, my role?"

"At the moment, it's just to keep tabs on everything. You're strictly hands-off and out of sight. Mostly, anyhow. Watch out for any difficulties. Fix them before they become problems. Give the others their instructions. That sort of thing.

"The stuff comes in hidden inside the furniture. George and Leggy take it out and cut and package it down in the basement. Day to day, they look after sales and deliveries. They're very busy guys and valuable, so we pay them well. You help George do the books and make sure he isn't screwing us. John D is different. He's a kind of freelance consultant we have on tap. Helps us out when we need him."

Drugs. That's what you cut and package. Listen to the boy. Learn.

"Sound good?"
"Sounds risky. I need to sleep on it."
"I think I was wanting something a tad more positive from you, Jack. But whatever. You've been through a lot. I can see that."
Hamish stopped speaking for just long enough to drain his glass. Then he took a phone from his jacket pocket and held it where Jack could see it before placing it on the table.
"Here again tomorrow? We'll get you back on the steak."
Without waiting for a reply, he got to his feet and walked out of the bar. Jack sat for a while and finished his pint. He needed to get home before he fell asleep again. He made sure to take the phone with him when he left.

That night he went to bed early and slept fitfully, his dreams a wild and disjointed patchwork of plane trips, car wrecks, violence and a woman in high heels called Stella.
In the morning, he found large chunks of his memory had returned, just as the doctor had told him they might. In truth, they weren't the kind of memories he'd been expecting, and maybe not the kind he would have chosen to have. But it was too late now to make choices about his past.
Sitting at the kitchen table in the early light, he examined the phone Hamish had left him. He logged

into the password manager on his laptop and found a note of the PIN. It worked. His phone, then. Obviously.

He spent an hour looking through the contents and learned that if he did have any kind of social life, he was keeping it well hidden. The names Stella, Hamish, Freddy and Junior cropped up from time to time. Names he had found amongst his emails. Not a vast circle of friends and acquaintances. So be it. It fitted in with the way he felt.

He had a light breakfast of buttered toast and made himself an espresso to sip as he sat and watched a few more of his memories begin to click back into place.

He put out more cat meat as Madge and Nancy pretended to hunt each other on the sofa and then shook the contents of their tray into the bin in the yard.

He took a walk through the estate, where his semi blended in amongst countless look-a-likes, and on past the park with its usual quota of dog walkers. He got as far as the village centre. It was all looking reassuringly familiar as he made his way home with his groceries and a spare bag of cat litter.

He spent the rest of the morning putting everything in order around the house. Then he took a shower and found himself a clean, black polo shirt before climbing into his crumpled blue suit and heading off to the Railway.

Hamish was waiting at the bar, nursing a half of something golden.

"Table sixteen," Hamish told the bargirl. "Steak and chips twice and a pint of whatever I'm drinking. For my man here."

He left Hamish to pay and went to find number sixteen.

As soon as Hamish sat down, he got straight into explaining how things needed to change over at the Project.

"Having you out of action these past few weeks has put me back in touch with exactly what's going on down there. And you know what? We need to rethink our operation. Reconfigure it."

"Like how?"

"Like close down the furniture importing side, or most of it. It's far too cumbersome and labour intensive."

"And replace it with what?"

"Something much more elegant and easier to operate. Artwork. I've been talking to Freddy about it. Remember Freddy? Our money guy? He's an artist. He paints. I got the idea from him."

"Freddy... yes. I think I remember being at his place. A garden full of rocks and walls full of paintings."

"That's him. Freddy Davidson. Painter and money launderer. You need to go over there and talk to him about the artwork thing. Get interested in what he can tell you about paintings, about shipping and packaging canvases. All that. He's sold a piece or two in his time, so he's familiar with all that crap."

"And our supplies? So we're aiming to bring them in with the artwork in future?"

"No. We're not. We're going to rest all that side of the business for now. We'll use a local importer instead and buy direct from him. We're going to use our facility at the Project to cut it and package it and ship it out in wholesale lots."

"Disguised as artwork?"

"Correct. We mostly dump the antiques and turn our salesroom into an art gallery. Product comes in from our importer, looking like crates of paintings. It goes down to the basement and gets split up, weighed out and packaged. Cooked or cut as necessary."

"And goes out crated up likewise."

"Exactly. There's enough interest in art these days to provide a credible cover. Some of our deliveries will be legitimate artwork going to genuine art lovers. The rest will be hiding our stuff. It'll look good."

"And if we're not importing our own supply, then what?"

"John D's put me onto a source with a yard down by

the docks. Crazy Horse, would you believe? Shortened to Horse, if you want to stay on his right side and keep all your teeth. Real name's Morris Wiseman."

"Sounds nice."

"He's not as bad as his rep. And as long as we treat him well and pay him on time, he shouldn't be a problem."

Jack sighed.

"So my private investigator thing? And the semi I'm living in, all that's just a front?"

"It's a great cover. It works well for us, and it's authentic. It's your recent past. Anyway, I've discussed all this with Dad, and he thinks we could be on the right track."

"Your dad? Is he in on this? Have I met him?"

Hamish looked around, making sure there was no one within earshot.

"Try to remember. My dad's dead, right? My uncle, Gus, murdered him. Set him up to fall into the cellar at the nightclub that night."

More pieces falling into place.

"I think I do recall that. Gus is dead too. Gassed himself in Stella's apartment. Right?"

"You're getting there, buddy. I knew you would. And we have work to do."

This has come up before. He imagines talking with his dad's ghost. Tried to kill Gus with a grenade. Hamish is dangerous as fuck. But then...

"And me. I killed someone, didn't I? Lawrence White."

Jack was nervous now. He, too, was looking around, checking for eavesdroppers. But there was no one close enough in the bar to hear a thing above the lunchtime conversations and the clatter of cutlery.

"You did, buddy. But you needn't sweat it. It was in a good cause. The best possible. You were saving me. Remember that."

"I shot him."

"You had no other option. It was him or me."

Jack was silent for long moments, assimilating this newly remembered past. It was coming into view thick and fast now. And none of it was what he'd expected.

"I'd like you back at the Warehouse keeping an eye on things asap, since you're getting better. You'll be safer there anyhow. Stella's got her minders guarding the place."

"And the kittens? I have two kittens."

"Kittens? Jesus. Since when were you a cat lover? We're big-time now. Dump 'em with that old couple next door. Or move the little buggers down to the Project to keep the wildlife under control.

"But, for now, you need to get yourself over to the Canaries. You like it there. Talk to Freddy about the art thing. And you can recuperate at the villa in Honda for a couple of days before you fly home. Okay?"

"Maybe. It might be okay. I'll think about it."

Back at the semi, he let himself in at the front porch and went through to the kitchen in search of his new house guests. He found the cat food and the water, but no Madge and no Nancy. Then he noticed the door was open, the lock forced.

The Ruskie. That Russian bastard again. Probably a Vladimir or Leonid or some such. What the fuck is going on here?

He armed himself with a hammer from the toolbox full of bits and pieces he kept, covered in cobwebs, under the sink and made a cautious tour of the premises.

He found nothing.

No Vlad. He'd settled for 'Vlad'.

No kittens.

No clues.

Apart from the forced lock, nothing seemed to have

been disturbed.

He checked outside in the garden. But there was no sign of the missing Madge and Nancy.

How do I explain this to Tooth?

The lock was shot, but the bolt was still intact, so he bolted the door and wedged a chair under the handle. He piled glassware and crockery onto the seat to act as a makeshift burglar alarm. It wasn't much, but it should help. Just about. He phoned a locksmith and arranged to have a new lock fitted later that day. Then, keeping the hammer close by, he booked a flight from John Lennon to Lanzarote and packed a bag for a few days in the sun. He could do with the break, and he would be safer out there than holed up at home, waiting for Vlad to return. Anyway, Hamish seemed to think talking to Freddy was important.

He spent the evening reviewing his now rapidly emerging memories and getting his life back into some sort of perspective. Here on the Point, living out the pretence of his semi-detached, suburban lifestyle, he was under threat from at least one dangerous Russian gangster. And that for reasons he did not understand. Meantime, down in Liverpool, in the Baltic, he was involved in money laundering and wholesaling illegal drugs. Also dangerous. But in the Canaries, he would have the use of a pleasant villa on Lanzarote and the opportunity to chat politely with Freddy Davidson on nearby Fuerteventura about marketing and shipping artworks.

He took the hammer to bed with him that night and wedged the bedroom door with a chair he'd carried up from the kitchen.

Late the following morning, he went to put his bag in the Qashqai and found a small package waiting for him outside his front porch. As far as he knew, he had nothing on order, and the delivery, in any case, was unaddressed. There wasn't much time to spare before he needed to drive down to John Lennon for his flight, but he carried the package, little bigger than a shoebox, through to the kitchen and placed it on the table. It was covered in thick brown paper and well secured with string, but it took only a few seconds to open it up using the bread knife.

It was little Madge, mercifully dead, wrapped tightly in a strand of barbed wire. Had he still been capable of such a thing, he would have cried.

3

Walking out of the airport on Lanzarote gave him the sudden boost of light and colour it always did. If it had been possible to live for light and colour alone, he might have moved out here for good and had done with it. But it wasn't like that. Some sense of purpose and achievement was needed too.

On the taxi ride out to Honda and Hamish's villa, he opened the ebook he'd downloaded. The book that promised to teach him all he could want to know about art. He'd attempted to get into the thing on the plane but had failed to engage with the subject matter and fallen asleep instead.

Between periods of staring through the taxi window at the sun-drenched rockscapes and clumps of cacti hurtling by, he tried again to tune in to the world of art. Could it be he was approaching this in the wrong way? 'Art' was a pretty big topic, and who could hope to know everything? Maybe he should specialise a little.

So, the simplest way into all this crap?

Abstracts. Obviously. After all, any idiot could splatter paint onto a canvas and call it a painting, right? He skipped through the book to the chapter on abstract painters and browsed through it until he found a section dealing with someone called Jackson Pollock. The guy had been a big name in the world of paint-splattering back in the day. It seemed as good a place as any to start.

At the villa, he let himself in through the large wooden gate in the perimeter wall, using the pin Hamish had sent him. Once through the garden, he used the key he had been given to get into the building itself. It was a while since his last visit, and it felt good to be back. All it would take to cut himself off entirely from the rest of the world would be to turn off his phone. It was a comforting thought.

He unpacked in the guest room and then went outside again with a freshly made espresso to sit under the shade of the awning covering the patio area and swot up some more on Jackson.

Art, he would readily admit, had never been his thing. No worries - Freddy would tell him everything he needed to know.

He phoned Davidson.

"Jack? Hamish said you'd be in touch. You all better? After your accident?"

"Fully recovered, thanks. I'm here in Honda. You're going to turn me into an art expert."

"I can try."

"Tomorrow okay? Your place?"

"Come for lunch. You're at the villa?"

"Where else?"

"Text me when you get to the ferry terminal in Playa Blanca. I'll send the car to collect you from Corralejo. That's where you'll be getting off, in case you've forgotten. I know about your memory issues."

That evening, he walked a couple of blocks along the beachside to get a meal at an Italian restaurant he remembered. Here in Honda, he felt safe and more like his old self. He ate well and enjoyed a half-bottle of Rioja with his food.

It was a pleasant evening, and he found the stroll back so relaxing that he extended his walk for a mile or so along the oceanfront toward the lights of nearby Arrecife, listening to the sound of the ocean. Then he turned around and headed for the villa.

The following morning, he got a taxi down to the ferry port. He texted Freddy and spent the thirty-minute crossing to Corralejo standing on deck looking out for flying fish. He spotted three and felt strangely pleased with himself.

Ashore in Fuerteventura, he found Davidson's Mercedes waiting for him in the car park by the dock. He tried to engage the driver, Miguel, in conversation, but Miguel was a man of few words, and they passed the journey in silence.

Once they had left the bustle of tourist-ridden Corralejo behind, he settled into enjoying the landscape of lava fields and scrub, quiet settlements, carefully cultivated plots and the occasional tribe of foraging goats.

Sooner than he had expected, the Mercedes was climbing the narrow track up to the finca. Freddy met him at the door and showed him into the gloomy lounge he had visited twice before. Back then, they'd had reason to be wary of each other. Not now, though. Now, they were both on the same team. At least, he had to hope they were.

"Welcome once again, Jack, to my humble abode. You've done well. Ana's almost ready to serve."

"Ana?"

"Anastasia. My housekeeper. Hungry?"

"Pretty much. Lunch smells terrific, even from here."

"Just fried fish with some locally grown potatoes and beans. Nothing fancy. But Ana's an excellent cook.

"And you can relax. No guns this time." Freddy laughed.

He remembered the visit he had made here when they'd both been serving opposing interests. Back then, Freddy had made sure he'd seen that he was carrying a pistol and that whatever Jack Charnley might have wanted to believe, he, Freddy Davidson, was the one in charge.

Well, he thought, you might still be in charge of the money-laundering side of things, Freddy boy. But the drugs? He felt sure that had always been just him and Hamish.

Ana was not the same woman he had previously seen wielding a duster at the finca. She was a good deal younger and very much more attractive. And he couldn't help but notice that, unlike her predecessor, she was not wearing an apron. Instead, she wore a tight-fitting blouse and a light, knee-length skirt as she served up the food.

"You changed your housekeeper?" he asked when Ana had left the room. "This one's nothing like the woman I remember seeing here before."

"All things change, Jack. Ana's a newer model, that's all."

"Does she live in?"

"Maybe. Does it matter?"

"Not to me. Not at all. Didn't mean to pry. She has a nice line in smiles, though. That's for sure."

Over lunch, Freddy began to tell him what he felt he needed to know about the art market.

"Basically, the type of person I imagine you guys will be selling to will simply be looking for something colourful to hang on their walls, in their offices or their homes. Stuff to pretty the place up a bit. And maybe you'll get one or two customers wanting a painting with a little more depth to impress their friends and business associates."

"So we aren't talking about anything too highbrow in the main?"

"Not really. Nothing highbrow."

"So, kittens playing with balls of wool? Dogs playing poker?"

Kittens? Poor Madge. God knows what's happened to little Nancy. Vlad. Has to be.

"Probably not," said Freddy, laughing. "Maybe too lowbrow."

"So definitely not highbrow, and probably not lowbrow either. So I'm just guessing here, but middlebrow, maybe?"

Freddy chuckled, but not in a way that suggested he found Jack's remarks amusing.

"I hope you're taking this seriously. Hamish seems to think you're the one to get a grip on all this."

"I'll get a grip. Don't worry yourself. I was thinking we might be heading in the right direction with a few simple abstracts. Jackson Pollock, you know. That sort of thing."

"You're a fan of Pollock?" Freddy seemed surprised. "His drip paintings?"

"I'm a long-time admirer of the man's work. His stuff is just so accessible. You ever tried using his technique?"

Careful. Best not push it. This is Freddy's area. Let the man do his thing.

"No, I haven't. I'm not really into action paintings as such. I used to prefer my work to be more representational than anything, but just lately, I've begun to feel my way into more abstract territory."

"Of course." He took care to adopt a friendly tone. "I've looked at the stuff you have hanging around this place whenever I've had the chance. I'm familiar with your style."

"You can easily get to understand the market by looking at what's selling in the online galleries. I'll point you at a couple of decent ones to start you off. Forget all about art history and all that guff. None of your customers will give a toss. Just look at what people are buying online. It's as good a place as any to begin."

"Okay. I think I can manage to cruise a few websites."

"Then there's the thing that really interests you, of course. The crating and shipping. There's a particular way of packaging artwork. And there'll be customs forms to get right if you're shipping internationally."

"You going to show me how to do all this? I need to

be able to train the boys we have working on the project to do a professional-looking job."

"Come and take a look in my studio," said Freddy, getting up. "I can take you through it. It's laborious, but it's pretty simple. You'll be an expert by teatime."

*

Much later, back at the villa, he texted Hamish, asking for a phone number for Fran, Freddy Davidson's long-time woman in Arrecife.

The number came through almost at once. Then his phone rang. It was Hamish.

"What's up? Why Fran?"

"Oh, I'm fine, thanks. Since you didn't ask. And, yes, I've learned all we need to know to make a start on moving some artwork around."

"So, s'up?"

"I was thinking that with the Fran woman being just a stretch along the road from your lovely villa down in Arrecife, I might pay her a visit. That's all."

"And you're interested in seeing her, why? Exactly?"

"Just being sociable. And your wee doggy, Keith. He's staying there, isn't he? While you're away? I thought I could check on him for you. Take the little bugger for a walk."

"Yeah. Good idea. Anything else?"

"No."

"So enjoy your break. Glad to hear it's all going well."

That evening, he stayed in, ate one of the ready meals Hamish kept in his freezer and managed to restrict himself to a single bottle of wine. As usual, it was a warm night, and he went to bed with the windows open, falling asleep to the sound of the surf breaking against the rocks down by the walkway.

In the morning, he visited the local mini-market and stocked up on a few supplies for his stay. Then he breakfasted on scrambled eggs and smoked salmon. Around ten, feeling relaxed and at peace with the world, he phoned Fran's number.

"Señora Rimmer."

"Buenos dias, Señora. It's Jack Charnley. Remember me?"

A short pause.

"Yes..." She sounded uncertain, tentative. "You're the man who was spying on Freddy and me a few months back. I understand you work for Freddy now."

"I can imagine he might have put it that way. His sense of humour, I think."

"He doesn't really have a sense of humour. Not so's you'd notice. So what do you want, Mr Charnley?"

"Nothing, really. Just being sociable. I was over in La Oliva yesterday, seeing the man himself on business. Maybe he mentioned it to you?"

"No, he didn't."

"No matter. Thing is, I'm back on Lanzarote now, in Honda. I've a couple of days before my flight home, and I'm at a bit of a loose end. Wondered if, perhaps, we might do lunch, as they say. Walk the dog, even. No pressure if you're busy. It's just a thought."

Another pause. Longer this time.

"Well, I don't know. I'm not doing anything in particular today. So maybe there's no harm."

"Great. How about one o'clock in that tower block across from your place? Star City? Up in the Gran Hotel."

"I might think about it."

"Good idea. I'll be in there anyway, so you can join me or not as you see fit. And please forget the Mr Charnley. Just call me Jack."

He rang off.

She was, he reasoned, pretty much sure to turn up. Her curiosity would be piqued, and maybe she wouldn't have a great deal else to interest her this afternoon beyond walking Keith and sunbathing on her terrace.

Would she want to clear it with Davidson first? A lot

would depend on the nature of her relationship with Freddy and how much she valued her independence. Her freedom of action. All this he hoped to find out soon enough.

But what exactly did he expect to gain from the meeting? He wasn't a particularly social being. Far from it. What he was hoping for could only be information. It was like gold dust. Accumulate a few grains here, a few more there, and gradually, you build your little hoard into something useful.

Twelve forty-five found him at the familiar table by the window, looking down onto the rooftops of Arrecife and remembering how, not all that long ago, he had sat here and spied on Fran and Freddy through the telephoto lens on his camera. Watching as the couple sunned themselves on the roof terrace of Fran's apartment.

A lot had changed since then.

Suddenly, she was there, the waiter pulling out a chair for her and handing her a menu.

"You took a chance, Fran. I'm glad."

"I was curious. I wanted to meet my spy."

They ordered sandwiches, cakes and coffee, and before long, things were going well enough to risk sharing a carafe of the house white.

"So you've been to see Freddy on business? Anything interesting? If you don't mind my asking."

"No particular secret. It's just an art thing we may be going to start up back in Liverpool. He'll be our art expert, and I needed a few tips."

"You're an artist? I thought you were some sort of private detective."

"Not now. I'm transitioning from private dick to art dealer," he said, laughing. "Hamish and I are aiming to open a commercial gallery down in the Baltic Triangle. We already have the premises."

When lunch was over, and they found themselves once again at street level and out in the bright sunlight of the early Lanzarote afternoon, Fran suggested a stroll along the beachside.

"It's time I took Keith out, anyway. He'll be ready to go. The dog, I mean."

"Hamish's Yorkie. It'll be a pleasure to walk him with you."

"Well, be my guest."

The food and wine seemed to have removed any serious reservations she might have felt about him. "Would you like to come and get Keith with me?"

They crossed the road to Fran's building and took the lift up to the floor below her rooftop apartment. A short staircase got them to her front door. Once inside, they found Keith ready and waiting to take them straight back out again.

The French windows onto the terrace were standing open, and while Fran searched out Keith's lead, he went outside to check out the view.

Just as hot up here. Nice, though. Much better than that gloomy old finca Freddy boy hangs out in.

They walked up past the Gran Hotel and on along the broad, beachside walkway. They walked as far as the small lagoon, used as an inshore harbour for small boats and known locally as El Charco, the 'Puddle'.

Fran took the opportunity to question him about what he knew of the situation up at the finca. Her questions were pretty innocuous, but he suspected he had a good idea of what she was leading up to.

"You don't get up there much yourself, then?"

"Not really. Not these last few years. Freddy says he likes to keep the finca for work and the apartment here for R and R. Keeps the two separate. You know how some people are."

So it's 'the' apartment, not 'my' apartment. Freddy pays the rent. Or owns the place.

"So, you're retired? Over here for the duration?"

"Retired a long time ago. I used to be an actress. The odd supporting role. Theatres, films. Television mainly. I've been over here for years. Ever since I've been with Freddy, really."

He could see how she would have pleased the camera. Her well-rounded figure, even features, and clear complexion would still, he imagined, stand her in good stead if she ever chose to resume her career. Her dress sense, too, was noticeably more stylish than that of your average British expat. Freddy, he decided, was lucky to have such a charming companion to call on.

"So, these days? A lady of leisure, is that it?"

She laughed. "Not entirely. I keep my hand in by giving a class at the local drama school. I give English lessons at the same place. Keeps me as busy as I need to be."

They strolled slowly around the Puddle, enjoying the holiday atmosphere of the pavement cafes and the upbeat buzz of the tourists crowding the area.

"I know that Freddy has staff up at his place, but I do worry about him. I don't see a lot of his driver, Miguel, and he's not much of a talker in any case. But I used to chat with his housekeeper over the phone sometimes. I got to know her well enough in the old days."

"Not now, though?"

"No. There's someone else there now."

"You've not met the new girl? Ana?"

"Girl? Is she that young?"

"To me? Yes, she is."

"What's she like? I've asked, but he hasn't even let me see her photograph. Makes some excuse."

"Youngish, as I said. Blonde. Attractive. Dresses well."

He knew what he was doing. He was searching out any possible gap in Fran's relationship with Davidson. A gap that he might have a need to exploit at some point. You never could tell when that kind of thing would come in useful.

They walked on in silence for a while, Fran staring

down at the pavement as they came up onto the beachfront and headed down towards the Gran.

"You've eaten there? Is she a good cook?"

"I'd say so. I've certainly had a lot worse."

Back at the apartment, Fran served coffee out on the terrace while Keith lapped up most of the contents of his water bowl before heading back inside to doze on the couch.

They chatted at random for a while about expat life on the island before Jack, aware that he had probably already outstayed his welcome, made his excuses and left.

Once out on the avenida, he considered taking a taxi but, feeling adventurous, decided instead to walk the couple of miles or so up to Honda. He could use the exercise.

It was hotter than ever, with no shade to be had anywhere along the oceanfront. By the time he had covered half the distance, he wished he'd taken a cab. He knew he wasn't in great shape. He hadn't been in great shape even before the accident, and despite losing a few pounds during his recovery, he still managed to be overweight.

When he reached the villa, he was breathing heavily, with perspiration trickling down his face. He trudged through the garden and collapsed onto the lounger under the patio awning.

4

Two days later, he was back at the semi talking to Hamish.

"So, the kitten? Madge?"

"I buried her in the garden."

"The barbed wire?"

"I managed to get it all off her. Made a mess. I binned it."

"We're going to have to deal with this. Right?"

"I'm all ears. You have a plan? You weren't even keen on risking coming round here last time we spoke. And we've no idea where to find this Russian thug. He finds me."

"Maybe we can't get to the Russian," said Hamish, "but we know it was our sleeping partner, Craig, who set him on."

"But why?"

"Could it be because it was his business we burned to the ground and his family we helped put behind bars?"

"But he doesn't know all that was down to us. We give him a decent cut of our profits, and he's never cut up rough before. Why believe Vlad? Why would Craig be on our case?"

"Who knows how the idiot's angry little mind works? It could have something to do with the fact that I reduced his share of the take to ten per cent. I must say he did seem unpleased with the idea. Understandable, I suppose."

"And why the fuck did you do that?" asked Jack. "And why not discuss it with me first? I'm in the buggering front line here."

"You've been out of it, remember? Practically comatose? Things don't just stand still. Craig was getting pushy, and I had to deal with it. And I'm sure that Dad would have approved."

"Your dad's been dead for the best part of a year. And as I said, I'm the one on the front line here. No one ever knows where you are from one minute to the next. And you know what Craig's like. What kind of reaction did you expect?"

"Possibly some sort of negotiation. I didn't expect you to be attacked. Why would I?"

"Seems to me that if you go out of your way to wind up some angry gangster, he's going to react, isn't he?"

There was no response. Hamish simply waited for him to continue.

"Okay. So forget that for now. What's the plan? You have a plan for dealing with this, right?"

"The first thing is to move you away from here. I'd feel better if you were at the nightclub with Stella, keeping an eye on things. And it's easier for you to keep tabs on the Project from there. It's easy walking distance. And I need you to get on with setting up the art gallery and teaching our guys what you've found out about handling artwork.

"That all went well, right? Your session with our tame art guru?"

"Well enough. I think I can manage to teach the boys how to crate up a few paintings without too much trouble."

*

"Nice to see you again, Jack," said Stella, giving him a hug at the Blue Warehouse's side door. "Come on up. Hamish told me you'd be moving in today."

"You don't mind?"

"Of course I don't. I'm glad to have you."

He followed her through the bar and up the staircase at the back of the nightclub to the top-floor apartment.

"You can have Gus's old room. All his stuff's gone, and I've had it refurbished as a guest room."

It felt awkward. A lot had changed since that evening

they had spent an hour in bed together, back when husband Gus had been alive.

Had Stella become a little more distant? Was it the effect of losing Claude and then Gus in the space of a few months, of being widowed twice in quick succession? Or maybe it was to do with his own accident and his coma? That seemed more likely. Hamish would have told her all about his memory loss, and it was only natural that she would be wondering just how much he could recall about their once-developing relationship, now apparently on hold.

"It's okay, Stell. I haven't forgotten how things were. And whatever feels right to you. We'll play it your way. I realise I'm on your territory here."

It was all she needed. She turned, smiling, and moved against him so he could hold her as she kissed him.

"I'll make you an espresso, shall I? I know you love those Colombian beans."

"That'd be nice." He relaxed and smiled back at her. "It was Hamish's idea that I should move in here, and, as far as I'm aware, he doesn't know anything about how things were between us."

"I think I'd prefer 'how things are' to 'were', if that's okay. Let's just see where this takes us. Hamish'll cotton on soon enough. He'll get used to it."

"He's still using his room here, right?"

"Sometimes. Quite often lately. He comes and goes. But he'll be here tonight. He says he needs to talk to you.

"Mia casa è tua casa," she said, handing him a key. "My house is your house. Come and go as you please."

"Thanks. I appreciate it. Your security guys still around?"

"Hogan and Barry? They are. Don't worry. I've told them about you."

"I suppose Hamish has told you we've been having a bit of trouble?"

"He mentioned it. But you needn't have any concerns on that account as long as you're here. Whoever's been bothering you won't get past my two Rottweilers. Hogan and Baz are pretty tough."

He went out into the late afternoon sunlight and headed along Jamaica Street towards Baltic Antiques.

A middle-aged couple in the main showroom at the front of the premises, intent on a detailed examination of a faux distressed, early nineteenth-century sideboard, gave him no more than a glance as he arrived before deciding to ignore him completely.

In the office, Fat George, the on-site manager, was busy with some paperwork.

"Everything going okay?" he asked. "Any problems?"

"All good, Jack. You all better now, then? Back in business?"

"Fully functional and ready to roll. John D around?"

"Down below. He should be up here anytime."

"I'll go down," he said. "I need to talk to you both. Get closed up just as soon as those two leave, and we'll all have a chat."

He walked over to the large trapdoor standing open by the goods hoist at the back of the room and went down the staircase into the well-lit cellar. Beyond the cellar stairs was the door to the powder room where cocaine was retrieved from its various hiding places in the furniture they imported. Then it could be weighed out and cut as required before being packaged for delivery to their growing customer base.

The door opened as he reached it. John D stepped out.

"All right, boss?" he asked, grinning. "Long time no see. Hamish said you were back. What can I do for you?"

"We need to talk about a change to our business model. Upstairs with FG."

That evening, sitting with Hamish in the apartment at the Warehouse, he described how his visit to the showroom had gone.

"We've picked out a section of wall to begin hanging the artwork when we have some, and we've ordered some packaging and crates. So all we're lacking right now..."

"We have our first batch of canvases en route as we speak, Jack. Freddy's organised some of his own stock to be flown over, and he's been out today, sourcing more.

"He's aiming to get his grandson, Junior, on board. The boy has contacts in town from his time at art school."

"Okay, so we can start the switch just as soon as the shipment arrives."

"It's sounding good. Our next move will be to insulate ourselves from the importing side of things. You can work out the arrangements with our new supplier."

"And we could use a name for the new setup. How about 'The Art Shop'? Something like that."

Hamish moved across to the drinks tray. "Sounds okay to me. Want one?"

"Do you really need to ask?"

He poured two large whiskies and handed one to Jack.

"But there's still this other thing."

"Vlad."

"Yeah. Or, more precisely, Craig Smith. We have to make it crystal clear to the stupid little redneck that he doesn't call the shots anymore. We should pay him a visit and scare him shitless. We could even do it tonight and get it over with."

"Not to be picky, Hamish, but Craig isn't actually all that little. And Vlad certainly isn't. And he's a vicious bastard to boot."

"True. So where'd you hide our firearm?"

"The Makarov? It's down in the basement, behind some brickwork."

"You should dig it out again, along with some of the ammo you've got stashed. I'll phone John D and get him to meet us at the Gallery. We'll use your car and fit your fake plates before we leave. Hide our tracks."

*

During the drive north to Craig's place, high up on the Longridge Fell, Hamish made sure that the others understood the importance of the job at hand.

"So let's be clear. This is our business at stake here. Craig's obviously teamed up with someone dangerous, and I doubt he's intending to stop with resolving the argument over his cut. He'll want to take over."

"Maybe," said Jack. "He's never been the most reasonable of people. Maybe you made a mistake putting him on the back foot like that."

"And maybe I didn't. Stick to what you're good at. Leave the strategic thinking to me, all right?"

So it's all gone. The equal partners thing. And he isn't the sanest person in this car either.

It wasn't too hard to find Craig Smith's cottage. It was just a little higher up the fell than the Smith family's rambling old barn conversion, now standing empty while the rest of the clan sat twiddling their thumbs on remand.

"That's the place," said Jack as they cruised slowly past with the car's lights turned off. "That's his Discovery in the driveway."

They drove farther up the darkened lane and left the Qashqai parked in a pull-in while they made their way back to the cottage on foot. Jack was carrying the Makarov.

They put on ski masks they'd bought for the purpose and pulled their caps down over their eyes.

"We don't know who else is going to be in there, so let's be careful," said Hamish. "And no names, okay?"

It was getting late, but there was enough moonlight as they crept up the driveway. There were lights in the cottage and the sound of some raucous comedy show on the television. Hamish motioned to Jack to move around to the back while he and John D went to try the front door. It was locked.

They were making their way around the side of the cottage to rejoin Jack when they heard a loud, angry barking from what sounded like a very large dog. Then a pistol shot, followed by silence.

They sprinted to the rear to find Jack standing over the body of a huge crossbreed, lying motionless on the ground in front of him.

Before they had time to react, the back door to the cottage burst open, and Craig darted out at a crouch, moving diagonally across from them toward the shadows at the bottom of the small garden. He got off a couple shots as he ran. Both went wide.

Jack fired three shots in return, more carefully aimed than Craig's, and the third shot found its mark. Craig fell to the ground, gasping and choking.

"Get his gun," he said. "I've got the bugger covered."

Craig was lying on his front in the grass, trying to lever himself up enough to allow him to turn and fire again. But he was too badly hurt. John D ran across the lawn and placed his foot on Craig's outstretched arm, bending down to snatch away the weapon.

Jack examined Craig where he lay, gasping for air.

"Mr Smith has a bullet in his chest," he said. "He's not going to trouble us. Better check the cottage."

Hamish followed the others as they made their way cautiously inside, moving quickly through the kitchen and a small hallway and into the tv room. Jack looked at Hamish.

"Check upstairs," he said. "And hurry up. We need to go."

Above the rustic stonework of the fireplace, a noticeably loud stand-up comedian on an enormous tv screen was doing his best to disturb the peace.

John D moved across the room and clicked the tv off. A low moaning sound was coming from behind a large armchair in the corner. Jack pointed the Makarov in the direction of the sound while John D dragged the chair out of position. A woman was crouched against the wall, hugging a shotgun close. But she offered little resistance when Jack pulled the weapon from her grasp.

"You Craig's missus?" He asked gently.

The woman nodded.

"What's your name, girl?"

"Monica." It came out as a whimper. "Don't hurt me. Please."

"Stay put and keep quiet. You'll be okay."

"We should kill her," said Hamish as he hurried back into the room. "We've already shot Craig. One more makes no difference, and she's a witness."

"To what? Three masked men?"

"She's still a witness. Kill her now, and we can get out of here."

"You know what? You don't get to tell me what to do this time. No one else needs to be shot here. It's enough."

He looked at John D. "Wipe down any door handles and whatever else we might have touched. We're leaving."

5

The day after, on an otherwise slow news day, Craig made the headlines.

"That went well, did it not?" asked Jack. "We were supposed to be putting the wind up the idiot, not doing an actual gangland shooting."

He and Hamish were sitting in the kitchen of the Blue Warehouse, nursing a breakfast espresso apiece, trying to think their way through their current difficulties. They were not seeing eye to eye.

"Just look on the bright side for once. Okay, maybe things went slightly wrong, but Craig has always been a pest. Now he's in intensive care."

"Slightly wrong? Slightly?"

"It's the nature of the business we're in. When the situation demands it, we need to be ruthless. Otherwise, we go under. You must see that. And, once we'd shot Craig, we should've made sure the bastard was dead."

"He could die anyway."

"But he might not and think how dangerous he could be when he gets back on his feet. We should have tidied up all the loose ends. We should have shot the woman too."

Were you always a psycho, Hamish? Did I miss that?

"Have it your own way. It doesn't matter now."

"It'll matter a lot if the cops get on our case about it. They're already interested in me, and it's not so long ago they interviewed me on record. That DI..."

"Slaughter?"

"DI Slaughter has already tried to link me to Craig

Smith. Think about that."

Jack took a sip of his espresso and then thought again and drained the whole thing at a gulp. These Colombian beans of Stella's were among the best he'd ever tasted.

"We can worry about that later if we need to. We still have the Russian to deal with, remember? And we've no idea where he is, so we're just going to have to wait for him to show up, aren't we? We should be ready. I've dug out the shoulder holster for the Makarov."

"You're planning on killing him before he smacks you in the head again?"

"I'm planning on opening some kind of negotiation, that's what. Maybe we can get him on board for now and watch for our chance."

"Our chance?"

"I hate to be the one saying this, but I think we'll have to kill the Russian too. It's unfortunate, but there it is. You should keep Craig's gun by you, just in case."

"John D has it," said Hamish with a shrug. "He seems reluctant to give it up."

"Perhaps it's better with him. He spends a lot of time over at the Art Shop."

"And what did you tell Stella about the night Craig was shot?"

"Only what we all agreed. That we were all over at the gallery with John D, putting in an extra shift to get things ready."

"I told her the same. Think she bought it?"

"Probably not. But she's not stupid. She'll stick to the script if anyone asks."

Hamish sat expressionless and stared at Jack.

"I know you're sleeping with her."

He said nothing. He got up to make himself another espresso. What did it matter if Hamish knew he was sleeping with his stepmum? Almost everyone was sleeping with someone at some time, so why not him?

Almost everyone. But not Hamish. Hamish didn't seem to do intimacy.

*

That morning, Stella had a problem of her own to worry about. It had been too long since she'd indulged in her favourite hobby, so she'd got Baz to drive her into town in the Lexus. It would have been an easy walk over a very manageable distance if her impractically tall heels had allowed it, but practicality did not rate strongly with Stella when it came to heel height. And in any case, she usually arrived home with so many bags and packages that walking back was out of the question.

She could have chosen to shop online. She could have played safe, stayed at home, and had her purchases delivered. But it was the whole shopping experience she wanted. The crowds, the stores, the cafes, the fawning assistants, the trying things on, all that. And the bags and packages were a part of it.

Baz had driven her to their usual multi-storey, next to the bus station in Canning Place, from where it was no distance at all to the vast array of shops of all descriptions in Liverpool One. The car park was busy, and he'd been lucky to find an empty space for the Lexus two floors up.

Jack was in the apartment kitchen, washing up the coffee cups after Hamish had left and wondering whether it might be a good idea to take a stroll down to the Art Shop to see how things were going, when his phone rang.

Stella.

"We went right into the wall," she explained. "The car's full of airbags and everything. And there must be some damage to the bodywork. To the front, at least."

"You're okay, though? And Baz?"

"We're both fine. Just a little shaken up. That's all."

"Tell Baz to phone it in to the breakdown. He can stay with the car until it's collected."

"Okay."

"Maybe you'd better get a cab back here. Soon as you can."

"I'm going to do my shopping first."

He thought for a moment. It wasn't necessarily anything more than a complete accident. But he felt sure it was. So, would it be a good idea to tell Stella that she'd come close to becoming collateral damage in a developing small-time gang war? Probably not. He would keep that to himself for now. Why ramp up the anxiety?

"Well, in that case, maybe you should get Baz to leave the keys with the guy at the barrier. He can go with you and carry your bags. I don't think you need worry too much about the car."

He knew that Stella's Lexus had been out for a full clean and valet only the day before. The usual man had turned up and got the key from Stella. Then had driven the thing away. Like always. Except not quite like always, by the look of it. The weekly cleaning session would have provided a perfect opportunity for some tampering.

But, if the result had only been a few dents and inflated airbags, they'd got off lightly. It could have been a great deal worse.

And now, there was a danger that the whole affair could spiral out of control. He had trusted young Hamish, the guiding hand behind their operation, to get things right. True, he'd solved all his financial problems and got himself some money in the bank. He'd even rediscovered a sense of purpose in following through on Hamish's schemes. But Hamish was proving himself to be careless. They were in a dangerous mess, attracting predators faster than a wounded rat in a piranha pool.

Just wait for your chance. Patience, like always.

After lunch, with Stella still out shopping, he found

Hamish back in the apartment.

"I'm going over to the gallery to check on how things are progressing with our first art delivery. The boys might need some help."

Hamish, sitting on the sofa and staring into space, said nothing. He simply grunted.

"There's a problem, though, Hamie."

"Another one?" Hamish's eyes were suddenly focused on Jack's face. "What now?"

"I think it could be our Russian friend again. Someone's maybe tampered with the Lexus. Stella and Baz bumped a wall in the car park in town. They're okay. Still shopping. It's nothing really, but it could have been a lot worse."

"How do you know it was the Russian?"

"Who else?"

"There's a bunch from Glasgow been sniffing around lately. Trying to cut in."

"And you didn't tell me about this because...?"

"Because I didn't want you to fret. Like you do. And I wanted to get some clarity first."

"And did you? Get some?"

"I did. It's John D. Our John has been dealing with these guys on his own account for a few weeks now. The deal the idiot thinks he's done behind our backs is to use our facilities at the gallery to process some of their stuff alongside ours and then move it on."

"Not good."

"To say the least. It's dangerous. Now he's got the greedy bastards pressuring him, trying to muscle in on our operation."

"And you know all this how, exactly?"

"Easy. John's not tech-savvy. I am. I'm into his phone and his laptop."

"You were spying on the idiot?"

"I spy, as you put it, on all our boys. It's one of the ways I keep us all safe."

Spying on me, too? Leave it for now. Just focus on

the John thing.

Jack walked over to the lounge window and stared out at the Baltic's panorama of old rooftops and repurposed buildings, currently warming in the late summer sun.

Had it been better when he was eking out a living as a small-time private investigator based in his semi, up on the Point? Broke, maybe, but not living in fear, carrying a firearm in a concealed holster. Not looking anxiously over his shoulder as he scurried between the relative safety of the Blue Warehouse and the Art Shop.

On that other timeline, he might, just now, have been standing in his garden, nursing a drink and thinking about nothing more threatening than the pile of bills on his kitchen table. The kind of threat to which he had long since become accustomed and, despite the bills, he would have been relaxed, in charge of his own life.

Who am I kidding?

He turned away from the window and looked directly at Hamish, trying to read more from his expression than Hamish was ever willing to give away.

"So, what do we do? You aren't going to suggest we shoot the bugger, are you? I fucking hope not. There's been too much of that already."

"No need to shoot anyone right now. I think, for now, we do nothing more. We wait, and we watch. I've been in touch with the Glasgow boys. I offered them a deal. Networking, as it's called. Standard business practice."

And never a word to me.

"But what about John D? Do we just leave him to get on with stealing our business from right under our noses?"

"I doubt he'll be in a position to be doing that for much longer. He'd led the Weegies to believe that he was the man who could call the shots for them south of the border. I made it crystal clear that John was no more than hired help.

"And then I told them that we would have been happy to facilitate their expansion plans if they'd approached us properly in the first place. Done their homework before helping John D to undermine us."

"So you came to an arrangement? With the Glaswegians?"

Hamish was silent for a while, considering his answer.

"I've been talking to some guy they call 'Tug'. Trying to come to an understanding."

"And you have an agreement with this Tug? A deal even?"

"Sadly, not quite yet. Tug's what you might call a bit of a hard case. Not the easiest person in the world to negotiate with. So, no, I don't think 'deal' is the right word to describe where we're at."

"So what, then? We're in negotiations? Is that it?"

Hamish pursed his lips and looked strained.

"You could put it that way. But it's kind of like the negotiations the British Government was having with Adolf Hitler before Adolf started invading all over the place."

Not the answer he had been hoping for. A war with a drug gang led by a hard case called Tug hadn't been high on his agenda.

"So what's his problem? This Tug? Isn't Scotland enough for him? It's big enough."

"It's big, yes. But outside of London, Liverpool is the drug capital of the UK. Tug needs representation and facilities down here to help him expand. I told him we'd be happy to provide both. At the right price. And, of course, on our terms. And, as a token of their good faith, I suggested they might consider correcting the mistake they'd made."

6

John D was worried. Tug had not struck him as the type to be in any way slipshod in his business dealings, but the delivery he had expected from his new friends up in Glasgow had failed to materialise. So he'd given it a day and then phoned the man himself.

"Yeah?"

"Nothing arrived yesterday. Is there a problem?"

"There was, but it's getting sorted. Loose end to tie up."

"Anything I can help with?"

"You could explain?"

"Huh?"

"Why you lied to us."

"Lied? How?"

"Told us you were the main man down there, and now we find that isn't so."

"Crossed wire probably, Tug. It's all a matter of perspective."

"Not really. It's all a matter of trust."

And Tug had cut the connection.

He had tried phoning back. Twice. But the man wasn't answering, and now he was even more worried than before. But then, he reasoned, perhaps that was all there was to it. The end of his Glasgow link. That would be a pity, but he'd find others. No way was he going to spend his life working for Hamish Beard when he could just as easily be working for himself.

And then again, maybe that wasn't all there was to it. Tug had mentioned a 'loose end' that needed tidying up. Him? Surely not. After all, what would be the point?

*

Jack was at the apartment, thinking hard. Hamish was out somewhere. God alone knew where, but he was glad to have the time to himself. It was easier to think when the boy wasn't around, and he needed to clear his head. Come up with some kind of plan.

It was true that the accident had affected his memory, but he was over that now, and he remembered, clearly, that Hamish had sold the drug dealing idea to him as something to be kept between the two of them. But then, it seemed, Freddy had become involved, and Hamish was increasingly failing to keep him in the loop.

Worse still, he was pretty sure that the boy was becoming unhinged. From his beginnings as the aimless young dropout who had begun his career by filling in with odd jobs around his stepmum's nightclub, he had come to see himself as some kind of ruthless, international gangster, able to view murder as a simple matter of expediency.

And then there was the whole issue with Hamish's father, Claude, whose death didn't seem to have disqualified him as the boy's personal consigliere, his trusted advisor. More than once, he'd heard him seemingly discussing business with Claude behind the closed door of his room. These discussions, often heated, were always noticeably and inevitably one-sided.

*

John D's phone rang. It was Tug.

"Where are you right now, John?"

"I'm at the gallery. Working late. Getting ready to close up."

"Of course you are. Guess where I am?"

"Glasgow?"

"Not Glasgow, John. I'm outside with two of the boys."

He skirted around the crates of artwork in the process of being unpacked and climbed onto a stool to peer through the high window by the main door. Across the street, he could see a large, black Bentley Mulsanne, complete with darkened windows at the rear. The headlights flashed as he looked.

"That's right, Johnny, dear. You see us. Want to let us inside? Get this over with?"

"Get what over with?"

"That loose end. We're here to tie it up." Tug chuckled.

There was no doubt now that he was the loose end that Tug and his boys had driven all the way down to Liverpool to deal with. The guy had a worrying reputation as being something of a sadist, and John D's personal mental theatre began to play out a series of scenes depicting interesting ways in which a loose end such as himself might come to be dealt with. He knew at once that attempting to reason with Tug would be hopeless. He just wasn't coming across as a reasonable kind of guy. And why would he have troubled himself with such a long drive to look into a matter that could have been addressed much more easily over the phone?

He watched as two men climbed out of the Bentley. They were big. One of the men was hugely overweight. His slimmer companion had a highly visible scar down the side of his face. Both enjoyed a complete absence of facial expression.

They were joined by a third individual, Tug himself, who leaned casually against the vehicle and lit a cigarette while the first two ambled towards the Art Shop.

The place was closed, and the door was locked. Nevertheless, he took the precaution of sliding the bolt into position before hurrying back into the office to unlock the drawer and lift out the handgun he had taken from Craig after the shootout. It was a revolver, a Ruger, small and powerful.

When fully loaded, the Ruger's cylinder held only five

rounds, and John D knew there were only three rounds left in there. But then, he reasoned, his Glaswegian visitors weren't to know that. Not that it mattered anyway. The Ruger had gone.

He went through to the loading bay at the back and let himself out into the yard. There was no one there. He ran out into the alleyway and swerved off to the left, almost colliding with Hugely Overweight, hurrying down to block his exit. The man, wearing highly polished city shoes and a smartly tailored suit over a white tee shirt, was already panting and beginning to sweat.

John D sidestepped the Glaswegian and easily outdistanced him, fleeing up and out of the alleyway into the gathering gloom of the Baltic evening as Tug and Scarface began their pursuit.

The gallery was on the edge of a sizeable area of semi-derelict properties awaiting demolition, where the only lighting was moonlight. If nothing else, the darkened streets and buildings would provide good cover.

His three pursuers broke into a determined trot as they followed their prey into the approaching night. None of the three was built for running, but Tug and Scarface, at least, looked as though they spent long hours working out at the gym.

Not since leaving school had John D made the slightest effort to keep himself in shape.

He was running up a gradient now, and he realised his initial attempt at a fast sprint had been a big mistake. The adrenalin was still there, along with the fear, but the lung capacity and the muscle power were rapidly nearing exhaustion. The two fitter Glaswegians were gaining on him steadily.

At the end of his strength, with his legs about to give up the struggle, he turned a corner and spotted a dark opening into a building on his right. He ran inside, his breath now coming in great, heaving gasps. He knew that if his pursuers had seen him taking cover in this derelict terrace, he was done for. But he could run no further.

Stumbling blindly over piles of rubble, he found a wall to lean against. It took an effort to keep the sound of his breathing down as he gasped for breath. Fighting off his rising panic, he pulled out his phone and turned it off.

He could hear the Glaswegians as they ran up the street, looking into doorways and window openings, calling to each other as they went. One came into the room where he was hiding, using the light from his phone to check the place out. John D shrank back into the corner by the chimney breast and held his breath as his pursuer stumbled, cursing, over the rubble. Then a shout from his companion farther along drew the man away.

When he felt reasonably sure that the pair had moved out of earshot, he lowered himself cautiously onto a pile of bricks and leaned against the wall, listening.

He stayed there for the rest of the night, not daring to move except when he felt compelled to urinate. Try as he might, there was no avoiding that. Drifting fitfully in and out of a troubled sleep, patched with anxious dreams, he made it through to the dawn.

In the early grey light, he picked his way, on aching legs, back across the rubble and peered cautiously through the open doorway into the street. There was no one in sight. The only sounds were from the distant traffic beginning to move through the city morning. But in this derelict part of the Baltic Triangle, nothing was moving. It seemed unlikely that his enemies had hung around here all through the night, but he intended to take no chances. If he could make it as far as the Art Shop, he could help himself to some of the cash hidden away downstairs in the powder room. After that, he would need only to cover the mile or so through the town centre to reach the rooms he rented above a restaurant off Dale Street. Once there, he could pack a bag and grab his passport. He had relatives in Dublin, and he could be there in next to no time.

Choosing his route carefully through the empty streets, past the looming hulks of once-busy warehouses and padlocked redundant goods yards, he found his way back. He checked ahead as he moved, keeping next to the walls to minimise his profile and peering around corners before going forward. At the last, he made sure that the Bentley had gone before he dared to cross the street and walk down the alley to the rear entrance.

The door was unlocked, just as he had left it. He tiptoed inside to check things out.

7

Jack had long regarded Tuesdays as a kind of dead zone. A hiatus in the otherwise more toned-up sequence of weekdays.

As if to prove his point, the Blue Warehouse was always closed on Tuesdays, and after lunch on this particular Tuesday afternoon, everyone, apart from him, was out.

Baz was out carrying bags and guarding Stella, who was shopping in town. Hogan, the other security heavy, was out, taking his mum to the chiropodist. No bar staff were due in until the following day, and the cleaners had done their thing and gone. Hamish was simply somewhere else, as he so often was.

Which left Jack alone in the apartment, enjoying some quiet time reading the Mail. He was partway through an interesting article about some duplicitous politician when his phone rang.

Hamish.

"Yeah?"

"Where are you?"

"In the apartment. Why?"

"You alone?"

"Yeah."

"Stella out shopping? Anyone else in the building?"

"Yes. And no, there's no one here."

"Praise be to God. Only something's come up."

"Yeah?"

"There's a delivery en route. It's for me, but there's no way I can be there."

"Because?"

"Because I'm not even in the country right now. You'll have to take it."

That could well be true, thought Jack. The lucky

young psycho could be back in his villa in Lanzarote.

"Okay. So what is it, exactly?"

"Can't be specific at this point. I'm not entirely sure. Let's just say it could be on the dodgy side."

"There's a surprise. Is it going to the gallery? I can be there in fifteen minutes if I rush."

"Better not there. The boys will be there, and it's best they're kept out of it. Best everyone's kept out of it."

Hamish was sounding worried. This was unusual.

"Apart from me, obviously."

"There is only you. We're partners, aren't we?"

"Fucking right we are. Doesn't seem to stop you forgetting that when it suits you, does it?"

"Not now, buddy. There really isn't time. I'm directing them to the Blue Warehouse car park. It's Tug. He's got your number. I'll get off the phone now."

His phone rang. Unknown number.

"Yeah?"

"And you are?"

Glaswegian accent? It must be Tug.

"Charnley. You're Tug, I expect. I've just finished speaking with Hamish."

"Okay then, Charnley. Wanted the organ grinder for preference, but needs must. I'll make do with the monkey."

Keep calm. Don't react.

"Well, maybe you should just fuck yourself. You Glaswegian twat."

"Sorry. No offence." Tug chuckled.

"I'm assuming you're in the Warehouse, so if you'd care to take a look out onto the car park…"

He grunted, got up from the sofa, went over to the window and looked out. The car park was empty, but then a black Bentley cruised in from the street and came to a halt, almost dead centre, in the rectangle of dark grey tarmac.

"You see us?"

"I see a Bentley."

"Good."

Tug ended the call.

As he watched from the apartment window, a big man wearing a smart suit and a large facial scar emerged from the driver's side and climbed into the back. He slammed the door closed with an expensive-sounding clunk, which echoed around the yard.

Inside the car, the radio was tuned to BBC Radio Two.

"And now," said the presenter, in a voice oozing with cheerful enthusiasm, "a real blast from the past. You wanted it. We're playing it."

And Whitney Houston began to sing, 'I Wanna Dance With Somebody'.

"This is nice," said Tug, sitting in the front passenger seat. "I love this. You ready back there?"

"Ready, Boss."

Behind Tug, jammed onto the rear seat, were Scarface and Hugely Overweight, who, along with Tug, had chased their victim through the derelict Baltic streets. Wedged between them, pale and breathing rapidly, sat John D himself. Hugely, on his left, was holding a pair of heavy-duty garden pruners. They were of the type used for trimming surplus branches from shrubbery. They were large and awkward to manoeuvre in the confined space, but they were manageable.

"You make any mess back there, and you'll pay for the cleaning."

"Don't worry, Boss," said Scarface. "We'll sort it. We won't spill a drop."

He took a strip of leather and a short length of wood from the pocket of his jacket.

"It's the left hand you want, yeah?"

"It's the left," said Tug. "You hear that, Johnny? I'm going easy on you. You're right-handed, yes?"

Scarface had pulled up John D's sleeve and was applying the leather tourniquet, with what some might have considered excessive force, to his forearm.

"Yeah," he said, his voice failing to conceal a tremble. "Look, Tug. I'm sorry if I misled you. It was an accident. Really. There was no harm intended. There's no need... anything you want..."

Tug chuckled softly. His voice was gentle. "It's all right, Johnny. This won't take a minute. And it's nothing personal. Just business. You know. We have standards."

John D began to moan quietly.

"You stay still now. The boys are going to be busy. You have to help. We don't want a mess in here, do we? You be good, and you get to keep your right hand. Okay? I think that's only fair."

Scarface tied off the tourniquet and held John D's arms in a grip that he simply couldn't quarrel with while Hugely arranged some plastic sheeting and a bin bag beneath John D's hand. When this was done to his satisfaction, he picked up the pruners.

"Can't get the whole thing in one, Boss. I'm going to have to nibble at it a bit."

"I don't care how you do it. Just don't take all day. I need to be back home by teatime."

At the first cut, John D began to scream and to struggle. Tug turned up the radio.

From all the way up in the apartment, Jack could hear the din through the closed window, albeit faintly. And he could see the car swaying rapidly from side to side. Then the movement stopped. Someone turned down the radio, and the nearside rear door swung open. A bin bag was held out and dropped onto the tarmac. At the same time, Scarface climbed out of the other side and got back into the driver's seat.

Then the Bentley cruised gently out onto the roadway and disappeared.

He gave it a minute or so before going down to the front door and out into the car park. He circled the bin bag cautiously, checking the yard entrance over his shoulder to make sure that Tug and his gang weren't sneaking back in. Then he picked up the bag and looked inside.

Jesus!

It was a hand, messily severed, lying in a pool of blood. It was all he could do to stop himself from vomiting as he tied off the bag and took it around to the row of bins at the rear of the building.

Stella had been preoccupied when she got back from her shopping trip with Baz. She'd been trying on various combinations of the new clothes and shoes Baz had carried up to the apartment in the collection of designer carriers provided by her favourite, expensive retailers. She had seemed so happy, fussing about with her purchases, that Jack couldn't find it in himself to tell her about the severed hand. So he went along with the chitchat for a while and then got busy concocting a Spaghetti Bolognese to go with the bottle of Chianti he was already working on. He opened another bottle with the meal.
As far as the drinking went, it was beginning to seem more like old times.
By bedtime, the Chianti had made him feel a little more relaxed about sharing the story with Stella.
He waited until she was settled, lying with her head on his shoulder. He was trying to find the right words. In the end, he realised that there was no gentle way of doing what he was about to do.
"Something a little bit disturbing happened while you were out."
"Well, I know there's something on your mind. You've got that look."
"I was in two minds about telling you, but it is your nightclub, and maybe it's a health and safety issue."
"Always keen to do my bit for health and safety. What's the prob?"
"I'm not sure it's actually a problem, more contextual.

For future reference."

"Okay, so you have my attention. Why not tell me what's troubling you?"

"It's a Hamish thing involving some chaps from Glasgow and one of our guys. John D."

"Okay. And?"

Possibly, he realised, it might have been better to leave this until the morning. Then, at least one of them would be able to get a good night's sleep. Too late now.

"There's been some trouble, some violence."

"Serious violence?"

"Pretty much, Stell. It's just that John D lost his hand."

Stella sat up abruptly and flicked on the light above the bed.

"What do you mean lost his hand? How, exactly?"

"Some Glaswegians cut it off. It's out the back. In a bin bag."

It was due to the sedative effect of a bottle and a half of wine that he was the first to fall into a fitful sleep. But even that was not until the early hours. It took a while longer, and a pill from the box of Sleep Nites Jack kept in the bathroom for Stella to fall asleep herself.

Over a late breakfast at the kitchen table, he tried to move the conversation along.

"It's just the way things are now. The way Hamish is running his business, our business, the violence is only going to get worse."

"I'll have a talk with him. Get him to see sense."

"You should try to get your head around the fact that this isn't simply some unfortunate one-off we're talking about here. Your stepson, not to put too fine a point on it, has developed his psycho side to a pretty scary extent. You must see that. You must have heard him chattering away to himself in his room."

"Maybe he was phoning someone. Chatting online."

"You know that isn't it. The boy has no friends to chat with. And you know that he thinks he's getting serious advice from his dad's ghost. And it's not like we could ask the authorities to deal with him. We're too heavily involved. I am for sure. And he's playing around with some very worrying people."

"We have Hogan and Baz."

"Yes, we do. And they're good to have. But at best, they're a couple of ageing nightclub bouncers."

"I still have Claude's old handgun, and I know you have a gun. I've seen it in that shoulder holster thing you have."

He got up to make himself an espresso and poured a glass of apple juice for Stella.

"Is that really the way you see our future? A brace of heavies backed up by a couple of semi-automatics?"

"If you're suggesting that we run away, I've told you before, I'm not leaving this place. It's my life. It's who I am."

"We could go elsewhere for a while, that's all. Until all this blows over or gets resolved somehow. These things have a habit of ending badly. You can read all about it in the Echo most evenings."

"Go where?"

"Wherever you like. You name it. Thanks to Hamish, I have money in the bank. I can put that to his credit, at least. Somewhere abroad? Somewhere nice. They say Italy can be good for shopping."

"I don't know anywhere abroad beyond the odd beach resort or two. Nor do you, right? We'd be like fish out of water."

He reflected on his one trip to Italy. To Naples on business. He had stayed in a run-down high rise by the docks and left a body pushed under the bed, oozing blood from a throat wound. He felt it was unlikely that that particular travel story would sell the idea to Stella.

"How about the Canaries? I sort of know a couple of people over there. It's quiet, and it's sunny. And they have beaches you could lie on. They even have shops for tourists."

"I'll think about it."

8

There was no doubt in Jack's mind about the danger he was in. He had trusted Hamish to get things right. But Hamish had been going quietly crazy all along. And now there was no reasoning with him. Hamish Beard was a lost cause.

And there was Stella to consider. It was a long time since he had had anyone else to think about, and maybe if he let Stella go, it might be a very long time, if ever, before he found a replacement. It was worth making the effort. So he stuck it out at the Warehouse while she made out like she was actively considering his Canary Islands suggestion, though he was pretty sure she was doing no such thing.

Such is life. Or death even, if it all goes tits up. Which it very well could. But then, what the hell else would I do?

Time passed, and nothing much happened. He had to visit the Art Shop almost daily now that John D was no longer on the scene. God alone knew where the poor bastard had ended up. He didn't feel like phoning Tug to find out. On the plus side, the transformation of the antique furniture salesroom into an art gallery was practically complete. And in the meantime, there was the drug operation down in the basement to supervise. So much for keeping his distance and being hands-off.

All the hard work, day to day, was done by the two permanent staff, Fat George and Leggy. The pair divided their time between the gallery and the drug operation, and so far, things were going relatively well.

"So, even with these new deliveries coming in from over the border, you're managing okay?"

Fat George put down the screwdriver he'd been using to uncrate some artwork and straightened up, exposing an unappetising expanse of pie-fed midriff in the process.

"Well, Boss," he began, pushing his hand down the front of his jeans to facilitate a searching scratch around his genital area, "it was a bit easier when John D was here, but we learned a lot from him. We can manage until he gets back on the job. Is he due back soon or what?"

"Off sick, as it happens. An operation he doesn't really want to talk about."

"An extra pair of hands would be a good idea, though. The way things are going."

Keep it zipped.

"Still," Jack persisted, "you'll be finding the artwork simpler to handle than all that furniture.

"And you'll both be getting some decent bonuses in future. At least until I can find you some suitable help."

Fat George remembered that he had left his hand stuck down the front of his pants. He pulled it out and gave it an absent-minded sniff.

"The gallery's looking good now, though, don't you think?"

"It looks the business, George. A credit to the two of you. Had any customers yet?"

"Some. Leggy deals with them. He can talk about paintings and such. Not my expertise."

"So, really, do you think we should make the basement more your area and let young Leggy front things up here? He could wear a fancy jacket and ponce about a bit. What d'you reckon?"

"Suits me just fine. And I'm sure Leggy will be made up with the idea. This whole art gallery thing, it beats humping antique furniture about, any time."

"Nice to hear you're so on board with it all. Keep up the good work."

Minutes later, he was making his way back along Jamaica Street to the Warehouse. It was a fine day, and he had to track through a crowd of Japanese tourists clustered around a painting on the wall by the footpath. It was a particularly popular image. A large pair of wings with a gap between them where a body could stand and pose for a photograph. It was rumoured that no less a person than Camilla Parker-Bowles had done so, although he doubted it. Maybe one day, when he felt more relaxed, he'd get a photo of himself standing there.

As he closed on the Warehouse, he wondered when he would see Hamish back there again. He had no idea where he was. Whenever he asked, the only answer he got was 'abroad' or 'out of the country'. Was he plotting to bring an end to Jack's career, just as he had with John D's? It seemed unlikely. Hamish needed him. He needed him here, in the Baltic, keeping an eye on the Art Shop and the powder room and watching out for Stella and the nightclub.

His phone rang. Freddy.

"Hi, Freddy. S'up?"

"Just touching base. Don't hear much from Hamish these days, so I thought I'd go straight to the source. How's it going with the gallery?"

"It's all fine. We're a man short right now, but we're coping. Your artwork shipments have arrived, and we've got most of the paintings up on the walls. The place is starting to look the business."

"Glad to hear it. I've got Junior on the case, too. Checking out his art school contacts. We can buy one or two of the better pieces from some of the students. A few of them are more than adequate."

"But why? Don't we have enough artwork already to keep us going for a while?"

"We do. But it'll be good for our image. Links into the local community and all that. It'll help set the scene for our opening night bash. I wish I'd thought of it earlier."

"Opening night?"

"Didn't Hamish mention it? My idea? It'll all help. You'll see."

"That's as maybe. And I'm sure you're right, but organising glittering social events isn't really my thing."

"Don't worry yourself about it, Jack. You just keep doing what you're good at. I'll sort all that myself. I might be an expat, but I think I can still manage to push the right buttons if I put my mind to it. Back by the weekend. Watch and learn."

"Can't wait."

"And don't fret yourself about your staff shortage. I'll get Junior to put in a bit of time. He can put in a few hours in the powder room most days."

"So, who is this Freddy Davidson, exactly?"

It was after closing, and Stella was sitting at the bar in the otherwise empty nightclub, listening to Jack's update on how things were progressing at the gallery. He'd been telling her about Freddy's suggestion of an Opening Night event.

"A business associate of Hamish and myself. Fancies himself as a painter and something of an art expert. Some of his stuff's not bad."

"So he's a gangster who paints. That it?"

"As much of a gangster as your stepson and myself. And your two dead husbands. If I can be pedantic about it."

"It's a type I seem to attract."

Stella sipped daintily at her glass of white. At least, she hoped her sipping came across that way.

"Anyway, Stell, gangsters apart, you want to come? You could help me appear socially acceptable while I get pissed."

"As long as I'm back here by closing. It's not far, and I can keep in touch with Baz by phone. They'll manage without me for two or three hours, and I could do with a night out."

"That's a relief. I'd be like a fish out of water at a thing like that on my own. Put it in your calendar. A week on Thursday."

"And if I'm going to be standing next to you in public, I think you'd better get yourself a new suit and a haircut."

And then, suddenly and unheralded, Hamish was back. He found him sitting in the apartment when he got in from the Art Shop that evening.

"So, you're not just a figment of my fevered imagination. You do actually exist. Where the hell've you been?"

"Away."

It was Hamish all right. Same outfit, same tan, same beard, same long hair. But it was a Hamish transformed. He now wore the inscrutability of an android in place of a grin. Inscrutable, it seemed to Jack, until he held his gaze for a moment and saw a universe of dangerous possibilities.

Jack managed a smile. "Good to see you back, anyway, buddy."

Suddenly, the android was gone, and something like the old Hamish was there.

"I'm here for the opening night you and Freddy seem to have arranged for the gallery while I was away."

"Nothing to do with me. All Freddy's doing. He wants to establish some credibility with the locals, apparently. Good idea, really.

"Coffee?"

He got them both a coffee and described to Hamish how Freddy had provided just about every local media interest he could think of with information about their brand-new gallery.

"And he's been busy phoning local celebs and bigwigs and a few arty types to invite them to sample drinks and nibbles at the opening."

"Sounds fairly tedious."

"I might agree with you, but then why come back for an event you aren't interested in?"

"Because the gallery side of things wasn't anything much to do with Freddy beyond him shipping us some artwork to get us up and running. It was our territory, remember?"

"It was supposed to be ours. But I wasn't the one who suggested involving Fuerteventura's answer to David Hockney. It was your idea to rope him in."

"He was going to provide you with some background info and some expertise in shipping paintings. That was all. But now it looks as though you're happy to sit back and let him take over. Can't say I care much either way. He could be useful."

There had been a time, not so long ago, when he would have found it easy to take Hamish's side in any tussle for control of their business. Hamish had often been his house guest at the semi. And now he was living and sleeping with the boy's stepmum at the Warehouse. They had been serious drinking buddies on more than one occasion. Any question about allegiance should have been a no-brainer. But Hamish had changed. Or maybe he had simply grown into the person he was always going to be.

*

In the event, the opening night proved to be nothing to worry about.

Baz ferried Stella and Jack over to the newly named Art Shop. Stella had made a special effort and had raised her game from glamorous nightclub hostess to truly elegant socialite. The experiment with daintiness had been found wanting and ditched. Elegance was back.

Jack, in an inexpensive and ill-fitting blue suit, bought in a hurry off the peg, was impressed. Her elegance wasn't just a matter of clothes and makeup; it seemed to come from somewhere inside her, an expression of her essence.

He felt a compliment was in order.

"You look nice."

It was the best he could deliver at short notice. It was little enough. But she wouldn't have expected anything more.

"Glad to see you made an effort with the suit, Jack. And I'm not wanting to be critical, but for future reference, you do know it's a wee bit too big, don't you?"

A waiter glided by with a tray of drinks. Pale and fizzy in fluted glasses. He grabbed a couple and handed one to Stella.

"I thought I might need the growing room. It's always this way with me and suits. It'll look better when it's had time to crumple itself to my shape."

The place was busy and becoming crowded. In a far corner, a trio was making agreeable noises of a kind which fell puzzlingly between chamber music and jazz. People were forming into little groups and chatting. Or listening intently to their companions while they sipped at their wine or nibbled on their catered canapés. He glanced desperately around the room and spotted a bar through a gap in the crowd.

"Give me a minute, Stell, and I'll get us a couple of proper drinks."

The bar was set out on a long trestle table at the back of the room. The white linen with which it was covered, the sparkling glassware and the gleaming golden optics on some of the bottles promised salvation.

He asked for three large whiskies and downed one immediately before carrying the remaining two over to where he had left Stella. It wasn't enough. He would need a few more to feel comfortable in the midst of all this highbrow socialising.

He found her in conversation with a distinguished-looking older man wearing a suit that actually fitted him. She was sipping demurely at her wine and seemed to be listening intently to what the man was saying.

"Got you a scotch."

She waved it away. "Haven't finished this yet. This gentleman is Gordon Donnelley, the art critic.

"Gordon, this is Jack Charnley, my partner."

Partner?

"Pleased to meet you, Jack," said the art critic, in a tone which suggested he really meant it. "Stella here was telling me how you've been the driving force behind this project. It's good to see someone making an effort locally on behalf of the arts."

"Oh, you know how it is, Gordon. One just feels one has to try to do one's bit. But it isn't only me. This was Stella's stepson, Hamish. His idea. And the artistic side of things is all down to that bloke over there." He waved his scotch in the direction of Freddy Davidson, who, at that moment, was stepping onto an upturned beer crate on the other side of the room.

The musicians fell silent as Freddy rapped on his glass with a fork. Gradually, the chatter faded away as those present turned to look at Freddy, smiling back at them from the top of his crate.

"Friends," he began. "Fellow art lovers. For those amongst you who I might not yet have had the pleasure of meeting, my name is Freddy Davidson, And on behalf of myself and my team, I want to welcome you all to the formal opening of our modest contribution to the cultural life of this great city…"

The audience was attentive as Freddy made his speech. Jack drank the contents of both of the glasses he was holding and threaded his way quietly over to the bar to get a couple more. By the time he got back to his little group, he was beginning to feel much more at ease. He tuned into what Freddy was saying in time to hear him announce the establishment of the Freddy Davidson Award. This, he explained, would be a prize of five thousand pounds, awarded to the art school graduate whose work attracted the most votes from visitors to the gallery during the year.

He wound up his speech to a round of applause. The Freddy Davidson Award had scored a hit.

For a couple of hours after that, Jack drank slowly enough to avoid looking too much like a drunk but just quickly enough to become one. As a result, he actually enjoyed the second half of the evening. Booze had its uses.

He took care to stay firmly by Stella's side as the proceedings gradually became a bit of a blur, and a succession of individuals and couples came and went. He said as little as possible whilst maintaining a show of polite interest in the conversation. He left most of the talking to Stella.

Once or twice, he caught a glimpse of Hamish moving around the room on his own. Against Jack's expectations, he didn't come over to join them for a chat.

Freddy came over briefly to say hello and get himself introduced to Gordon.

"I was impressed by your generosity there, Freddy. Five grand should make a big difference to one of these arty student types."

His speech was becoming slightly slurred now. But what could he do?

"We needed to make an impression. That's the thing. And we can put the prize money down to expenses against the tax bill for this place. I've cleared the arrangement with Hamish."

After a few minutes of small talk, Freddy moved on.

"I need to work the room and grab some social capital for our five grand while we have all these good people in our sights."

And then Gordon was there again, introducing a journalist who had a photographer in tow.

"Would you mind?" asked the journalist as he gently ushered the pair into position. "Just a couple of shots of you and the lady?"

So they posed obligingly and grinned into the camera.

"You seem to be enjoying yourself," said Stella when they found themselves alone. "You're drunk again, aren't you?"

"I might be a little bit pissed, dear. But I'm still vertical. And I'm doing my best to be nice."

9

Hamish was back at the apartment talking to Jack, who was pretending to be interested in the copy of the Mail he had found on the sofa. He was hoping that Hamish would go away and leave him in peace.

"I have to go abroad again. Just for a while. It's business. A new area I'm investigating. I'll need you to step up here while I'm gone. Things are quiet enough just now."

He looked away for a moment and sighed. He didn't like the sound of 'stepping up', and he didn't like this talk of a new area. It sounded like something onerous and possibly dangerous was in the making. He put the Mail aside.

"You don't think we might have enough on our plate at the minute? You want more?"

"I've told you before. The idea is to stash as much loot as possible as quickly as possible and then bail out and enjoy it while there's sufficient time left to get the maximum benefit."

But he felt sure that Hamish was never going to 'bail out' as he put it. He was hooked. Only some kind of disaster was going to release him from his gangster lifestyle. After all, what else had he?

Go with the flow? Just until I can figure out some way to get some control over all this shit.

"So, this 'stepping up', then?"
"A bit of routine stuff, that's all. Like you're good at."
"Okay, so?"
"So I want you to go and talk to our new supplier, the importer guy. Arrange for regular supplies. Regular

payments. It's all been a bit random up to now. And we need to move things up a gear and get everything onto a proper business footing."

"Why? We're already running near capacity. Fat George can't do too much more, and Leggy is tied up with the Art Shop thing."

"We'll get FG some reliable help. Freddy tells me that Junior's available and anxious to get involved. So that shouldn't be a problem. We're about to open up a whole new outlet. We're going online."

"How?"

"I've been busy. While you've been here looking after things, I've been building us a website. In future, we'll sell online. Big deals only, to users and dealers who have the cash and who know what they're doing."

"We can't advertise cocaine on the Internet, on a website. Are you nuts?"

"Yes, we can and no, I'm not. I've worked my way into the dark web. You must have heard of that, yeah?"

"Of course I've heard of it. I used the interweb all the time as part of my PI work. Not the dark bit, though. I never had the right connections for that. Are you telling me you've built a website on the dark web?"

"Exactly. You needn't fret yourself about the technicalities. Lucky for you that I'm geek enough for the both of us. I've got a special set-up somewhere safe, and I'm training FG to use it.

"And don't worry. I've steered well clear of using Encrochat. A fortunate accident of timing."

Despite his reservations about just where all this might be leading, Jack was impressed.

"I've spent time and money setting this up. That's one of the main reasons I've been off the radar occasionally."

"And it works, does it? This website of yours?"

"It works. We can now sell and ship our product across the country. Largish quantities to regional dealers, disguised as crates of artwork."

He had to admit that the scheme did have a certain elegant simplicity. The Art Shop project provided the perfect cover.

"We take the orders online using a system that makes it practically impossible to trace anything back to us. We make up the deliveries in the powder room, using the same type of crates we use to ship our paintings."

"And we get paid how?"

"Either payments into a special offshore account or cash where appropriate. Junior can move any surplus down to Giuseppe like always."

"So, if we're on the dark web, I imagine you're thinking, why stick with the UK? We could go global, right?"

"Try to think like a businessman. Supply and demand. Risk. All that.

"The problem isn't going to be demand. Demand for our product is growing all the time, right here at home. So you'll need to chase up our supplier and get all that sorted. Like we talked about. We're really going to need to leave the importing side to a specialist for now."

"Okay, Hamish. What the fuck difference can it make? We're in over our heads anyway. Let's do it. But this is as far as it goes. For me, at least."

"Excellent decision, Jack. You won't regret it. And now, if I know you, you'll be feeling anxious and in need of a drink to calm yourself."

"You read my mind."

Hamish was already at the drinks tray, opening a bottle of scotch.

"Tomorrow, you should get onto that importer I've lined up for us. Make sure he's up to speed."

*

He called the man on the number Hamish had given him. His call was answered by silence.

"Horse?"

"Maybe."

"Hamish will have told you about me. I'm Jack. We need to talk. Your office? Two o'clock?"

"See you then."

The call was terminated.

The previous night's drinking had extended, predictably, into the early hours, and he'd decided to walk down to the meeting at Horse's place by the docks to clear his head.

Despite the damp and gloomy October afternoon, the fresh air helped, and eventually, following the directions provided by Hamish, he located the yard - Horse's centre of operations.

At first glance, the place looked almost derelict. The yard occupied a space between two ancient, red-brick warehouses, their windows long ago filled in with cement blocks. A high, white wall ran across the rear of the area. Across the front, running parallel to the little-used access road, the enclosure was completed by a substantial, if rusty, chain-link fence topped with razor wire. The gates were chained and padlocked.

Obviously, something inside required protection.

In the yard, there were four deep-blue shipping containers, a black Porsche Cayman and a trailer home. The trailer looked as though it had seen better days. On the wall, above and behind, was a large painted sign, done in long-since faded red. It said, 'Containers - Conversions - Hire or Buy' and gave a landline number.

If the padlock had not been enough to deter Jack from going inside, the two large Alsatians barking and snarling at him through the fence would have decided the issue. He stood by the gate and waited for Horse to respond to the commotion caused by the dogs.

"There's a good boy," he crooned to the nearer of the Alsatians, now throwing itself energetically against the fencing in its enthusiasm to reach him. "Try to calm down. Think about your blood pressure."

He smiled at the dog, which redoubled its frenzied efforts to make his acquaintance.

"Ah well," he said. "Have it your own way. If you don't want to be nice, why don't you fuck off and leave me alone?"

He wasn't sure how long it would be seemly to wait before he began to appear pathetic to whoever must surely be examining him now from inside the trailer.

He reached for his phone.

As he did so, the door to the trailer opened, and a man stepped out onto the gravel of the yard. The man walked slowly towards him. He was smartly, if somewhat flashily dressed, and his black hair reached down to his shoulders in a profusion of tangled, well-oiled curls. It was only when he stood facing him, unlocking the padlock, that he bothered to look at Jack directly. Removing the padlock, he turned to speak to the dogs. He could not hear what the man said, but the dogs reacted at once. They put their heads down and trotted away toward the containers, silent now.

"Horse?"

"Maybe."

"Do you ever say anything other than 'maybe'?"

"Maybe."

He stepped inside the yard with a nervous glance in the direction the dogs had taken. Horse padlocked the gate behind him and led the way, in silence, back to the trailer.

Horse sat down at a table, indicating the chair opposite for Jack. There was a jug of coffee and two cups.

"Help yourself."

He poured himself a cup.

"Milk? Sugar?"

"I like mine black, thanks."

He felt relieved at this touch of civility.

"Your boss said you wanted to come over here to talk business. Now's your chance. Talk."

"Last time I checked, I didn't have a boss. If you're talking about young Hamish, we're partners. Just so you know."

"Sorry, Mr Charnley. My mistake. No offence."

Horse grinned as he said this, just to let him know that if Jack had felt in any way offended, then he, for one, couldn't have cared less.

"No worries. I don't take offence easily. And call me Jack. There's no need for formality, especially as the only name I have for you is Horse.

Horse took a sip of coffee. Then he put his cup down on the table and pushed it away. He folded his hands in front of him and looked Jack in the face.

"So. What did you want to talk about?"

"About how we conduct our business. The whole thing. We're expecting, in the near future, to be able to take all the stuff you can get for us and we need to regularise the way we do things. No glitches in the supply chain."

"I don't do glitches. So you can relax. Just tell me what you want."

"What we want is something secure and regular. We aim to order at the same time every week. We'll text two pieces of information to your mobile phone from a number that will be changed periodically."

"Go on."

"The first text will be the number of kilos we'll need to collect from you on the same day the following week. From a safe collection point."

"Which is where?"

"There'll be several. The second number we text you will tell you which collection point to use for that delivery. There'll be vehicles parked in various places. You'll be provided with the numbered locations and sets of keys.

"You going to be okay with all this? Might not be the way you're used to doing business."

"And I get paid how?"

"We leave the cash in the car at the agreed rate for the quality you're supplying. You collect it when you drop our stuff.

"Any surplus cash you generate and need to get cleaned up can be processed by us."

Horse was silent. Jack took another sip of coffee. Instant. Nothing like Stella's Colombian.

"All good? You can manage all that?"

"If I try really hard, I think I can do it."

"And don't forget. We're expanding our operations, so you can expect the size of our orders to increase over time. If it begins to get so you can't handle it, make fekking sure you let us know before it becomes a problem."

10

He was in the office at the back of the Art Shop, going over some accounts with Fat George, when Leggy came in from the gallery where he'd been hanging some new artwork.

"Man out front says he knows you. Wants to talk."

"Who?" He was preoccupied. Numbers really weren't his thing. They weren't proving to be one of Fat George's strong points either.

"Gordon somebody or other. He was at the opening."

He sighed and opened the desk drawer. He slid the paperwork into it and closed it up as Gordon came through the door.

"Good to see you again, Jack." He looked across at Fat George.

"Sorry to interrupt. Didn't realise you were busy, but I just needed a quiet word. It's kind of urgent."

"I'll get back to work, then, Boss. We can try again later."

Fat George eased himself slowly onto his feet, his chair groaning in gratitude. He ambled over to the cellar stairway and creaked his way noisily down the steps. Jack motioned to Gordon to take a seat.

"Thanks. Hamish is out of town. He said I could speak to your good self in his absence."

"About?"

"Buying some stuff?"

"Stuff? You're looking to buy some artwork?"

Gordon smiled uneasily.

"No, not artwork. The other thing you sell. You know."

What the fuck has Hamish been blabbing about?

"I'm afraid I don't know, Gordon. You best take it up with Hamish if it's important. The only stuff we retail out from here is art. And the odd antique commode or suchlike. Can I interest you in a commode?"

Gordon was tapping his foot rapidly and frowning.

"This is all very awkward. I would have hoped young Beard would have had a word. I wouldn't be so pushy, but I have a bit of a soiree arranged for this evening, and my guests will be expecting to enjoy themselves."

"And I'm sure they will," said Jack, giving Gordon a beaming smile.

His phone rang. Hamish.

"I'm in the office at the Art Shop. Gordon's here."

He moved away from Gordon and went out into the gallery to find a quiet corner out of earshot.

"The art critic from the opening night."

"It's okay. He's a friend. I told him you'd fix him up with some of our excellent product."

"Oh well, that's all fine then. Maybe I should just get a sign on the wall outside and put a few ads in the Echo. You know the kind of thing, don't you? Something like 'best quality snort at great prices - support your local dealer'. That would do it, right?"

"Just give the man what he wants. He could be useful. He's got influence with the council."

"I hate to say this, but you're losing it big style. Why the fuck would I want to risk bringing our operation to the attention of the authorities. Are you nuts?"

Over at the far side of the gallery, he could see Leggy hanging the latest exhibits, adding a little more detail to their carefully constructed cover.

"You're far too cautious to make a successful entrepreneur. You know that? You're lucky I'm on board. A bit of influence will be good for us, you'll see."

"So we take a chance?"

"Like I told you, it's all about calculating risks against rewards. Give the man what he needs. And as a freebie. No charge."

"And how can you be sure we aren't being set up?"

"Because I can. You'll just have to trust my judgement."

"Ah…"

He wandered slowly back into the office, where Gordon was waiting, an ingratiating smile on his face.

"Give me a minute, will you, and I'll see what I can spare? How much did you need exactly?"

Later that afternoon, in the apartment, he sat in an armchair by the window, watching the gulls cruise through the blue October sky, and he brooded.

In a way, he knew Hamish was right. He was often over-cautious. Left to his own devices, he would most likely still be plying his trade as a bargain basement private investigator, his business slowly failing as he sank deeper into debt. Hamish had changed that, and he well knew that he owed the boy that much.

But Hamish himself had changed. Never content to reach a limit and stay within it, he seemed driven to stray over boundaries and stake out new territory. It was in his nature. And in the end, he was certain Hamish would push things one step too far and bring everything crashing down around them.

He should bail out now. While he still could. Go away to relax somewhere warm and sunny. But then he'd be on his own again. Aimless and friendless. Pathetic.

If he could have persuaded Stella to go with him, his prospects would be entirely different. But he had to face the fact that she'd never willingly leave this place.

He phoned Freddy Davidson and told him he needed to talk.

"Is there a problem?"

"There could be. Maybe. Let's discuss it. Just you and me."

"My hotel's down by Stanley Dock. Come for dinner. I could do with the company."

Freddy, he realised, could well become a problem in his own right. But then, Hamish was already becoming a cause for concern, and of the two, Freddy might be the easier one to come to terms with. He knew that Freddy would be thinking hard about how to get some leverage on their drug operation. He had wasted no time inserting Junior into their day-to-day activities.

That evening, he climbed into his new suit and took a cab out to the Stanley Dock, where he had an enjoyable meal at Davidson's expense. They made small talk as they ate. Trying to assess each other's mood and motivation. The meal over, they carried their drinks out onto the terrace, overlooking the water, and found a secluded table.

"We can talk here or up in my suite if you prefer. I don't really mind which." He was staring at Jack quizzically, obviously hoping that he would get to the point.

"Let's just stay out here," said Jack, sitting down. "It's a fine evening, and I could use the air. Nice hotel, by the way. I haven't been here before."

"It's okay for now. I'm looking at one or two apartments here in town. Pricey, but who's counting the pennies? I even have my eye on a yacht."

Jack savoured the single malt in his glass and took in the view of the nineteenth-century docks and warehouses silhouetted against the setting sun. He had yet to broach the subject he had come here to raise - it felt like a betrayal of the person he had trusted and relied on for so long. But that was just a feeling, and feelings could be disregarded if need be. He began tentatively.

"The thing is, Freddy, that I'm not sure whether I should be worried about the way things might be going with Hamish."

Freddy looked across at him, waiting for him to continue.

"The money laundering side of everything seems fine. Junior looks to be handling that with no problem. And Hamish is content to leave well alone."

"And so he should be. As you say, we've had no problems with the cash."

"It's the drug thing we've got into. Me and him."

"The business you excluded me and Junior from and kept to yourselves?"

"As I said, it was me and him. Junior's involved now anyway, so you're hardly being excluded."

"So what's your problem? And why should I care about it?"

"Not to put too fine a point on it, I think Hamish is in danger of getting in out of his depth. And sometimes, I get the impression that he may be losing the plot. Either that, or he's playing some much bigger game that I'm completely unaware of."

"And this is a problem for me... because?"

Jack stared down at his whisky glass. It was empty. Just when he needed it.

Freddy noticed his disappointment at once and signalled to the waiter who was busy clearing tables along the terrace. The waiter hurried off and came back almost at once with two fresh whiskies.

Jack sipped gratefully at the scotch.

"Because?" Freddy repeated.

"Because, as I've just said, Junior is now becoming increasingly involved. And I'm sure that you wouldn't want him to be caught up in the mess if everything went tits up."

"Junior's there because we're very interested in what you and Hamish, our two partners, are up to."

"Okay, like I said..."

"It was me gave you guys your start, if you recollect. And no disrespect, but without me, you'd likely have stayed the two no-marks you always had been. And what you'll most likely be again if you don't watch out."

"If that was meant as a threat, then you're making a mistake. I'm here to offer you an understanding. An arrangement."

"So what is it you want?"

"I want peace of mind, and I want you to help me get it by helping me solve our Hamish problem. I'm concerned that the boy's trying to run before he's learned to walk."

"And so?"

"Talk to him. Get him under some sort of control before it's too late. He'll never listen to me, but he has to have some respect for an experienced operator like yourself."

They sat in silence for a while as the sun sank below the horizon and let the night-time in.

"Let's say I do talk to him, and I get him to behave himself, as you put it. What exactly are you offering?"

"I'm offering to cooperate in bringing you and Junior on board with our coke operation as smoothly as possible."

"Go on," said Freddy. "I'm listening."

"I'm offering to do whatever I can to help you take an interest in our drug business. To get everything properly rolled into the partnership, along with the money laundering. So we can all be full partners again, right across the board."

"And what's the catch?"

"No catch. This whole thing is growing by the week, and it all needs bringing under control. I can't do it on my own."

Freddy Davidson sat quietly for a moment as if carefully considering Jack's words. Then he got abruptly to his feet.

"I'll give some thought to what you've said. For now, though, it's getting late, and I need my beauty sleep."

*

In the cab on the return trip to the Warehouse, he got a call. It was Tooth.

"Alan?"

"You might want to get back here. I've called the police."

"The police. What the fuck for?"

"It was the banging. I thought it was a break-in or kids messing, so I looked out the window. Someone round the back of yours. I saw him leave."

Vlad?

"You sure about this, Alan. It's pretty late."

"I told you, I've phoned the police. Marj is worried. We both are."

He heard a woman's voice in the background. Then, "The police car's here now. I'm going out to them. I'll tell them you're on your way."

By the time he stepped out of the cab outside his house, the two uniformed officers, a man and a woman, were getting ready to leave. The policewoman came over to speak to him while Alan Tooth stood in his open doorway, watching.

"Mr Charnley?"

"That's me. Is there a problem, officer? Next door phoned me. Something about a burglar?"

"We've spoken to your neighbour. He thought he heard some kind of disturbance coming from the rear of your property. This is your property?" The officer waved her notepad in the direction of his semi.

"That's my house. Did he get in? The burglar?"

"We've had a good scout round. No sign of any attempt at a break-in. Everything's secure. Would you like me to come inside with you to make doubly sure? Just for your peace of mind?"

"If you say it's secure, I'm more than happy to take your word for it."

"Might be best if I come in while you have a look around?"

"If you feel it's necessary."

He waved at Tooth and let himself in through the front door. The policewoman followed and waited in the hallway while he made a quick tour of inspection.

"Nothing out of order. Everything looks fine. Thanks for waiting."

Tooth wandered over as Jack stood out on his drive, watching the patrol car pull away.

"I think the coppers thought I'd imagined it," he said. "But there was a lot of banging for a minute or so. Marj heard it too. I didn't imagine it."

"Maybe it was just someone else further along the row. Sound echoes all around this brickwork."

"Could be." Tooth was sounding less certain now. "Hard to be sure. Still, better safe than sorry, eh?"

"No harm done. You did the right thing. I should probably put in some kind of alarm system, shouldn't I? What with me being away so much."

"Maybe you should. You're hardly ever here these days."

"I've been staying in town with a friend. I've got interests down there now, in the Baltic."

"I know. I saw the photograph in the Echo. She looks nice, your friend. Never took you for the arty type, though. Surprised me."

"You're right. She is. She's even nicer than me. And I'm not arty at all. It's a business thing."

It was some time since he had been at the semi, and he decided it would make sense to spend the night at his own place. Just in case.

If it had been Vlad making a noise out there, and he returned to try again, he felt sure that the Makarov, nestling in his shoulder holster, would be enough to scare him away.

He wished Tooth goodnight and went back inside, locking and bolting the door behind him. He saw no point in taking unnecessary risks.

He phoned Stella to let her know he'd be staying at the semi overnight. There'd been some problem with vandals, kids probably, he said. For a while, he sat slumped on the sofa, reviewing his situation. He was hoping the review would lead to some kind of plan, but it didn't. Strategic planning had never been one of his strong points. Perhaps that was why the highlight of his brief time in the British Army had been standing guard on the stores through rainy Berlin nights rather than working on contingency plans to deal with a possible invasion from the East.

As to what might come of his approach to Freddy Davidson, he had no idea. He feared that Freddy saw him as weak and ineffective. Clueless. Should he simply have waited for events to unfold and taken his chances?

He was at an impasse, waiting, as usual, for others to do their thing. Waiting for Hamish. Waiting for Stella. Waiting for Freddy. Waiting for everyone or anyone to make their next move.

A drink. A good way forward. He hadn't drunk too much back at the hotel, so maybe he could allow himself a little more before turning in. Otherwise, his mind would go rapidly into overdrive as it sifted through all the imponderables currently cluttering up his mental horizons.

He wandered through the lounge and kitchen in search of something suitable. He found a few bottles of wine and a small amount of whisky.

Not wine tonight. Feels more like a whisky night. Like the old times.

He searched out a clean, cut-glass tumbler and emptied the whisky into it. Not a huge measure. Maybe a double. He held up the glass and admired the look of the thing. It was part of a set of four he'd had as a birthday present from his mother-in-law, Beatrice, years before. God alone would know what had happened to the other three. He certainly didn't. He drank it in one and then reluctantly considered the wine.

No alternative suggested itself. The stores would all be closed now, and in any event, he didn't feel like going out again.

He was considering the possibility that he might, after all, have to resort to the wine when he remembered that there had been a half case of scotch in the shed. He would have had a bottle or two from there at most.

As usual, the door was jammed tight shut, and he had to apply considerable force to yank the thing open. Flicking on the light, he saw the object of his desires at once, wedged between a pile of old Sunday magazines and a bucket of long-neglected gardening tools, home to an impressive array of spider webs.

He bent over, brushed the dead leaves off the lid and opened the box. There were four bottles still in there. He thought he could hear angels sing as he picked up a bottle. The rest would be best left in place to cover future emergencies.

As he turned to leave, he noticed something odd hanging on the back of the door, something he had failed to see on his way in. He took a closer look.

Nancy.

She had been nailed to the planking. A nail protruding from each of her paws. Thankfully, the tiny cat was dead.

He found a claw hammer from somewhere and yanked out the nails. Then he carried her gently into the house, along with the whisky, and wrapped her in the only clean pillowcase he could find. He placed her carefully on the sofa where he had last seen her alive, practising her pounce with her sister.

He would have shed some tears if he hadn't given up on tears a long time ago. Instead, he spent an hour or so teetering on the edge of depression as he drank his way into the whisky bottle.

11

When he managed to open his eyes, he was immediately dazzled. The morning sun. Bright. Slanting in through the garden window. The depression was gone. In its place, the usual post-whisky brain fog. His phone was ringing.

Horse.

"Yeah?"

"There's a problem. Where can we meet?"

"Is it urgent? Not sure I should be driving at the minute."

"The problem's up your way. I'll come to you."

His mind clicked up a couple of painful gears.

"Like you know where I am?"

"Well, you aren't at the nightclub in town. I called them when you weren't answering. Thirty minutes ago. So I'm assuming you're at your place up on the Point."

"It so happens that's exactly where I am, but how come you even know I have a house up here? I never mentioned it. Did someone at the Warehouse tell you where I lived?"

"You came to speak to me on business, remember? How long would I last if I didn't check out the people I dealt with?"

"Give me an hour."

It was just enough time for him to shower and to take little Nancy out into the back garden and bury her under the old laburnum next to Madge. He was too rushed and too hungover for the sadness to reach him again. No sign of Tooth. Thank the Lord. He couldn't have handled Alan Tooth this morning.

Eating breakfast was out of the question, but he was into his second coffee when he saw the Porsche park up.

"You'd better come in."

Horse was at the door. Same sharp suit. Same shiny locks of curly hair.

"Coffee?"

"I'll have one while we talk. You look like shit."

The whisky bottle, its contents well down, stood on the table.

"Thanks, but if you're aiming to worm your way into my affections, then I have to tell you, it isn't working."

Horse followed him into the kitchen and waited while Jack poured him a coffee and topped up his own.

"Nice place you have here. Classy."

Was the man trying to needle him? Or was it simply in his nature to be pointlessly offensive? He didn't have the energy to care.

"Why don't you just tell me what the problem is?"

Horse pulled out a chair and sat at the table with his coffee. Jack sat opposite.

"So, the problem?"

"The thing is that despite my instinctive caution, there've been a few times down the years where things have gone wrong. I've always dealt with those incidents quickly and thoroughly."

"I'm listening."

"And that's what I'm doing right now. This very morning. And you, Jack Charnley, are going to help me."

"So, are you going to tell me what this is all about before one of us dies?"

"The first thing to know is that I have a partner, a business partner, called Paul. We've worked together for a long time. This morning, Paul went off to take care of our latest shipment."

He paused and took a thoughtful swig from his cup. "Nice coffee, by the way."

Nice coffee. You see? Not everything about me is shit.

"I grind it myself."

"Paul isn't answering his phone, and he really should be. I need to find out what the problem is, and I need someone to watch my back. Normally, that would be Paul. So I thought you might want to help me out."

"And that would be because...?"

"Because if we don't find that shipment, you don't get your stuff, your customers don't get supplied and so on. You lose money, and you get a rep for being unreliable. I'm guessing you have no other sources of supply?"

"Not sure. I'd have to talk to Hamish."

"You have to clear it with the boss?"

"I told you already. I don't have a boss. The boy's my partner."

He tried to think it through. The chances of them finding a suitable supplier to stand in at short notice for the quantity they needed were going to be slim, whatever Hamish might have to say on the subject. Maybe this was a good opportunity for him to begin making his own decisions. Maybe it would be best to keep Hamish out of it.

"Okay, so supposing I'm willing to help you out. What's the plan? Where do we start?"

"We start just up the road from here, in the pinewoods by the beach."

"We can walk up there in less than twenty minutes."

"We'll take the Porsche. I don't want to waste any more time. And make sure you're armed. You'll be watching my back, remember?"

It was less than a mile to the car park in the pinewoods. From there, they set off on foot along one of the paths laid out by the wardens for the use of day-trippers and nature lovers. Then Horse took the lead as they veered off the path and into the pines. In under ten minutes, they were well away from the beaten track. Horse led the way through a gap in a seemingly impenetrable bank of brambles and ferns into a hollow, surrounded by more brambles and towering pine trees.

"The stuff comes in by ship en route to the docks. It gets dropped over the side and collected by a guy on a jet ski. Last night, that guy should have left it here."

He pushed aside a clump of bracken fronds to reveal a shallow hole in the sandy ground, in amongst the brambles.

"This morning, Paul would have been up here at first light, dressed like a nature lover and carrying a backpack. He should then have backpacked the shipment out to the car park and delivered it to my yard at the docks."

"And I'm assuming that that wasn't what happened."

"I haven't seen him. I've spoken to the shippers, and they say everything went off as normal."

"Have you received any threats or demands?"

"No."

"Had any unusual contacts?"

"No."

"So you think some rival or competitor has been watching you and your partner, sussing out the situation? Watching how you operate. And that someone has intervened?"

"Could be, but there's obviously nothing here that's going to tell us anything."

"You were expecting to find your guy lying here with a hole in his skull? Something like that?"

"Half expecting it. It can happen in this business."

Horse stood in the centre of the little clearing, scratching his head as he rotated slowly around, taking in the whole scene as if looking for clues. Jack felt sure there were none to be found and waited for Horse to accept the inevitable.

"There's nothing more to be done here," he said, his inspection completed. "Come on to my place. We can talk over lunch."

As a commuter town, serving Liverpool's multitude of city-centre businesses, Gunner's Point had grown up around a small farming community, with farmsteads dating back to the time when Norsemen had grounded their longboats on the wide beaches and settled their families inland. Thatched cottages and crazily contrived Tudor constructions from the centuries in between could still be found sprinkled at random throughout the area.

But such properties were in the minority.

Jack's semi, at the lower-value, southern end of town, was situated in one of several brick-built estates erected from the fifties onwards. The northern part of the settlement, known locally as the 'Money', was where the wealth was concentrated. Composed initially of ornate Victorian piles with huge gardens, the Money was now as built up as it was possible for it to be while still having the look and feel of a very leafy suburb. Expensive properties in every conceivable style, from faux Spanish villas, via restrained bay windowed family homes, through to ultra-modern architectural dreamscapes, standing, mostly, in their own grounds bounded by substantial and secure walls.

Horse lived in a modernist palace on one of the more expensive roads. The high gates at the end of the drive opened automatically as the Porsche growled its way in and closed securely behind them.

"Didn't realise we were neighbours," said Jack. "I'd imagined you living in that trailer home you have in your yard. Rich bastard, right?"

"I suppose I am. As I imagine you are yourself, underneath that veneer of 'just about managing' that you hide behind."

The Horse residence was impressive inside and out.

"This hallway has a bigger floor space than the entire ground floor of my semi."

"I like a bit of space. Here..." He opened a door which Jack, at first glance, had mistaken for an abstract artwork. It lead into a square, windowless room. "Come into my den. We can talk."

The lighting came on automatically and lit the place to the level of a bright midsummer afternoon. They sat across from each other, over a low table, on couches covered in the black-and-white pattern favoured by Friesian cattle. The far wall was entirely taken up by an enormous electronic screen displaying a series of open, rural views.

"Sandwich? Coffee?"

"Anything you have will suit me fine."

"Kirsty?"

A red light began to glow softly on the little console he could see sitting on the desk behind Horse's couch.

"Yes, Mr Wiseman?"

"Two of your BLT specials and two coffees. To the den."

"How do you like your coffee, Jack?"

"An espresso would be great."

"Make that two espressos. Doubles. Okay?"

"Yes, Mr Wiseman. Right away."

"Thank you, Kirsty."

The red light went out.

"Hiring out the odd cargo box or two must pay well. I'm impressed with your set-up."

"The shipping containers pay well enough. At least on paper. And no one is going to bother to look too closely as long as I appear to behave myself and the taxman gets his cut."

"But right now, you have this problem."

"*We* have a problem. You and I. We've already agreed that you're a part of this."

Jack said nothing. He sat back on his Friesian couch and glanced around the room. There were expensive-looking paintings on the walls. The desk on which the little console stood seemed to be made out of hammered metal of some sort. There were two more couches, computer equipment on a glass table and a carved stone statue, a metre high, that looked as if it could have belonged in some museum's collection of Aztec sculpture.

"So, I bow to your no doubt extensive experience in this area. What do you suggest? How do we proceed?"

"How do you think?"

"With caution, I imagine."

Jack's phone rang. Unknown.

"Better answer it."

"Yeah?"

"Surprise, surprise, Jacky boy. Guess who?"

"Tug."

"Correct, first time. It's probably the hint of Glaswegian in the old voice there that gives me away. Am I right?"

"Can we do this later? What the fuck ever it is. I'm busy just now."

"Of course you are. You're trying to work out what might have happened to that big fat delivery you had in the pipeline. Am I right? Tell me I'm right."

"You? It was you?"

He glanced across at Horse and pressed the speaker button on his phone.

"Might have been me. Might be me who's taking good care of your goods and your errand boy right now.

"You can have your man back, safe and sound, more or less, once you're clear about the way we do business."

"Don't think I'm following you. What way do we do business? Beyond the fact that we move along some of your product, as a favour to you?"

"I thought I'd laid all this out for that weirdo partner of yours. Beard."

"Hamish? Heard nothing from him for a while."

"Well, here it is then, Jack, for the avoidance of doubt. You work for us now. We supply. You distribute. You're lucky. We've chosen you as our North of England distributor. Good, right?"

"First I've heard of it, Tug. You've got me on the back foot here."

Hamish? What the fuck is Hamish playing at? Trying to get me killed?

"Well, you know now, okay? And to be quite crystal, you work for us exclusively. You can tell that Crazy Horsey friend of yours to piss off. No offence. But he's out of it."

He thought quickly. The situation was spiralling rapidly out of control on all fronts. What to do? Stall?

Or do something decisive - for once?

"I'll talk to some people and get back to you."

He terminated the call just as Horse's housekeeper, Kirsty, came in with a tray of sandwiches and coffee.

"Thank you, Kirsty," said Horse. She left, closing the door carefully behind her.

"Do help yourself."

Jack suddenly realised how hungry he was. He had eaten nothing since yesterday. He grabbed a sandwich and ate.

"So, this Tug, then. Friend of yours?"

Regretfully, he put his sandwich on hold.

"Pain in the backside, more like. One of our boys went off-piste and got mixed up with these Glaswegian bandits. We ended up handling some of their stuff as a favour. I'm simply trying to keep the peace."

"Think he's dangerous?"

"I know he is. He's a fucking psycho. This business seems to have psychos everywhere you look. How he found out about you, I've no idea. Unless Hamish mentioned you."

"We might get to worrying about that later, but right now, we need to get Paul back. Plus our delivery. So, I think, for the time being, we just have to go along with the guy. Make him think you're giving him an exclusive to your distribution network."

Jack parked the discussion for the moment and focused on the sandwich. He was hungry. It was good. The coffee likewise. Life would be impossible without coffee.

There had been a time, not very long ago, when he might well have decided at this point that enough was enough. That Hamish and Tug and all the other drug-dealing, murdering psychos could just go and play with themselves while he took himself off to some quiet corner elsewhere.

But this time? Something, he had to admit, almost grudgingly, to himself, had changed. He'd begun to entertain the idea that he himself had wants and needs.

He wanted to hold on to his newly found aims and ambitions. Wanted to continue sleeping with Stella. Wanted to be somebody.

It wasn't that he craved a house like this one. And he didn't feel the need for a Porsche to replace the Qashqai. But he was no longer the Jack Charnley he had been when all this had started. He wanted a life.

"Nice sandwich," he said. "My compliments to the chef."

"Yeah, she's a real gem. But more to the point, do you need to talk to your partner Hamish? We have to do something to get my guy back."

"I know. Don't worry. I'll call Tug now and reassure him that I'm going to discuss the matter with Hamish just as soon as I can locate him. I'll see what kind of accommodation we can make. And then you and I'll decide how to fix our Tug problem."

12

There was a social at Horse's place. He was invited, making this a dizzyingly busy year on the Jack Charnley social front. First, the Art Shop opening night and now this. Two events only weeks apart.

Stella was delighted.

"A house party up in the Money? I didn't think you were so well connected. Anyone I know?"

"Probably not. Unless you happen to know someone called Morris Wiseman, otherwise known as Horse."

"One of your gangster friends?"

"He rents out shipping containers."

Much as he disapproved of the idea of lying to Stella, his years working as a private investigator, poking his nose into other people's doings, meant that lying had become painlessly second nature. And, anyway, for all he knew, Horse actually did rent out a container or two.

"The man's perfectly respectable. He's just someone I happened to meet when I was searching for storage options back in the antique furniture days. Google the guy if you're worried."

She gave him a playfully suspicious look.

"Okay, I'll buy that for now, and we'll see how it goes."

And then, in a more serious tone, "But if this Horse is in any way dodgy, I expect you to keep it all away from here. No more gangster games around the Warehouse. There's been enough of that already. Okay?"

"No worries, Stells. I'm an art dealer now, remember? You can relax."

Horse's party was on a Friday night, and Stella had arranged suitable cover at the Blue Warehouse. They arrived at the house in the Lexus. Baz driving. They were screened at the gate by two polite but dangerous-looking types in dinner jackets and bow ties. Baz dropped them off at the door, circled around the forecourt and then drove out and down through the Point to wait at Jack's semi until he was needed again.

Jack, his new suit now doing its best to crumple itself more fittingly to his shape, and Stella, who was very much dressed for the occasion, were ushered in through the doorway by a distinguished-looking man with grey hair, who had been engaged to act as butler for the event.

Then they were in the main hall. A lot of activity, a lot of light, a lot of guests and over in the far corner, a group of musicians backing a well-known female singer in a glittering evening gown. Jack, no expert on music or musicians of any kind, felt sure, nevertheless, that he had seen the woman on television more than once.

Horse was at his side now, smiling.

"Glad to see you could make it tonight. And I can see that you're wondering about our star."

"I am?"

"I think so. Judging by your expression. She's exactly who you think she is. Had her flown in specially from Manhattan for the party. But you haven't introduced me to your lovely partner."

He made the introductions, and then Horse ushered them toward the bar at the end of the hall.

"Grab yourselves a drink, people, and feel free to mingle. Or just wander around if you'd rather. Most of the place is open. Anywhere I don't want folk to go is locked, so you can't go wrong if you want to browse. Right now, I have to network, but I'll be back.

"And Jack, try not to get too pissed up right off. There's someone I want you to meet later."

He disappeared into the crowd.

"Well, you heard what the man said, Stells. Let's hit the bar. What do you think? Impressed?"

"Pretty much. I have to say this is all a lot posher than I expected. I never suspected you had such classy friends. Do you know anyone here, apart from Horse?"

"Not that I've seen so far. Seems unlikely."

They got drinks at the bar and stood gazing around the room. In the end, not knowing quite what else to do, they wandered out of the hall and down a long corridor, pretending to admire the expensive-looking abstracts hanging on the walls.

"They speak to my inner art dealer," he said, grinning.

They passed the dining area, where a buffet was being set out, and went out onto a garden patio.

There was a pool with submerged lighting. Two girls, naked, were splashing about in the shallow end.

"Fancy a swim?"

"Maybe not. But you go ahead if you want. I'll sit here and mind your drink and watch you make a fool of yourself."

He drained his glass and said nothing.

"Perhaps we should just find ourselves a seat and hang out here for a while," suggested Stella. She was taking pity on him. He could see that. "Watch and learn."

"Good idea." He was relieved. "I'll go and get us some more drinks. It might help."

He left her sitting on a bench by the patio and hurried back along the corridor to the bar. He asked for four doubles, drank one immediately and poured a second into the glass he had earmarked for himself. Then he made his way outside to rejoin Stella. It would all be all right, very soon now. The scotch would see to that.

But Stella wasn't alone. There was a man sitting next to her on the bench. He was sitting with his back towards Jack as he approached, and it wasn't until he was standing in front of them handing Stella her fresh drink that he recognised Gordon.

Donnelley. Again. I look away for a minute, and there you are. Drooling all over Stella.

"Gordon. Fancy seeing you here. You're a friend of Morris's?"

"Hello, Jack. I was just telling your lovely partner here that our host and I go back aways."

"Small world."

"Isn't it?"

"Morris wants to see you in his study for a few minutes, Jack. So Gordon's come to keep me company for a while. Isn't that kind of him? He says you know where it is. A business matter. It would only bore me. Apparently."

"Oh."

"Off you go then. I'll be fine here with Gordon. He's been explaining all about the abstract expressionists. It seems that's what those paintings in the corridor actually are."

"Of course they are. I knew that."

Something about Stella's tone told him that she wasn't altogether buying into the idea that this new social world had come about by chance. He felt sure, though, that however much she might suspect that there was a whole lot more lying hidden beneath the glitzy veneer presented by the party that night, she was happy to go along with it. She would feel that this was a step up socially. And whatever else, Stella loved glitz. It was a world, he knew, to which she would very much like to belong and in the interests of which she might be prepared to overlook a multitude of sins.

Once again inside Horse's den, he found his host standing and drinking with another of his guests. He recognised the man at once.

"Jack." Horse greeted him enthusiastically. "Come right in. Close the door behind you. I believe you already know Detective Inspector Slaughter here."

"We've met," he said, puzzled at the police presence.

"It would be difficult to spend all those years as a private investigator hereabouts without running into the good inspector here at some point. How are you, Inspector? You're well, I hope?"

Slaughter stared across at him. He was expressionless, as if unsure what manner to adopt.

"Charnley. Glad to see you're keeping the right sort of company these days and staying out of trouble."

Cheeky bastard! What the fuck is he up to?

"Always striving to stay on the straight and narrow, Slaughter. I must admit that I'm surprised to find you here. Wouldn't have thought this was at all your kind of affair. Or are you here on business?"

Slaughter looked questioningly at Horse, who seemed to be enjoying the exchange.

"It's okay, Jack," said Horse. "Clive's a friend. He's here to help us with some info about our Scottish problem. I suggest we make ourselves comfortable and talk the thing through."

They sat. Jack and Slaughter facing each other from opposite Friesian couches, Horse equidistant from both, on a swivel chair dragged over from the desk.

"I've told Clive here all about the difficulty we've been having with our good buddy, Tug, and he's assured me that he'll be pleased to help."

This guy is fucking amazing. A senior cop, no less. On our team. How can we possibly fail?

"I'm all ears. Help how, exactly?"

"He's offered to ask his colleagues north of the border to provide him with Tug's address."

13

"I don't want to make a big thing of it, but you invited me to come with you, and I didn't expect to be left to fend for myself for a full hour with that man Gordon breathing down my cleavage."

They were in the apartment the day after the party.

"I asked you because I thought you would enjoy it. There was no way I could have known that Horse had set up a business meeting in his den. And I'm sorry if you didn't enjoy Gordon's company, but you seemed happy enough when I left you with him."

He didn't really want to be talking about this just now. He was preoccupied. He was expecting an important phone call, the one where Horse would tell him that Slaughter had managed to come up with the address they needed.

"I was okay about you disappearing for ten minutes or so. You were gone for a long time. And listening to Gordon droning on about abstract expressionism made it seem even longer."

He was about to make a second apology when his phone rang.

Horse.

"Everything good?"

"Not sure. I've just had a call from our friend, telling me if I want Paul back, I should get up to the drop spot in the pines asap."

"And?"

"And I need you to go up there and see if you can find the poor bugger. Find out what's happened."

"Paul's your man, Horse. Not mine. It's up to you to help him."

"It was my connection with you got me and Paul into this in the first place. I've explained all that already. You deal with me, or you deal with Tug. You choose."

He could see Stella looking at him via the wall mirror where she was adjusting her make-up, taking an interest in this sudden turn in the conversation. He went into the bathroom and closed the door.

"And you can't go up there and collect him yourself?"

"I'm at the yard, and there's a Bentley, complete with darkened windows, parked outside my gates. I'm looking at it now."

"Shit."

"They're in there just waiting for me to make my move. You wanted to partner up with me. Now's your chance to show me what that's good for."

It was apparent to Jack that his choices here were limited. If Tug succeeded in removing Horse from the equation, then he might well become Tug's man from here on in. And Tug was a violent psycho.

"If I do this, you owe me, right?"

"Throw your lot in with Paul and me and we're solid. Remember, I have Clive on the payroll. For whatever that turns out to be worth."

*

"More storage problems?" Stella had asked as he searched around for the keys to the Qashqai. He grunted something noncommittal and ignored the question.

"And don't forget what I said. None of that funny business gets back to the Warehouse. None of it."

Another grunt, affirmative this time, as he left.

He took the Makarov with him and drove up to the Point. The day was uninviting with a light drizzle falling as he parked up on the pinewoods car park. There was only one other car. A small hatchback. Probably a local giving her dog a run on the beach. Some people didn't seem to mind the rain.

Rather than walk directly to the hollow in the brambles, he skirted carefully around it, listening and watching.

There was no one about, so he took out the Makarov and made his way in through the undergrowth. In the hollow, he saw nothing at first. Then he spotted the feet, minus shoes or socks and covered in mud, poking out from under the brambles.

What the... Good God! A corpse?

"Paul?" he asked, keeping his voice low. "I'm a friend. Horse sent me."

There was a muffled sound in response.

Alive, at least. Praise be.

He could see no one else in or around the hollow, so he holstered his gun.

"Paul?" He asked again, more loudly this time. "Horse sent me. I'm here to help."

He was answered by a gasp and what sounded like a groan from within the tangle of undergrowth. Obviously, the man was in no condition to extricate himself. He grabbed hold of his ankles, bound together with gaffer tape, and pulled.

Paul was heavy and, judging by the sounds he was making, in a great deal of pain. Eventually, he had the man clear.

He was a mess. His torn city suit had bloodstains. His face was bruised and covered in cuts. His hands had been taped behind his back, and a thin cord had been tied securely around his head and drawn in tight against his opened jaws.

If he had had a knife of some kind, it would have been much easier to remove the tape and the cord. But he had to make do with a sharp piece of stone. It took a few minutes.

Paul struggled to speak. "Water," was all he could manage to say when Jack pulled the cord from his mouth. After that, he was coughing as he tried to sit up and then, with difficulty, to stand. It was obvious to Jack that he needed medical attention and just as obvious that there was no way he could chance getting him any. It would be too risky to attempt to explain away Paul's injuries.

"Lean on me, Paul. I'll give you some water as soon as I can. We'll take it easy, and I'll get you to my car. I'm going to take you to my place for now."

They met no one on the way to the Qashqai, and there was no one about as he helped Paul from the passenger seat and in through his front door. Unlike most days, Tooth's car wasn't on his drive. He guessed that the Teeth must be enjoying their weekly trip to the supermarket. It was the only time, most weeks, when their ancient but immaculate Toyota ever moved.

"Sit yourself down on the sofa there, buddy, and I'll fetch you a drink."

He got a cup of water from the kitchen and watched his bruised and bloodied guest glug it down to follow it up with a fit of coughing.

"There's nothing else on the agenda just now, so you lie yourself down there and rest. Then you can get a shower while we put your stuff through the washer-drier."

"Thanks. Who the fuck ever you are. I owe you."

Within a very few seconds, he was snoring quietly.

Thank you, Horse. This is great. Your half-dead henchman snoring away on my sofa, and you boxed in by Tug's boys down at the yard. Absolutely pissing marvellous.

He poured himself a scotch and reviewed his options. They seemed limited.

Stella would surely not welcome the presence of a badly beaten gangster over at the Warehouse. The Art Shop basement was a possibility, but that would only invite questions from Fat George and Leggy. He decided to keep Paul at his place and under wraps until he could take him safely to Horse's gated mansion up in the Money. So, for now, he was stuck with the problem.

He called Horse.

"How's it going? They still there?"

"Still here. Haven't even shown themselves. Paul?"

"A bit of a mess. Safe, though. He's at mine, resting. So what's the plan?"

"Best I can do is wait it out. I have the dogs. I'm tooled up, and I have food in my fridge. I'm good for as long as it takes. I doubt they'll risk trying to get in."

"Maybe they'll decide enough is enough and go home soon. They must have more productive things to do than sit outside your yard."

"You'd think so. Is Paul okay?"

"I'd say 'okay' was pushing it, but he'll recover. He's had some pretty rough treatment by the look of it."

It was mid-morning of the next day when Horse dropped by to collect Paul.

"They sat out there until the early hours. Two of them, I think. I watched them climbing out for a pee against my fence. They even had a takeaway delivered. And then just drove off. I reckon they'd decided I'd got the message."

Paul was sitting at the kitchen table eating breakfast, wearing his newly laundered but unironed clothes and a pair of Jack's socks.

"You're looking a little beat up, there, Paulie. Like literally. You good to go or what?"

"I'm fine," he said. "Jack here makes a lovely nurse. Even cleaned up all my stuff."

Horse placed a bag on the table.

"Shoes and socks. Jack told me you had none. If you're sure you don't need the vet, I'm taking you back to my place."

"I'm pretty much A1. It only really hurts when I laugh."

"So what do you think went wrong on the Tug front?" asked Jack. "I'm not sure what to make of all this."

"I don't think anything went wrong as such. It looks as though Tug was just playing us. They're anxious to make it clear who they think should be running things from here on in."

"We'll have to hope that as long as Tug thinks you're out of it and that I'm cooperating, he's going to leave you alone from now on."

*

When he got back to the Art Shop, he found Hamish already there, sitting at the desk in the office going through some documents on his laptop.

"Nice of you to drop by. I was wondering when you'd show up for work."

"I've been otherwise occupied. Horse and I have had a problem to deal with. And I couldn't rely on you to sort things, could I? Since you hardly ever bother to show up these days."

"I thought I'd made it clear that I expect you to be keeping an eye on things here? You're supposed to be sorting some help for the boys. And what was so much of a problem that Horse couldn't fix it himself?"

Maybe now's the time to put the boy straight?

He said nothing. He took a look back out into the gallery where he'd passed Leggy on his way in, busy stacking canvases. Leggy was still busy.

He closed the office door, walked over to the open trapdoor leading down into the basement and peered down the staircase. The lights were on, but there was no sign of Fat George. If Fat George was on the premises, then he must be working in the powder room. It was a good opportunity to clear the air.

He sat down on the chair on the opposite side of the desk to Hamish and cleared his throat. The throat clearing was meant to attract Hamish's attention, but he didn't even look up from his laptop.

He reached across and snapped the laptop shut.

Hamish looked up suddenly, startled.

"We need to talk."

"Okay. I'm all ears. What's up?"

"You tell me, Hamish. You tell me why I always have the feeling that I'm not being kept fully in the loop. And why it's beginning to feel like Freddy Davidson is more involved in the decision-making around here than I am?"

"I'd been meaning to speak to you about all that. Freddy wants us to cut him in on the drugs side. Full partners."

"And you told him what?"

"That it seemed only reasonable, and I'd think about it. The Davidsons already handle all the cash. Junior's getting well involved in the powder room side. And now Freddy's doing a lot to build up some social credit for the Art Shop."

"And you were going to consult me about all this when?"

"I'm telling you now, aren't I? Junior's on the payroll. Freddy's an equal partner. Just like you. Just like me."

"I'm fine about Freddy being brought on board. I was going to suggest it myself. But let's be clear about something, Hamish. We need to reach an agreement about who does what around here. You don't get to tell me what to do. All right?"

Hamish's startled expression vanished as quickly as it had appeared, and he now looked across the desk at Jack with what might have been thinly disguised contempt.

"Watch yourself, Jack," he said. Then he grinned. "You should realise that you were never anything more than a foot soldier. You're never going to be a player, and without me watching out for you, you'll go straight back to being the no-mark you were when we first met."

"Whatever I was back then, I'm not that now. I've been running everything around here and carrying you for weeks. I'm the one who's been taking care of business while you've been off swanning about fuck knows where. Doing fuck knows what."

Any response from Hamish was pre-empted by the creaking of the basement staircase as Fat George emerged, pushing open the trapdoor.

"Coffee, anyone? I'm parched."

By the time Fat George had made four coffees and gone out into the gallery with one each for himself and Leggy, the confrontation between Jack and Hamish, which had seemed on the brink of flaring into a blazing row, had died down to become no more than a smouldering ember.

"So," asked Hamish, "what was the problem? Serious?"

"Yeah, I'd say it was. Someone muscling in and trying to take over our business is serious, right?"

"First I've heard of it."

"It's that bunch of tossers from Glasgow again. The ones that John D got himself involved with. Remember that? You passed the guy on to me when things started to look dangerous."

"Tug? We gave him what he wanted, didn't we?"

"Yes, we did. Turns out that wasn't the best thing to do. Now he wants more."

"Like?"

"Like, basically, he thinks we should be working for him. Exclusively."

"And he's been acting up?"

"Just a little. He's putting a lot of pressure on Horse. Lifted his last delivery right out of the drop and kidnapped his man, Paul, to boot."

"Not good, then."

"He's given Paul back, a bit the worse for wear. But no sign of the stuff. So now he's trying to pressure Horse himself."

"Why didn't you tell me about all this? We could have dealt with it."

"I am telling you about it. And anyway, you'd disappeared again, like you do. So I'm telling you now that if you have any bright ideas to contribute, I'm all ears."

Hamish's look of contempt made a fleeting re-appearance before being replaced by one of concern.

"We need to deal with this at source. Just like we did with Craig."

"I couldn't give you an argument there, buddy. Let me know when you can spare the time."

"For what? We don't even know where to find the twat."

"Yes, we do. Horse has his address."

14

They drove in over the Clyde in the late afternoon of the following day and found the city centre hotel they'd booked. After checking in, they got themselves a quiet corner in the hotel's largely empty dining room to eat an early dinner.

"Okay. If we can keep our voices down, no one is likely to overhear us," said Jack, fingering the drinks menu. "And, as we're in Scotland, it might be fitting to stick with the scotch. There's a pleasant-sounding single malt here if anyone's interested."

"Can't you think of anything other than booze?" asked Horse. "We're on an important mission here. Serious stuff."

"Certainly I can. It's just that sometimes I need to have a drink in my hand to help me do it. Don't worry, I'll keep it well within limits."

Once they had ordered their meal and Jack was holding a large scotch, they began to organise their thoughts for the night ahead.

"Okay then," said Hamish. "We're agreed that we do this tonight?"

"I think what we decided on the drive up was that we reconnoitre the address we got from Clive Slaughter and assess exactly what's possible," said Jack. "We have the option of leaving the hit itself for a day or so if need be."

Good God, I'm actually talking about carrying out another hit on someone. Maybe just one more whisky.

*

The satnav took them on an easy ride of a few miles out to the road they were looking for in Bearsden. An avenue of substantial properties in the heart of another leafy suburb. They had to cruise up and down a couple of times to track down Tug's house, a large pre-war detached at the end of a gravel drive behind high, iron gates.

It was getting late and already dark, and there were lights showing in several rooms. The grounds were well-lit by security lighting at the front and sides. Only the rear was in darkness.

"Best not make a show of ourselves," said Horse. "We're a bit obvious, sitting here like this."

He drove around the corner and parked up under a clump of beech trees. "This'll do."

"Now what?" asked Jack. "This was your idea, Hamie, old boy. What next?"

"We scout the place out. There's nobody about, and most of the good people hereabouts will either be tucked up in their beds or quietly getting pissed in front of their tv."

"So we're going to creep up through the shrubbery like James Bond and peer in at the windows? That kind of thing?"

"Exactly. We find Tug and teach him some manners."

"And then we're aiming to get ourselves out of there. Rapido. Yeah?"

"Sort of."

"What does that mean? Sort of."

"Only that once we've gone to all the bother of getting ourselves safely in there, we'll be keeping our eyes peeled. See what comes up. We make our point as forcefully as we can."

Horse was in the driver's seat with Jack on the passenger side. Hamish, sitting alone in the back, pulled two black ski masks and two baseball bats out of a large bag. He handed Jack one of the bats.

"And me?" asked Horse. "What do I do?"

"Like they do in the cop shows on tv. You stay here in the car, ready to speed us away at the first hint of trouble."

Jack and Hamish climbed out of the car and moved in amongst the trees next to the grounds of Tug's house. Hamish handed Jack his mask and quickly pulled on his own.

"I'm not sure I can wear this."

"What? Doesn't it go with your outfit? What the fuck are you talking about?"

"I have an issue with some fabrics. Wool isn't good. It can make my skin itch, and then I get a rash. It can be quite bad sometimes."

"How many whiskies did you manage to neck back at the hotel? This is no time for jokes. Put the fucking thing on, right? It's acrylic. Look at the label."

Carrying a baseball bat each, they climbed easily enough over the perimeter wall. They moved quickly through the shadow of the trees, skirting around the edge of the lawn towards the rear of the house.

And if there are dogs? wondered Jack. What then? He felt for the Makarov, sitting snugly in his shoulder holster. He knew Hamish had the Ruger. Silencers would have been a good idea. Too late now.

In the event, they found no guard dogs in their way as they emerged from a stand of ancient rhododendrons close to a small, paved yard. Judging by the row of bins and the extractor fan set into the wall, they were standing outside the kitchen.

Hamish ducked below the sightline of the unlit window as he moved quietly across the yard to the doorway. He tried the door. It was locked. He turned toward Jack and shook his head. Then he pointed to the roof of the single-storey extension running out along the side of the yard. It was a flat roof, and there was a window directly above it. It would be easy to reach.

Hamish held one of the bins steady and crouched down, allowing Jack to clamber over him and onto the bin with a minimum of noise. It was quite an effort for Jack to haul himself up onto the roof, but once there, he was able to reach down to help the younger, fitter Hamish balance himself on the bin. In less than a minute, they were both crouching on the roof of the extension, examining the window. It was an old-style sash. It looked promising. But, like the door, it was locked.

He watched as Hamish put his finger to his lips, took a long-bladed knife from inside his jacket and went to work on the window lock.

Checking quickly around, he noticed a small skylight behind them. He took hold of Hamish's arm and pointed toward it. It seemed to be open slightly.

He moved over to the skylight, slid his hand into the gap, found the latch and freed it. A simple matter then to pull the thing open wide and lie it flat on the roof.

It was easy to hang down through the opening and drop onto the floor. They each made a dull thud on landing, but judging by the dark and empty silence of the place, no one would be close enough to hear.

They pulled back the bolt on the yard door, freeing up their escape route in case they needed to leave in a hurry, before moving through the spacious kitchen toward the main body of the house. The door into the area beyond was closed, and they opened it cautiously into a darkened hallway. Edging slowly forwards, feeling their way in the dark, they heard the click of a switch behind them as the place was flooded with light.

"Welcome, gentlemen, to my humble abode." The words came from a heavily built man sitting in a padded armchair at the far end of the hall.

"I'm Tug, as I'm sure you're aware. Me and my friends here have been expecting you." He chuckled. He was flanked by two men wearing business suits and serious expressions. Jack recognised one of the men from the incident in the Warehouse car park. Scarface.

"I'm so glad you felt able to visit. Saves us a tedious drive down the M6 to fetch you."

He paused and stared silently for a few long seconds at the two masked intruders.

"Please, tell me I've got this right." He looked at Jack. "You there, in the crumpled suit, you'll be Jack Charnley. And you, the other masked superhero, you would be Hamish Beard. Am I right? Tell me I'm right."

The pair stood stock-still, saying nothing.

"Tongue-tied, are we? Well, not to worry. I expect my wee laddies here will be able to help you with that. Not that I need you to say too much. Just say yes to my generous offer to bring you into our little family, and all will be well. After you've been punished, obviously. Discipline is so important, ye ken?"

Tug's two flankers moved toward them, and from behind was the sound of more movement.

"Time we fucked off, then," said Jack. "Hamish!" he shouted. "Let's go!"

He whirled around, his bat raised, and saw a short, broad, muscular individual coming calmly towards him. The man was holding a roll of gaffer tape in his left hand. In his right fist was a shining metal knuckle duster.

No time to think about this. Go for it!

He flung his baseball bat at the man's face with all the force he could muster and then dodged to his right. On his left, Hamish ducked down to avoid the oncoming metallic fist and took a swing at their assailant's right knee. It was enough. There was a loud crack as the man went down. They fled back the way they had come, with two heavies in pursuit, to find yet another heavy blocking their exit. The man lunged at Jack and managed to grab his arm as he tried to push him away.

Another loud crack sent the thug reeling aside as Hamish's bat connected with his skull. Then they were out through the kitchen door and running, before their pursuers could reach them.

They were across the yard and all but over the lawn, heading for the trees, when they heard the dogs coming up behind them. They were growling as they ran, getting closer with each second.

Jack was turning and fumbling for the Makarov when he stumbled and fell onto his knees on the lawn. He saw the outline of the dogs, Dobermans, as he tried again to reach his gun. He knew he didn't have time. No time to pull and fire his weapon. No time to get to his feet and run. Nevertheless, he tried to retrieve the Makarov. It was his only hope.

The first dog was onto him just as he freed his weapon from its holster. As it lunged, he instinctively blocked the snarling animal with his right arm. The Doberman locked its jaws onto his forearm and held on, making it impossible for him to fire at anything but grass. Within seconds, he knew, the other Doberman would be on him too, and it would be game over. Then, somewhere over to his right, he registered the flash and crack of a gunshot. And then again, as the dog collapsed into a whimpering heap.

He managed to raise his gun and fire just as the second Doberman reached him. The animal simply dropped in its tracks.

He wasted no time in resuming his sprint toward the trees as he heard shouts and the metallic clatter of silencer-suppressed gunfire coming from behind. But he knew he would present a poor target against the darkened tree line, and Tug's men would no longer be running in pursuit. They would be taking cover or crouching down to protect themselves.

Crashing carelessly through undergrowth and low-hanging branches, he reached the wall and vaulted over it without a pause. He saw the car, a little farther along, its engine running, and heard Hamish calling him, telling him to hurry the fuck up.

The passenger door was open, waiting, and then the car was accelerating away as he collapsed into his seat and jerked the door closed. He was sweating heavily, his breath coming in deep gasps. For a minute or so, he was afraid that having escaped the dogs and the gunfire, he was about to succumb to a heart attack.

Horse accelerated the Porsche through the network of roads leading out of the area and then slowed to avoid attracting attention.

"Thanks, Hamie. I'd have been a goner back there if not for you."

"Couldn't let them get you, could I? They'd have had another hostage. Probably mailed you back to us piece by piece. And you'd have told them everything they needed to know, too. Anybody would."

It was late, and they were driving along dark and largely deserted roads.

"So," began Horse, "where are we going. The hotel?"

"Not such a good idea," said Jack. "We're on their territory, and they might well find us there before too long. We should accept that we fucked up and head for home. Rapido."

"Did we leave anything in the rooms? Anything important?" asked Hamish. "Anything we need to go to the hotel for?"

"Just a bit of laundry, I think. Best we get back down the motorway."

"I'm not sure I'd call this a total fuckup," said Horse. "We've let them know that we're capable of fighting back. They'll have to take that into account, right?"

"We ran," said Hamish. "That's never a good look, is it? I mean, what kind of impression do you think that's going to make?"

"We killed two of their dogs in the process," said Jack. "Not much in the great scheme of things, but it should count for something."

"Like you said," said Hamish, "it's not much. How's the arm?"

"Well, since you ask, the pain's beginning to kick in. Maybe we can stop and get some painkillers and something to clean up the wound. With any luck, I can avoid a visit to the doc and bypass any awkward questions. I think my sleeve got the worst of it."

Back in the city centre, they found an all-night pharmacy, and Horse went in to get the pills, antiseptic and dressings needed to deal with Jack's wounds. The woman behind the grill gave him a questioning look.

"It's for me," he joked. "When the missus has finished with me. I'm going to be very late getting home."

The woman only glowered in response as she pushed his change through the narrow slit in her fortifications.

They pulled up again at a large, brightly lit supermarket car park to allow Jack to take off his badly torn jacket and clean and dress his dog bites.

Horse climbed out for a smoke and to stretch his legs.

"What do you reckon Tug's neighbours will have made of all the gunfire tonight?" asked Hamish. "Think he'll be getting a visit from the cops?"

"Well, there wasn't really that much shooting. Maybe fewer than a dozen shots in quick succession. I'm guessing they don't have a great many shoot-outs up in Bearsden. They'll put it down to some late-night fireworks or something like that."

"And what do you imagine Tug'll be thinking about our little incursion?"

"I'd guess he'll be pretty pissed at the way his guys botched it. Probably, he'll be making things unpleasant for them for a while."

"But about us, I mean. What do you reckon he'll be thinking about us now?"

"Well, he's going to be even more pissed off with us, isn't he? What with us spoiling his little surprise. After all the trouble he'd obviously gone to. Most likely, he'll want to do a revenge trip down to our patch."

"So. Not quite the result we wanted."

Horse got into the driving seat and turned on the ignition. "Home then," he said. "With all speed."

"Maybe not," said Hamish. "How's the arm, Jack?"

"Okay, I suppose. Sore but functional."

"Well, then. I'm thinking that the last thing our friend Tug will be expecting tonight is any further trouble from us. I say we go back there and make it clear to him that he's not dealing with a bunch of quitters."

Silence. Then, "You're joking, yeah?" asked Horse. "Aren't you?"

They were cautious enough on their second trip to Tug's place to park farther away from the property. Just in case. Once again, Horse remained in the car while Jack and Hamish climbed over the wall and moved in amongst the trees. The area immediately surrounding the house was floodlit. Whether he was expecting a return visit or not, Tug was taking sensible precautions.

They made their way around the edge of the trees, wearing their ski masks and staying in the shadows. Rounding the side of the house, coming from the back, they found themselves opposite a large, well-lit window. The blinds were drawn, but from time to time, it was possible to make out the shapes of the people moving about inside.

No doubt Tug and his lieutenants carrying out a postmortem on tonight's cock-up. Good.

It would do. It would be enough to let their opponents know that they weren't cowed by tonight's experience. That they weren't interested in admitting defeat. A few rounds fired quickly at the window, and they could be off and on their way home. There were no dogs around. Most probably, thought Jack, they had disposed of the only canine residents on their previous visit. Sad, really. He liked dogs. But mainly little, friendly types like Keith. Maybe not huge Dobermans intent on tearing him to pieces.

They took up positions, side by side, on the edge of the trees and took aim. It was a large target, and from this range there was no way they were going to miss. He glanced at Hamish briefly to make sure he was ready.

"Now," he grunted.

They fired off a few rounds apiece as the glass of the well-lit window shattered and collapsed into the room, leaving the blind still in position and newly decorated with grey-rimmed bullet holes. It might not be long before Tug and his men came charging out with their weapons drawn to chase them down. Or maybe, thought Jack, they would be learning to treat them with more respect and be a little more cautious.

Either way, they had no intention of hanging around to find out.

They reached the Porsche unchallenged, and Horse accelerated the car out of the area as fast as he dared. When they felt they had covered enough distance, they slowed and made their way back towards the Clyde.

In well under four hours, they were back in the Baltic. The adrenaline rush brought on by the night's excitement had gone even before they'd reached the M6. Too tired to sit down to a fry-up in one of the early cafes off Jamaica Street, they dropped Hamish at the Warehouse before Horse and Jack headed north along the coast.

"I could drop you at your semi unless you think you'll feel safer behind my gates for a while?" said Horse, as he swung the Porsche off the by-pass and onto the Point. "I have room. You'd be welcome."

"Well, it's nice to know you care, buddy," said Jack, grinning. "But I'll risk it at mine. I could use a few hours of peace and quiet before I head back into town, but I've got some ammo for the Makarov stashed in my loft, and I need to get some over to the Warehouse and the Art Shop, just in case."

15

"It's as if Tug was ready and waiting for us," said Hamish, "when we went up there to teach him a lesson. So how did that happen?"

They were down in the basement at the Art Shop an hour after closing, reviewing the stock levels and making sure everything was in order. Jack was checking through newly made-up batches of coke awaiting delivery.

"I've been asking myself the same question. They had their security lights turned off at the back of the house and the dogs out of the way. They were probably watching us on their cctv. I spotted the cameras on our return visit."

"Like they wanted us in there, with them ready to pounce. We walked right into it."

He wrote a figure on the pad he had in front of him and switched off the scales he'd been using to check the batch weights.

"So," Hamish went on, "how the feck did they know we were coming? Someone must have tipped the buggers off, yeah?"

"Good a theory as any. Who would you put your money on?"

"Not likely to be you or me, is it? Since we were the ones they were using for target practice. So, working outwards from there, how about Horse?"

He ushered Hamish out of the powder room, locked the door and led the way up the staircase into the office.

"Hugely unlikely. Horse was safe enough, sitting it out in his car like he was. But someone needed to be ready to drive, and he had a lot to lose if Tug had managed to muscle his way in."

Jack lowered the trapdoor into position and locked it. Then he dragged the heavily upholstered armchair over it, its castors squealing, and sat down. He motioned towards a bottle of scotch, as yet unopened, standing beside Hamish on the desk. It was a relief to have the old Hamish back on board. The boy's strangeness and his unexplained absences seemed to come and go. But, whatever else, it was some time since he had hit the booze in any significant way, so why not this evening? And Hamish could make an excellent drinking companion when he was in the mood.

"Correct me if I'm wrong, but as far as we're aware, wasn't Clive Slaughter the only other one who might have known? According to Horse, it was the good DI who got hold of Tug's address for us."

Hamish took a couple of glasses out of the desk drawer and poured them each a large measure.

"We already know that Slaughter is bent," he said, handing Jack his drink. "Maybe he sees Tug as just another revenue stream to plug into his pension fund."

Jack sipped gratefully at his scotch and gave Hamish a quizzical look. "But we've no proof either way, have we?"

"None at all. And seeing that that's the case, I suggest we proceed on the balance of probabilities. We make Slaughter our prime suspect. Our only suspect. Fitting, really. Him being a plod and all."

"I'll drink to that," said Jack. "Let's have a big one. Then we can lock up and drink our way into town and back to the Warehouse. It's been a while."

He regained consciousness early the following morning, lying on the couch in the apartment. Apart from his shoes and jacket, which were in a heap on the floor, he was fully dressed.

Again? I did this again? God, I'm thirsty.

He made it to the kitchen and found they were out of bottled water. He could bring some up from the bar later, but for now, he glugged down a couple of cupfuls from the tap. He wasn't keen on tap water, what with all the additives and lead that might be in there.

But the water didn't help. His thirst was still raging, and he had the beginnings of a headache. What was it that made him drink like he did? It was just that sometimes, and sometimes frequently, it seemed so necessary.

There was no sign of Hamish. Most likely, he'd managed to get all the way to his bedroom and wouldn't surface until noon.

He managed a shower and a shave and the other thing. Then he found himself some fresh clothes and sat down at the kitchen table to a second coffee.

His phone rang.

Stella.

"You're back on your feet then, are you? The condition you were in last night, I'm surprised, frankly. The pair of you, staggering in, singing and out of your heads. You disappoint me."

"Where are you?"

"Downstairs in the kitchen behind the bar, trying to source some lemons. Gordon is here. He wants to talk to you."

"Why?"

"No idea. Are you in a fit state? I'll send him up."

So I can't get a little bit pissed when I feel like it? And we aren't even married.

There was a light knock at the door, and Gordon came in. He strode over to where Jack was sitting.

"Nice to see you again, Jack," he said, giving him a beaming smile. "That coffee smells good."

"It's there on the worktop, Gordon. If you want to get yourself a cup. You can pour me a fresh one while you're at it."

This was puzzling. Gordon was an art critic with connections in the city and, as such, was to be carefully cultivated. But if he had come barging in uninvited like this, being so smilingly friendly, just to score more coke for himself and his posh friends...

"I'm not exactly feeling at my best right now, buddy. And I can't spare you any more coke. Not now or ever. That was a one-off. A favour. You need to understand that."

"Don't worry," he said, sitting down opposite Jack. "Here's your coffee. I'm not looking to score."

"Then, please pardon my French, but what the fuck do you want? As I said, I'm not feeling particularly great, and I have things to attend to."

"I understand. But this is important. I was hoping for a friendly discussion about a person of mutual interest. And to offer you some help."

"What person of mutual interest? And why would I need help? Unless you're talking about more publicity for the Art Shop."

Gordon reached across the table and pulled the sugar bowl towards him.

"Do you take sugar?" He scooped two heaped spoonfuls into his cup and stirred it in slowly.

"No, I don't. And I don't understand why anybody would want to ruin the taste of a perfectly fine beverage by adding sugar to it. Can we please get to the point of this chat? Is there a point?"

"I'm looking for information about a mutual acquaintance. Clive Slaughter."

"And you're interested in Slaughter because?"

"I'm interested in his growing network of connections with drug dealing and serious organised crime."

Suddenly, he understood the true meaning of the term 'grim foreboding'. He was flooded with it.

"You're a cop?"

"No, I'm not a cop. And I'm not a gangster. You can relax. Slightly, anyway. I'm simply a journalist."

"I know that. You write stuff about art. Stuff that nobody reads. No offence."

Gordon took a swig of his coffee, got up and strode across to the window. He leaned on the low windowsill and looked out over the yard at the rear of the nightclub.

"For reasons which now entirely escape me, when I was young I did a BA in Art History. And I'd always fancied becoming a writer one day. Hence the art critic."

"This is fascinating stuff. Truly, it is. But, like I told you, I'm busy today."

Gordon ignored Jack's sarcasm and continued. "But writing about art doesn't really do it for me, as it turns out. As you yourself don't hesitate to point out, it seems marginal at best, and I want to do something meaningful. Something that would impact on the world around me."

"So?"

"So I've been looking for a project I could work on to help me raise my game. And I've found one."

"You've decided to write about serious crime."

"Exactly. I'm perfectly placed. Connections to the media, connections across society in the city and beyond. And at the same time, I'm regarded as being someone of little real consequence. No one gives much consideration to their local art critic. Apart from artists, of course. So I'm practically invisible."

Now what? Jack wondered. How much did Gordon know? How much was it safe for him to say? Just let the man talk. He would get to the point of all this eventually.

"So? I'm listening."

"Drugs seemed to be the obvious way to go. And your friend, Hamish, provided me with an easy intro. He got pretty high at your opening night bash. And then he got drunk to boot. And we got friendly and had a nice chat."

He sat down again.

"He wanted some good publicity for your new project, and I let him know that, in return, I needed to score. And score heavily enough to satisfy a group of my socially important friends."

"And that was when the idiot put you onto me."

"Exactly. All at once, I had a connection to what appeared to be some fairly significant local drug dealers. So I took an interest. To me, it was obvious, pretty quickly, that your Art Shop wasn't enough of a business to keep you and Hamish and your boys afloat."

"Really?"

"At least, not in the style to which I assumed you were aiming to become accustomed, as they say. So, I'm thinking it's some kind of front, yeah?"

Can't argue with that. This guy would know.

"You're the one telling this story. Not me. And just to be clear, we fixed you up with some stuff as a favour. Out of our own personal stash."

"Right. Anyway, I get around, and I keep my eyes open, and next thing I notice is you and your good lady hobnobbing with the gentry up in the Money."

"We went to a party. If that's what you mean. Lots of folk do. I don't think that marks a person out as some kind of serious criminal, does it? Which is what I imagine you're leading up to."

"But it wasn't just any old party, was it, Jack? Some of the people there were pretty dubious types. And what exactly, so I asked myself, would you and young Hamish suddenly find you had in common with a guy who rents out shipping containers from a yard down at the docks?"

"He's an acquaintance. Is acquaintanceship morally questionable as well now?"

"An acquaintance with connections to shipping. A very rich acquaintance. And one whose party guests were casually snorting coke like it was just so normal."

"And lots of folk sniff a bit of coke at socials. It's what they do nowadays, in case you hadn't noticed."

"But this particular social had a senior copper mingling openly with the other guests. And nobody so much as flinched. Odd.

"So I'm thinking about all this, trying not to jump to the wrong conclusions, when I call in at the Art Shop on spec one afternoon and find out from young Leggy that you and Hamish are off on an overnight to Glasgow in Horse's Porsche. Glasgow? Why Glasgow?"

"What can I tell you, Gordon? Sometimes a person needs a break. Work hard, play hard. Right?"

"In Glasgow? Okay, if you were wanting to look at the art at Kelvingrove or watch the footy at the Ibrox, but I seriously doubt either of those was the reason for your visit."

Jack finished his coffee. He was finding the conversation difficult to manage. He thought maybe he should go for broke.

"This is all totally fascinating. Not. Could you get to the point a bit more rapido? Only I'm struggling to avoid breaking wind here, big style. And after the night I've just had..."

Gordon retreated to his place at the window and turned to face Jack.

"I think I'll be safe enough over here. And the point is this. I know you lot are up to something seriously dodgy. You can either put me in the loop to help my project, and I'll do my best to keep the three of you out of anything I might produce, or you can continue to act dumb. If you do, I'll just carry on digging until I find something. And find something I will. Be sure of it."

He stared across at Gordon, saying nothing, willing him to continue.

"The point is, I want a bigger story than simple drug dealing. I want bent coppers on the take. And I want Slaughter, for starters."

*

"But the bastard's supposed to be an art critic, for fuck's sake!"

Horse was angry. He had been angry since the first minute Jack had begun to tell him and Hamish about Gordon. It was the sort of reaction he had expected. Who wouldn't be upset to find out that some nosey, smart-arsed journalist knew about your exceedingly illegal revenue stream? And not only knew about it but was quite likely to write about it unless something was done to prevent him.

But Hamish had taken the news much more calmly.

"So, what does he want? Must be something, or why else would he have told you this?"

"It seems he's more interested in investigating and writing about corrupt policemen than common-or-garden drug barons like ourselves. He wants us to help him with that."

"How?"

"He's got Slaughter in his sights, for starters. His connection with Horse was enough to raise his suspicions."

"So we feed him info about Clive, and he leaves us out of it?"

"He seems to be suggesting something along those lines. He tried to sell me a line about journalists protecting their sources. That kind of thing."

"This is a fucking nightmare," said Horse. "If the idiot starts blabbing about Clive Slaughter, then there's no way we can manage to stay in the clear. There'll be other journos and cops and politicians all over it."

"So what do we do?" asked Jack. He was looking at Hamish. "Any ideas?"

They were in the trailer in Horse's yard. An inconspicuous place to meet.

"The first thing is not to panic," said Hamish with a glance at Horse. "Gordon Donnelley is obviously not the brightest specimen on two legs. He can be handled."

"How?"

"There are quite a few ways we might do it. He's already lost the game by giving his position away. He's given it away for nothing. Just relax. Both of you. Let me think about it for a bit. You'll see."

The following lunchtime, they were back in Horse's trailer, sitting around the table over the three take-away pizzas that Hamish had taken the trouble to bring.

"Okay, guys. You sit there nicely and eat your lunch, and I will explain how we can deal with our Gordon problem."

"Before you start," said Jack, "I'd like to make it clear that shooting the idiot in the head would not be my preference."

"There's absolutely no need for anything so extreme," said Hamish between mouthfuls. "That would be amateurish, and we're no longer in any position to behave like amateurs. This is a great pizza, by the way. You can get me this one when it's your turn. I love anchovies."

"So, anchovies, but no shooting. That's good. I like anchovies, too. So what do we do?"

"Three options spring to mind. One way would be to involve Slaughter himself. We could let him know what Gordon was planning and leave it to him. We might choose to help him out with a sizeable bag of coke to plant on our favourite journalist as evidence."

"Sounds promising," said Horse. "I like the sound of it."

"Except," said Hamish, "that it involves Slaughter as a third party and removes control of events from our hands. And if it goes wrong, and Gordon ends up being charged, anything could come out."

"And your second option?" asked Jack.

"The second option is much simpler, much more direct, and keeps the entire thing under our control."

There was a pause while Hamish dealt with a particularly chewy mouthful of deep-pan pizza.

"I have to say, I prefer a thin pizza base myself," he said. "You know, crispy."

"Do you think you could cut the dicking about and just get on with it?" asked Jack. "We need to get this sorted."

"Okay. So, keep your hair on. The second option we have is to threaten to kill him if he doesn't keep quiet and forget all about writing about anything other than art."

"That's no good," said Horse. "He might go to the cops for protection and call our bluff. And it'd put us right in the frame."

"Which is why," said Hamish, grinning, "I'm suggesting we go straight for the jugular. He has a wife and a young daughter, doesn't he?"

"Yes," said Horse. "His wife's called Janet. And the daughter's Mia. Nice little girl. Six or seven years old, I think."

"There you are, then," said Hamish. "We tell Gordon that unless he forgets about this whole business, we fix it so that if anything happens to us or to Clive, Janet and young Mia get kidnapped by someone not very pleasant and sold on."

The others fell silent at once.

"We make it clear that hiding them away or getting protection or whatever just won't do it. Our people will simply wait it out. All year if need be. Who'd take the chance? What d'you think? Good or what?"

"Making threats against someone's family?" asked Jack. "Is that really who we are now?"

"Well, we don't have to carry the threat out, do we? It's a threat. That's all it is."

"I think it's a good idea," said Horse. "And I think we should take steps to make sure he takes us seriously."

"Don't you feel making threats against Gordon's family is serious enough?"

Horse ignored Jack's question. "Gordon lives up in the Money, like me. I know which school Mia goes to. I'm wondering if, maybe, a couple of photos of the girl being collected by her mum at home time might help."

"You mean we send them to Gordon?"

"Right. We print them off and push them through his door. Scary, yeah?"

Jack didn't like what he was hearing. "This sounds way over the top to me. Couldn't we just threaten the man himself and hope for the same result?"

"Well, we could, of course," said Hamish. "But, for the reasons already outlined, that would have drawbacks. This is more likely to put the wind up our art critic friend and panic him into backing down."

"And if he chooses to go to the cops instead?"

"He won't. He isn't going to risk his family's welfare for a story, however good. There'll be other stories. Arty ones. And anyway, if we don't do something to stop him, he'll spill the beans at some point. We can't risk that."

"So that's settled," said Horse. "People know me up there, so I don't want to be the one hanging around outside the school in my Porsche."

He looked across at Jack.

"You've got expertise in this area, Jack, being an ex-snoop. So it should be you, I think. Telephoto lens and all that. You can drive us both up there, and I'll point them out to you. Easy peasy."

Jack had to admit the logic of what was being proposed, even though the idea disturbed him. But after all, it was simply photographs and a threat delivered to Gordon. He felt obliged to concede.

"All right," he said, pushing away his half-eaten pizza. "I'll go along with it, just this once. But try to remember next time, I don't like my olives black."

16

Life was all a question of balance, wasn't it? He was lying on his sofa after lunch, turning over a thought or two. It didn't feel as though he had the balance quite right. Money was piling up in his offshore account while his needs, when he considered the matter, were pretty small compared with some. His debts were gone. He had a new car. He had even bought himself a new suit - although he felt more at home in his old, crumpled one.

Likewise, his nineteen-sixties semi, here on an estate with a couple of hundred almost identical properties, felt like home. He liked the bare, painted floorboards and the sparse, elderly furnishings.

So why not give up his gangster lifestyle and do something a little less fraught, a little less dangerous?

A good question. But he knew he wasn't going to change. This was the first time since Wendy had died, and his old life had been snatched away in mid-flight, and he had banked and turned to begin that long, slow descent to nowhere that he'd had any sense of purpose. What did it matter that much of his new way of living was criminal? Laws, after all, came and went. Commodities that were illegal today might well be legalised and go on sale at the local pharmacy tomorrow.

And, in any case, it wasn't as though he forced anyone to take the stuff he helped to supply. It was all down to personal choice. Just as he himself chose to drink. No one forced him to do it. Alcohol and tobacco were highly addictive and potentially damaging substances but perfectly legal for all that. It was all just someone else's rules.

And without his gang membership, all his social interactions would be in danger of vanishing as well. What would he then have in common with Hamish? Or Freddy? Or Horse? Or any of the other people in his life? Nothing. That was what. He had nothing else to contribute. He amounted to nothing more.

There was Stella, of course, but he suspected that she saw him mainly as her tame, in-house handler for the various gangsters and criminal types who might otherwise happen to impinge on her nightclub lifestyle. Give up his gangland expertise, limited as it was, and she might well come to regard him as no more than a drone, a hanger-on in a crumpled blue suit who could soon find himself replaced.

It was better, clearly, to be a somebody on the wrong side of the law than a nobody on the right side of it.

Enough introspection. It'll only drive me to drink.

He got to his feet and belched. Maybe some fresh air would be a good idea. He went through the kitchen and out to his back garden, with a view to inspecting the weeds growing around his gravel patch.

Tooth was prowling by the fence.

"Hello there, Jack. How's things?"

"Oh, you know how it is, Alan. Ploughing on, as always. You?"

"Mustn't grumble. Bit of old age and dry rot."

He grunted something incoherent in response.

"Glad to catch you, actually. Been meaning to ask you about the kittens. They okay? Only the wife's been wondering."

Actually, Alan, their tortured little corpses are under that mound of earth next to the shed there. But I don't think Mrs Tooth would much like to hear about that.

"Oh, they're just fine. Re-homed them with a friend in town. What with me being away so often. Not practical to keep them around here."

"Right. Good. That's good, then."

"Okay. Got to get back to work now. No rest for the wicked and all that. Regards to Marj."

His phone rang. Hamish.

"The photos?"

"I'm doing it now. I'm about to go over to the school with Horse."

"Good. Get them printed off and pushed through Donnelley's letterbox tonight. Don't hang about, Jack. This is urgent."

There was a long road of prim semis at right angles to the playground. A better class of semi up here, he thought, as he fiddled nervously with his camera. The sort of area he and Wendy had once planned to move to. No point in doing anything like that now. No real point in a lot of things.

Photographing school pick-ups wasn't the sort of photography he was used to, and it made him feel uncomfortable. Still, as far as he was aware, he wasn't committing any crime, and with care, no one would even notice.

Horse was sitting next to him in the passenger seat, his collar turned up and a cap pulled down over his brow as the children came out into the schoolyard.

"You were spot-on about the time, Horse."

"Not rocket science, Jack. It happens every day. That's Mia there. The little blonde one in the pink top. And there's her mum, taking her hand now."

He found the address Horse had supplied easily enough. It was after dark when he parked the Qashqai at the end of the road where Mr and Mrs Donnelley lived with their daughter, Mia. It was no gated mansion, simply a small, red-brick Victorian house with a short driveway. There was no one about, and there were no lights visible, so he was reasonably sure no one would have spotted him as he pushed the plain brown envelope through the letterbox.

17

Horse and Jack were listening when Hamish phoned Donnelley the next morning. They were back around the table in the trailer in Horse's yard as Hamish clicked on the speaker on his phone.

He was using a voice changer and a burner phone, just in case.

"Donnelley."

"You got our message?" He sounded a lot like a Donald Duck cartoon.

"Who is this?"

"Someone with your best interests at heart. Your family's too."

"Tell me what you want?"

"Simple. Back off on that drug dealing, police corruption project of yours. That's all. Stick to writing about what you know. Stuff no one gives a shit about. Okay?"

Silence.

"There's a market for nice little girls like your daughter. And your wife even. We have contacts in the trade."

Silence.

"Last chance?"

"Consider me backed off."

"Don't make me have to call you again. Might be bad news next time."

He rang off.

"So that's that," he said, smiling. "He'll be no kind of problem now. Simple really."

"Much more civilised than blowing the idiot's brains out," said Horse. "Better all round if we could deal with all our problems so easily."

"Next on the agenda is our friend DI Slaughter," said Hamish. "So, for the sake of giving the matter some context and perspective, what have you been paying the guy?" He was looking at Horse.

"Just lately, he's become an expensive item. He's into me for a few grand a time."

"For what?"

"For his silence. And doing what he can to keep me and mine off the books. Plus, he gives me the odd bit of info from time to time. There are good reasons for keeping him on the right side of friendly."

"And doing in a plod, even a bent one, isn't an option, is it? The repercussions would escalate way out of control very quickly."

"I vote we keep him on the payroll," said Hamish. "Put the expense against our joint interests as a kind of insurance. Our tame cop. No knowing just when we might need someone like him to make a difficult problem disappear."

"I thought we had him in the frame for letting Tug know we were coming after him," said Jack. "Do we simply let him get away with that?"

"I think we should overlook it," said Hamish. "It's only a suspicion. We've no proof. And even if we had, I can't see what we could usefully do about it. Better we put it on the back burner for now and tread carefully. The time might come when we can play the situation to our advantage."

*

He was at the Art Shop, trying to get his head around why young Leggy's arrangement of the latest batch of paintings on the gallery wall looked so out of kilter. The artworks themselves, by and large, were good. Junior

Davidson had sourced much of it via his old art school contacts. The problem was with the way the pieces had been hung.

"I don't think it would be good to have them all set out in straight lines," said Leggy, standing back, with his left hand cupping his right elbow and the fingers of his right hand holding his chin. "You know what I mean? In a grid type of thing?"

He really didn't feel he had time to spend on this, but the youngster was obviously intent on making an effort to improve the look of the place.

"So, you're thinking, maybe…?"

"A kind of even more random arrangement, you know."

"Random is the way you have it now, is it not?"

"But it doesn't look right, does it? And I'm not sure why."

"Could be how the different sizes are grouped? Or maybe the frames? Or it could just be the lighting. Best thing might be to have a word with Freddy next time he's here."

"I've been meaning to ask you, actually…"

"What?"

"Whether you could give me day release. I'd like to spend a day a week at art classes.

He looked carefully at the youngster standing next to him. Was the boy developing a genuine interest in art?

"Day release?"

"It's where you get the day off to learn a skill. My Dad did it, out of Walton prison one time."

"I believe I know what day release is."

"You still pay me. For the day. That's how it works."

So this is me now, is it? The responsible, drug-dealing employer. Can't hurt, though. Freddy would approve.

"Okay. Find yourself a suitable course, and we'll talk. We've got Junior here most days now. He and FG can cope."

"Great," said Freddy when Jack told him about Leggy's day release idea. "It all helps with the image."

They were sitting in Maggie May's on Bold Street, having a catch-up chat. It wasn't their usual cafe, but Freddy had been keen to explore a few of his old haunts.

"Perhaps you could call in and have a word with him, could you? He needs to talk to someone arty about our gallery wall display."

"Not today I can't. I have to get over to the radio station. I'm giving an interview."

"About?"

"Our campaign against legalising drugs. I've been talking to Hamish, and we both feel it would be great for the image. The Art Shop is going to put up some cash to help fund it. Good idea, don't you think?"

"Why not? We're pretty much becoming a charitable institution these days anyway."

"Meaning?"

He lowered his voice.

"There's already the five thou' you promised we'd offer as a painting prize. And now we're subsidising the career of a senior copper. We're about to cough up to help pay for young Leggy to attend college. So why not pay out to fund your campaign as well?"

Freddy looked surprised.

"What senior copper?"

"Not in here, Freddy. Hamish is supposed to have told you all about it. Talk to him."

"I should have been kept in the loop."

"I'm keeping you in it now, aren't I? You know how it can be with these things. Circumstances change. Situations arise. Decisions have to be taken."

He was enjoying the role reversal, laying it out for Freddy Davidson.

"It's just another business expense. You know how it is. Like I said, talk to Hamish."

They were sitting at a table by the window overlooking the street, busy with shoppers. Davidson stared out at the scene for a while in silence.

"So," he continued, "you were going to tell me about this idea you have. This campaign of yours."

"Not my campaign. An Art Shop campaign. It's perfect. No one's going to legalise recreational drugs anytime soon. Not even cannabis."

"I agree. Seems unlikely. So why are we bothered?"

"Because plenty of people like to talk about doing it. All sorts of folk are putting in their tuppence worth right now. It's become kind of fashionable. We join in the debate and take a firm stand against the idea. More good publicity."

"Okay. I get all that. But the other thing we talked about. You given that any thought?"

"Hamish? I think you're worrying about nothing. I've spoken to him about his plans for the business, and I have to say they seem sound. As long as we can keep it all within reasonable limits."

"But the boy himself? You think *he's* sound?"

"It's true that he can come across as a bit of an oddball at times. Kind of moody. But the guy is what he is. You just need to be careful how you deal with him."

18

Things were going smoothly for once. Except that Hamish had taken to spending most of his days shut up in his room at the Warehouse, where anyone interested enough to stand by the door could sometimes catch the sound of a vigorously conducted, one-sided conversation.

"He's still talking to his dad's ghost in there, isn't he?" Jack had asked. "It's fairly obvious when you take the time to listen. It's not as though it's his girlfriend or anything because we know he doesn't have one."

"A girlfriend would be good, wouldn't it?" asked Stella. "But you're right. It's Claude. I know that for sure because he's told me. And before you ask, yes, it worries me. And, no, I've no idea what to do about it."

Stretched out comfortably on the bed after breakfast, he wondered whether there would be any point in going over to the Art Shop. After all, the Art Shop and the powder room seemed to run well enough without him most days.

His phone rang. Fat George.
"George. S'up?"
"Bad news, Boss."
"Like?"
"Like someone tried to burn the place down. There's a bit of a mess around the front entrance. A few of the paintings are spoiled."
He felt his heart miss a beat.
"And the powder room?"

"Fine. All that's fine. It didn't get going properly. The office is okay, and I've been downstairs with one of the firemen, checking things out. They never went inside the powder room, though; it was locked. You might want to get over here. We've still got the fire brigade messing about. And the cops."

He considered taking Hamish along but decided it would be simpler to leave him be. Walking quickly down Jamaica Street, he passed a fire engine and two police cars going in the opposite direction.

He found Fat George outside on the footpath, waiting. There was a second fire engine and a couple of firefighters loading up their gear. A man in a light grey anorak was taking photographs. Across the dressed stone of the wall, by the doorway, someone had spray-painted the word FREEDOM in white.

"The brigade was here when I arrived this morning. Some passer-by had spotted smoke coming from the edges of the doorframe and called them."

"So, not too much damage."

"Nah. Don't worry. Everything's cool. Fucking arsonist bag o' shite."

"Well, thank Christ no one found the powder room."

He looked across at the firefighters rolling up their fire hose in the road.

"Does anyone want to speak to me, do you think? I mean, police? Fire brigade?"

"I spoke to both lots. The fire bloke's offered to come back and check the place out properly. Sprinklers and whatnot."

"And the police?"

"The cops, for sure. It being arson. I gave them your number. Hope that's okay."

"No problem, buddy. You did well to steer everyone away from the basement. Thank God you did."

Craig? Putting two and two together, fighting fire with fire?

But even as he had the thought, he realised it could just as easily be Tug. And which outfit did Vlad work for? These days, they had a growing number of enemies to choose from.

The Art Shop, like many of the enterprises in the Baltic, was housed in an old-style, converted warehouse. The doors were big, verging on huge. And they were made of wood. One of the doors had a smaller, man-sized door built into it. The larger doors hadn't been opened since they'd finished doing the refurb and conversion work.

The man with the camera was packing his equipment away.

"You police?"

"Yeah."

"All right if we go in? Touch things?"

"Anything inside is okay. But not the outside of the door area. Forensics will be taking a look."

The fire engine was pulling away now as the photographer got into his car.

There was yellow tape across the doorway. Black lettering on the tape said 'crime scene - do not enter'. The door itself was hanging open and badly splintered along the edge, where the firefighters had forced it.

He ducked under the tape with Fat George and went inside where the charred and scorched woodwork made it easy to see where the fire had begun, just below the letterbox. It had worked its way upwards and outwards from there.

The wood was still wet from being hosed down, and three of the paintings by the entrance were water-damaged beyond saving.

"We've been lucky." He remembered how Craig Smith's antique furniture salesroom with the drug lab hidden within it had been burned to the ground after Hamish had planted an incendiary there. And now the thing had almost come full circle, and it was his own operation, cloned from that of the Smiths, which had been set ablaze.

Almost full circle, but only almost. The fire had been stopped in time to prevent the destruction of the business and the exposure of the powder room to the police.

"So who called the brigade?"

"Someone on his way to work who happened to see the smoke. Didn't give a name. Do you know who did this?"

"Let's just say I have a couple of likely candidates in mind," said Jack. "But as far as the authorities are concerned, we should go with the story that fits the slogan on the wall."

"Freedom?"

"Yeah, we can play the idea it was some random, pot-addled hippy taking against the stuff that Freddy's been putting out. The anti-drug thing. Any questions from anybody - you can refer them to me. Have the media been asking?"

"Some reporter got here just before the cops. She took a photo or two and asked a few questions. Like you'd expect. I didn't give her your number."

"Nice one. She can talk to Freddy. At least he'll welcome all the fucking publicity."

*

"Good job we have Slaughter on the payroll."

He was speaking to Hamish and Freddy in the Blue Warehouse bar. It was late afternoon and apart from the three of them, the place was empty. They were sitting around a table on which stood a whisky bottle. Jack was drinking.

"You've spoken to him?" asked Freddy. "Is he going to help?"

"As far as it's possible," said Jack. "It's not his case, but he thinks the guy they've got on it is suggestible enough. He reckons he'll be able to steer the enquiry towards putting the crazy-hippy slant on things."

"I can help with that. I've already talked to the media and told them I believe some left-wing extremists are targeting our anti-drug campaign."

"Maybe you should row back a bit on the politics there, Freddy. You'll be getting the press more interested than they need to be. We don't want the story ending up on the national tv news."

"And maybe," said Hamish, "we should be taking more care of our investment. This was a close shave, and we were lucky. Next time? Who knows?"

Jack poured himself another whisky. He made it a large one. He would sip carefully until the meeting was over.

"We can't afford to relax," he said, "until we've got on top of this. We've got Tug, Craig and this Vlad character on our case. And I'm beginning to wonder if the three of them could be in cahoots somehow."

"Could be," said Freddy. "No way we can be sure, though. Just tell us you've got everything covered over at the Art Shop."

"Should be okay for now. The door might be a tad charred, but it's sound enough, and the bolts still work. Once the cops take their tape away, I'll get a whole new doorway in place. We can use the opportunity to fancy it up a little. Metal doors would be an improvement."

"And the fire risk?" asked Hamish. "Didn't look as though we were too well prepared."

"Sprinkler systems are awkward where you have paintings. So there's gas. Possibly. I'm looking into that, but it'll be expensive. We'd have to make the place airtight for that to work."

"And until then? What if our arsonist friend comes back tonight?"

"We're going to need a full review of our security. In the meantime, I have Fat George sleeping there. At least until the new doors are in place."

"That's it? Our security system?" asked Hamish. "Fat George?"

"He'll want a weapon." He looked at Hamish. "You'd better let him have the Ruger."

"I might need it. Why not give him your Makarov?"

"Because I'm on call. George has instructions to call me at the first sign of trouble. I can be there in no time if I drive."

"If you happen to be sober enough to drive."

"Piss off, Hamish. Since when were you such a pillar of fucking sobriety?"

Freddy had been sitting quietly, just listening. "Maybe you could both be on call. You're both armed. And maybe, since we seem to be getting into some kind of fight right now, we should all be. Can't say I'm happy to be asking this, but can one of you fix me up with something useful?"

"I think I can do that," said Hamish. "And you're right. From now on, it would be good if we all had access to a firearm."

Jack considered taking another sip of scotch, but when he looked, his glass was empty.

After Forensics had finished doing their thing, and the tapes had been removed, and Jack had talked with the DI who was handling the case, he felt free to organise a local firm to design a new front entrance.

"For now, we still have a security problem," he told Hamish. "I've had some people in to check our arrangements, and they think we should consider installing a metal door at the rear and shutters on the windows. By the time that's done, the place is going to be as safe as Fort Knox."

"Sounds good," said Hamish. "And I think we can make it even better, security-wise. We have a loft area above the Art Shop that isn't being used."

"We do. So?"

"We can use it as a kind of unofficial studio apartment. Someone can be there overnight whenever we need a bit of extra protection. Every night if necessary. George can't camp in the office there forever. It's not even sanitary. I found his used underwear in the desk drawer yesterday."

It was two in the morning when Jack's phone growled him awake from beneath his pillow. He was lying in bed beside a gently snoring Stella, so he took his phone and padded through to the lounge. There was a text from Fat George.

```
someone downstairs
```

There was an agreed procedure, and if Fat George was following it, he would now stay quietly up in the loft, where he had been thoughtfully provided with a camp bed and a bucket.

He sent a text in response.

x

It meant that he was on his way. He pulled on his suit and shoes and retrieved the Makarov, in its shoulder holster, from its hiding place in the bedroom drawer. He checked his pocket for his keys and went in to wake Hamish.

"Text from FG. An intruder. Follow me down."

Hamish grunted and began to climb out of bed as Jack hurried downstairs and let himself out into the yard.

"Going somewhere?"

He froze. The voice was Tug's. He turned slowly as Tug stepped out of the shadows, holding a handgun aimed directly at Jack's chest. It was too late to reach for the Makarov.

One of Tug's men grabbed his arms while Tug stepped forward and took Jack's gun from its holster. Then they marched him through the yard gates to the waiting Bentley.

There was no way out. There were two of them. They were armed, and he wasn't. Nobody spoke while they drove the short distance to the Art Shop, where Tug pulled him out of the car in the deserted street and ushered him inside at gunpoint. He felt sick with the fear of what might be about to happen. As they closed the door and pushed him through the gallery and into the office, he could only hope that Hamish would not be far behind. And what about Fat George?

The first thing he saw as he was marched into the room was Fat George taped securely to a chair. His face was bloody, and one eye was closed and swollen.

"Sorry, Boss," he said, through lips badly split and oozing blood.

Jack was lost for words as he was pushed down onto a second chair.

"Nice to meet again, Charnley. Pity you ignore my warnings."

The voice came from behind, and he couldn't immediately see the speaker. But he knew it was Vlad.

"Pity your little cats. They die for no good reason. But this time is different. No cats. Only this fat man. And you."

Tug held Jack's arms against the armrests on the chair while his man, the familiar Scarface, taped them securely into position.

"You're a very foolish person, Charnley." Tug was speaking. "You haven't a clue what you're up against, have you? You and your crew are simply a bunch of amateurs who got lucky. I've tried to play nice, but you refuse to behave."

"Play nice? You tried to burn us down."

"Just a little fire as a warning. Another warning you chose to ignore. That's all. This place is going to be very valuable to us. Why would we want to destroy it? And who do you think called the brigade so very promptly?"

He knew his only hope now lay in Hamish somehow mounting a rescue. But that hope seemed a faint one. To stand a reasonable chance, Hamish would need help. But who could he call on? Horse was over thirty minutes drive away. Freddy was a good deal closer, maybe ten minutes, but Freddy didn't seem to be the type who would be much use in a fight. He might be more of a liability. Junior, just down the road at the Limo Hire, would be Hamish's best option.

Tug was speaking again.

"Look at your friend here, Charnley. He isn't looking too great right now, is he? Well, the bad news is that he's going to look a lot worse over the next couple of hours."

The panic in Fat George's eyes was unmistakable as Tug taped the man's mouth firmly shut.

"He'll be driven to scream, you see. Given what's about to happen, he simply won't be able to stop himself. And we wouldn't want any nosey passer-by interfering, would we?"

"You needn't hurt him," said Jack. "Just tell me what you want, and we'll do things your way from now on."

"Easy for you to say that. But how do I know you'll keep your word once we've gone? You killed my dogs. You shot up my house. You cheeky cunt."

Tug chuckled.

"Someone has to pay for all the trouble you and your pals have caused. Am I right?"

"There's no need. You win."

"I think there is a need. Like I said, someone has to pay. Mainly, that will be your fat friend here. And he'll serve as an example to the rest of you. When we've finished with him, it'll be your turn. Not so much for you. We need you in one piece. Lucky, eh? But not so lucky that you won't feel it. A lot."

He desperately wanted to believe that Tug was joking. That nothing of what he feared was actually about to happen.

"When you've learned your lesson, you can begin to cooperate. Vlad is going to stay with you. He'll be embedded into your little gang from now on to make sure you all behave.

"I really would like to stay here too and watch. Vlad is such a craftsman. Unfortunately, I have another meeting first thing tomorrow, and I need my rest, so we'll have to leave you to it. But I'll watch all the fun later."

Vlad stepped forward and set up his phone on the tabletop. It was pointing directly at George. He was going to record what happened next.

"Don't forget," called out Tug as he and Scarface left. "Look and learn. You're getting a second chance."

And then they were gone, leaving Vlad alone with his victims. He was crouching down on the floor now, ensuring that Fat George's ankles were tightly fixed to the legs of his chair before pulling off his shoes and his socks. Then he got to his feet and drew a leather pouch from inside his jacket. He laid the pouch on the table in full view of his audience of two and opened it up to reveal an eclectic collection of blades, pincers, spikes and other worrying implements.

He dug into his pocket and took out a small box from which he shook a tiny, pink pill.

"To help the fat man stay with us," he said, looking at Jack.

He felt as though he was about to vomit. He was becoming breathless at the horror of the scene now unfolding in front of him.

Vlad selected a blade from the array lying on the table and turned to Fat George. Holding his head tightly with one huge hand, he cut an inch-long slit in the tape covering his mouth. Then he pushed the pill in through the slit.

"Is good. Dissolve soon. Have a good trip."

Jack searched desperately for something to say. Something to keep Vlad from whatever he was planning to do next.

"Please," he began. "There's no need for any of this. We can pay you. We can give you enough to let you travel anywhere in the world you want and to live comfortably."

Vlad ignored him. He was sorting through his blades, holding them up, comparing them. Jack could hear Fat George whimpering now through the tape covering his mouth.

"You could even work for us if you like. What do you think?"

Vlad seemed to settle his choice on a long, thin blade.

"Hmmm," he muttered, looking down at Fat George's naked feet. "Good."

There was a creaking noise from the office doorway. Vlad whirled around to look.

"Put the knife down and get your hands against the wall."

Hamish.

And then Junior was there too, pulling the tape from Fat George's mouth before picking up the roll from the table and going over to begin taping Vlad's wrists together behind his back while Hamish kept him at gunpoint.

Once Vlad was secured and had been made to kneel with his forehead resting on the floor, Junior bent over him and searched him for weapons. He removed a gun from his jacket and a short-bladed knife from a sheath taped to his calf.

"You've had a busy evening, old mate. Time to have a little rest now," said Hamish as he pushed hard against Vlad's raised backside, sending him ungracefully forward to lie face down on the office floor.

"I was beginning to think you weren't going to save us, buddy. What kept you?" said Jack as Hamish pulled the tape from his arms.

"Oh, you know. More haste, less speed and all that. But seriously, there's no need to thank us. Just seeing you smile is more than enough thanks for me."

He was starting to shake as he stood up and leaned on the table for support. Fat George had already been freed by Junior, who was walking him slowly around the room, using up a little of the surplus adrenaline that was flooding his system.

"And yet," said Hamish, who had returned his attention to Vlad, kicking him back down as he struggled to get onto his knees, "sometimes it seems like you solve one problem only to find that it leaves you with another."

"I take your point," said Jack. "We have to decide what to do with Cuddles here."

"You let me go now," said Vlad. "Or is very bad for you."

"My vote would be to cut the bastard into little pieces with his own blade and then dump him the Mersey," said Hamish. "But maybe we could lock him in the lower basement with the rats. As a kind of bargaining chip until we work out what's best."

19

"Sorry, Stell. It's only for today. I can't just leave the poor bugger, can I?"

Fat George was sitting in the apartment and whimpering quietly. From time to time, he shouted out or screamed as he appeared to fight off an attack from some assailant only he could see.

"And where's Hamish?"

"He's had to take over at the Art Shop for now. Until we get our man here up and running again."

"Acid?"

"Could be. George isn't too sure. Someone gave him a pill. He wasn't making a lot of sense when we found him."

He was hovering by George's chair, hoping that Stella wouldn't put her foot down and throw the pair of them out.

"You can put him in the guest room as long as you're here to look after him. But I want him out of here by tea time. If he isn't okay by then, you'd better drive him up to the hospital as an emergency. I can't have him dying on the premises."

Jack sighed with relief and grinned. "Thanks, Stell. I owe you. He'll be no trouble. Promise."

By six o'clock, Fat George had recovered from the worst effects of whatever it was that Vlad had given him, and Jack had him safely back on his camp bed at the Art Shop with instructions to take things easy.

"So he's okay?" asked Hamish. Jack didn't think he sounded particularly concerned.

"As okay as might be expected for someone who's come within an ace of watching his own feet being dissected by a madman. A madman who's force-fed him some sort of unhelpful drug. That kind of okay."

"Just so we aren't caught out again, how did Tug manage to get in here, anyway? I mean, we had FG up in the loft there, and even if our fire-damaged alarm wasn't fully functional, he should have heard them breaking in."

"They didn't break in. George went out to buy some milk for his coffee. When he got back, they pounced. They pushed a gun in his neck and followed him in."

"And then what?"

"Then they hurt him enough, for long enough, to make sure that he was telling them the truth when he finally explained that we had no secret code that meant something along the lines of, 'they're armed and waiting for you, so do take care'."

"Like we should've had if we'd thought about it."

"Exactly. But if George had stayed inside when he was supposed to, it might have been okay."

He couldn't really blame Fat George. The man was amiable and hard-working, but he wasn't full-on gangster material. Not of the sort that could reasonably be expected to mount guard on a drug lab in anticipation of an attack from a psychotic gang boss and his crew. He knew that what had happened had been down to him. He'd been sloppy.

But their opponents could be equally careless. Hadn't Tug gone off into the night and left Vlad alone and vulnerable? Not that anyone in the know would be much given to thinking of Vlad in such terms.

"What have you done with our friend?"

"I have him taped to a chair in the lower basement," said Hamish. "Just as you suggested. And I've had his phone turned off since then. Tug will be wondering what's going on and fearing the worst."

"Good. I've spoken to the others. They're all due to be here by eight. Do me a favour and order the grub. I need to think. And see if FG is up to going out to fetch some booze."

*

The pizzas and the rest of the crew all arrived within ten minutes of each other. Promising, thought Jack. We've managed to plan and execute a successful takeaway meal.

After the usual, confused discussion about who owned which pizza topping, Fat George brought in two packs of lager as a prelude to a short bout of sustained munching and drinking.

They were gathered in the office, making use of whatever they could find to sit on. Jack, Hamish, Fat George, Junior, Horse and Freddy. Leggy, due to his youth and the fact that he had an art project to complete for his day release course, was excused and was safely at home with his mum.

Jack waited until everyone had finished eating before beginning to speak.

"Taking a positive view of what's happened, I believe it's a testament to the way we've grown our business that we're now attracting the attention of predators."

"Who we've seen off," said Junior.

"So we have. But we've been lucky. And we can't continue to rely on luck. We need to get organised. We need to be more effective, more proactive."

"Meaning?" asked Horse.

"Meaning it's pointless retaliating against Tug if all we succeed in doing is provoking the bastard. We have to act in a way that makes a real difference."

"Like we did with Craig," said Hamish. He was looking at Jack. "If we'd done what you suggested and let him off with a bit of a scare and a warning, he'd have done something ten times worse to us in return. Lucky for us, you put a bullet in the fucker. We should have killed him."

"Agreed," said Jack. "You were right all along. There's no point in retaliating unless our retaliation is decisive. Otherwise, it only risks making matters worse."

"So you're saying we should kill Tug?" asked Freddy, sounding nervous. "You're talking about murder?"

He stared silently at the group in front of him for a few seconds.

"We don't have to kill anyone. We can simply decide that this is all too much for us to handle and walk away. Find some other way of making a living.

"Or we roll over and do Tug's bidding. We do the work and take the risks, and Tug grabs the lion's share of what we make.

"Or we do whatever it takes to finish this."

"So you're talking about murdering our competitor," said Freddy. "Like I said."

"If we're going to stay in business, then there is no other option. Have I got this wrong?"

"You aren't wrong," said Hamish. "And I, for one, am not ready to bow out or roll over. Anyone here feel otherwise?"

"If only there were some alternative," said Freddy.

"Well, there isn't. Unless you can tell me differently. So, anyone not in favour of dealing decisively with this better say so."

No one spoke.

"In that case, I suggest we act quickly. We pay Tug another visit. We take every gun we can muster and get ourselves up there tonight."

"He'll be aware Vlad isn't using his phone," said Freddy. "How do we know he's not on his way back down here?"

"We don't," said Jack. "But my guess is that right now, he'll be feeling confused, to say the least. And he'll have to suspect that we're most likely trying to lure him down here into a trap. So he'll bide his time and wait for things to become clearer."

"I agree," said Hamish. "He won't be expecting us to risk going back onto his territory. So I vote that's just what we do. We take the fight to him."

"And this time," said Jack, "we go up there with a clear purpose. We go there with the aim, if possible, of killing Tug. Or at least inflicting serious damage. Much better to keep all the violence up there and leave Tug's boys to clean up."

"We can't snuff out the whole gang. That would mean leaving a big mess for the police to find," added Hamish. "We go there, as Jack says, with the intention of killing Tug. We do that, and we come home. That should be enough to get them off our backs."

"Not to be picky," said Junior, "but suppose it doesn't? Get them off our backs, I mean. What then?"

"Then we find a way to escalate. Every time they act against us, we do worse to them. Until they get the message," said Jack. "There is no other way of dealing with this. But I have to believe that our best option is to kill Tug. If we can.

"George, you'll stay right here. You lock yourself in, and you don't go outside again until we give you the all-clear."

Fat George, relieved to be left out of the operation, nodded in agreement.

"If you do happen to have any problems before we get back," said Horse, "you can phone my man Paulie. I'll text you his number and let him know the score. In an emergency, he could be here within thirty minutes."

"Tug's boys were thoughtful enough to leave my gun behind with Vlad," said Jack. "So we all have weapons."

He looked at Freddy. "Barring you, I think, Freddy. Take Vlad's. Make sure you all have ammunition for a firefight if it comes to it."

"And what do we do about our prisoner in the meantime?" asked Hamish. "I'm not too happy about leaving him here, even if he is locked in the basement."

"We'll be taking him with us. So I suggest we force-feed the dear thing vodka and sleeping pills to make him a little quieter and more cooperative. Then we'll get him into the luggage compartment in my Qashqai."

20

By two in the morning, Jack's Qashqai was in position, parked, once again, in the shade of the tree-lined street running by the side of Tug's Bearsden property. They were well out of any line of sight from the neighbouring houses as the five of them climbed out of the car and gathered in the shadows. They were all wearing dark clothing and ski masks and under strict instructions from Jack not to talk unnecessarily. Jack and Hamish were each carrying a large backpack.

Jack, Freddy and Hamish clambered, as quietly as possible, over the wall to be hidden by the trees and shrubbery around the edges of Tug's extensive and well-groomed lawns. Jack and Freddy stayed crouched by the brickwork as Hamish darted forward to check the grounds. Within minutes, he was back, signalling all was clear.

Hamish took two lengths of rope from his pack and climbed back onto the wall. He let one end of each down onto the footpath and passed the other ends to Jack and Freddy. At the same time, Junior and Horse opened the tailgate of the Qashqai and lifted out the chair to which the heavily drugged Vlad was still taped.

Once tied to the hanging ropes, it was simple enough to haul Vlad to the top of the wall and lower him down the other side. Junior and Horse followed him over.

They carried Vlad with them as they moved through the trees to position him upright on his chair at the edge of the lawn.

Jack reached into his backpack and retrieved an assortment of fireworks he had bought the previous afternoon. These he handed to Freddy, who began to set them out around their unconscious prisoner. Then he took out a knife with a six-inch blade, which he also offered to Freddy.

"Take it."

Freddy shuddered and backed away, shaking his head. Hamish stepped forward and took the knife and, as the others stood and stared, calmly slit Vlad's throat. Then, all at once, the little tableau broke up, and four figures moved off through the shadows, leaving Freddy with Vlad's bleeding corpse.

Keeping out of sight beneath the trees, they made their way around to the front of the property. They passed the window they had shattered on their last visit, now boarded up, and crouched down facing the house. On every side of the building, lights illuminated the grounds. Inside, the entire ground floor was brightly lit. They saw nothing of the occupants. Jack pointed out a large window on the corner, and each of them drew and readied his weapon.

They waited a long, anxious minute until the crackling and explosions of fireworks broke the silence, and rockets could be seen rising and exploding above the back of the house. At this, they each fired two rounds at their target and immediately ran towards the shattering glass. They had learned from their last visit how easily a few shots from a handgun could make a large pane of glass disappear.

In seconds, they were at the window bay, using stones from the flower border to remove any problematic shards left at the bottom of the frame. Then they were inside, running through rooms and passageways in search of the hallway. They could hear shouts from the rear of the house. From the upper floor, where they assumed Tug would be tucked up warm in his bed, they heard rapid footsteps and the banging of doors, accompanied by more shouting.

They reached the hallway, which rose to the full height of the building and was topped off by a gaudily chandeliered ceiling. A wide, central staircase gave access to a landing, from where further stairs branched off to either side.

Leaving Horse and Junior to secure their escape route, Jack and Hamish ran up the stairway to the landing, where they separated and took a side staircase each. As they sprinted up the remaining stairs, the sound of shouts and a dog barking, followed by gunfire, came from below.

When they reached the upper level, a door opened on Jack's right to reveal Tug dressed in shorts and clutching a pistol. Tug's first shot went wide, splintering the bannister rail next to Jack's shoulder. His second sent a bullet whining over his head, smashing through the glass chandelier on its way to knocking out a chunk of plaster from the wall.

Jack dropped to one knee and squeezed off two shots in quick succession as he heard Hamish begin firing behind him. He ducked instinctively to avoid a third shot from Tug, and when he looked up again, his gun at the ready, Tug had disappeared into the bedroom, and the door was slammed shut. He looked around as Hamish fired into an open doorway at the other end of the landing, warning whoever might be lurking inside to stay out of it. Then, from the far reaches of a darkened corridor in front of them, blasts from a shotgun began to splinter the wooden bannister rails.

"Okay, buddy," he yelled. "That'll have to do. Time to fuck off!"

He fired a further shot as he got up and ran down the stairs. Hamish followed close behind. On the ground floor, they found Horse and Junior crouched at each side of the staircase, returning fire from Tug's guards.

"Let's go, boys!" shouted Jack, waving the Makarov toward the door they had come through a few minutes before. They left at a brisk pace, making their way back through the house and out through the shattered window. They were almost across the lawn when the clattering of gunfire broke out behind them.

Almost at once, Hamish cried out and fell. The rest of the group reached the deep shadows of the tree line before turning to fire on two of Tug's men running across the lawn to reach Hamish, now crawling desperately over the grass. The pair broke off their pursuit and sprinted back to the house.

Horse and Junior made a crouching run to where Hamish was trying to crawl towards the shadows. They grabbed an arm apiece and pulled him along between them as they rejoined Jack to make their escape. When they reached the spot where Vlad was still sitting, flanked by the spent and smoking fireworks in Freddy's hastily built display, they moved off at a right angle through the trees.

Hamish was no heavyweight, but he was enough of a burden to slow them up and pose a further difficulty in getting back over the wall to where Freddy was waiting behind the wheel. The Qashqai's engine was already running as they dropped onto the footpath and crammed into the car. They wedged Hamish between Horse and Junior on the rear seat. No one followed them as they moved out of Bearsden, heading for home.

Cramped as they were, it was impossible to do more than tape a dressing over the wound in Hamish's calf as they drove.

"Looks like you were expecting injuries," said Horse, "with surgical dressings stashed in your glove box."

"Thought I'd take the precaution after what happened on our last trip," said Jack. "We don't seem to be able to visit friend Tug without at least one injury and one large, smashed window."

"Did you do the job?" asked Freddy. "Did you get Tug?"

"Hard to be certain, but I'm pretty sure I got a bullet into him. Two, maybe. We couldn't stick around there any longer without risking Tug's boys getting us bottled up."

"Did you enjoy my firework display?" asked Freddy, sounding happier than Jack would have expected.

"It was lovely," said Jack, grinning. "I always like a nice exploding rocket, and all that noise would've well hidden the din we were making."

"I don't want to worry anyone," said Junior. "It could be the light in here, but Hamish has turned a funny colour. And he's slumping a bit."

"I've some whisky in the door pocket," said Jack. "How about it, Hamie? Fancy a quick slug of the magic juice?"

All they got from Hamish in return was a low murmur, followed by coughing.

"I have to say," said Horse, taking hold of Hamish's chin and turning his face towards him, "he really isn't looking all that great. His eyes are closed."

Horse bent down and checked the wound in Hamish's calf.

"There's blood seeping through the dressing. But I don't think it's going to be life-threatening. He should make it okay."

"Probably just shock, right?" said Freddy. "But he'll be needing some proper help at some point. Why don't we leave him at the nearest hospital?"

"Way too risky," said Jack. "We need to get him back to the gallery. He can have a camp bed upstairs with Fat George. We'll take care of him ourselves."

*

It was almost seven a.m. when they parked in the alley behind the Art Shop. Horse and Junior pulled Hamish from the car and carried him inside. Jack and Freddy followed them in.

Hamish was semi-conscious and incoherent as they struggled to haul him up the backstairs to the loft. Fat George was waiting with hot water, soap and clean towels. They laid him down on the bed, carefully cleaned his wound and changed the dressing.

"No sign of an exit wound," said Freddy, "so the bullet's still in there, and he's going to need surgery to dig the thing out."

"I know someone who could help," said Horse. "The guy I used for Paulie after Tug had done with him. A friend of mine."

"A doctor?" asked Jack. "We can trust him?"

"He's a vet. With a drug habit. Pay him enough, and he'll sort Hamish and keep his mouth shut. He has a couple of rooms up on Rodney Street."

"How soon can you have him here?"

"I can go up there now and get him. He'll have anaesthetic and all the surgical gear."

"Okay," said Jack. "Probably our best option."

"Forget it," said Freddy, "I don't think we do have a medical problem, after all. I think the boy's dead."

"Dead?" asked Jack, striding over to Hamish's bedside. "He was shot in the calf. What do you mean, dead?

"I mean he's stopped breathing, and I can't find a pulse. Dead like that."

21

"So, did he say when he'd be back?" Stella was asking about Hamish.

"No," said Jack. "You know how he is. I don't even have any idea where he's gone."

"I was hoping he was done with all that disappearing stuff he does for weeks or months on end. I hoped it was all going to settle down. You, me, Hamish, this place and your art gallery thing. Nice and normal, like other people do."

"Maybe he'll be home soon."

"It's just that I'm getting too old to be worrying about what you two might be up to. I need life to be a little more predictable. More peaceful."

"Things are peaceful, Stell. You'll see. Trust me on that."

He didn't like lying to Stella. They'd begun to grow close these days, and he valued that. Why wouldn't he? He'd been a long time on his own. But truth could be an expensive commodity, and right now, it was a commodity he could not afford. One day, maybe, when he'd got well on top of it all and everything was sorted. Perhaps then things could be different.

*

When, two days before, Jack and the others had finally satisfied themselves that Hamish was indeed dead, they had been faced with the need to dispose of his body.

"There's nothing for it but to leave him here with FG for now," he'd said. "Get a few hours sleep and some food inside us. Then we can decide what to do."

They had left him there, on Fat George's bed, until the early evening when they had reconvened in the office downstairs.

"The river is the simplest way, I suppose," Freddy had suggested. "But maybe not too safe. We can't risk him being found."

"And having him dropped off a ship would mean involving others," said Jack. "So don't even bother suggesting it."

"So what then?" asked Junior. "We can't just leave him lying around in the loft."

"We'll bury him here, in the lower basement. No one's ever going to go digging down there. I stopped at the DIY and bought a pick and a spade on the drive over."

Only when they lifted him off the bed, wrapped in the sheet they were about to use as a burial shroud, did they see the pool of congealed blood where his back had rested on the mattress. And then they found the bullet hole between his shoulder blades.

"Oh, fuck," said Jack with feeling. "We've been looking at the wrong wound. No wonder the poor bugger died on us."

"I doubt we could have done anything, in any case," said Freddy. "Horse's vet would've needed a full operating theatre to have any chance of dealing with this."

They double-wrapped the corpse in the bedsheet and manoeuvred the bloodstained bundle down to the lower basement, where they took it in turns to work at a grave three feet deep. Even at that shallow depth, the stony, compacted earth made the digging hard going.

Later, when he left for home, Jack made sure to take Hamish's Ruger with him. He checked it was loaded and pushed it to the back of the sideboard drawer at the semi.

*

"It doesn't look to me like there's going to be any comeback from the Tug raid," said Jack. "Could be we've seen the end of the whole bunch of them."

"Could be you finished him," said Freddy, taking a sip of his flat white and smiling. "Let's hope."

They were sitting in Maggie May's.

"Don't know how you manage to drink that stuff, Freddy. You should maybe try an espresso. It could change your view of things."

"And why would I want to do that? Perhaps I'm happy with things the way they are. We've got everything running pretty smoothly for once."

"You're right. Horse has the stuff flowing in like a river. FG has turned out to be a technical whizz with Hamish's Dark Web thing. And the orders are growing as fast as we can deal with them."

"So we're all making money. And we're looking good. Regular pillars of the community. What more could we want?"

"Maybe, not a lot," he said. "Maybe I couldn't give you an argument on any of that."

It was true that there had been a lot of problems in getting things to this stage. He had been on a steep learning curve, largely forced on him by Hamish in his relentless drive to push beyond the limits.

But, for Jack, the raid on Tug's gang in Bearsden had been an epiphany. And now Hamish was gone, and all he was required to do was watch over Stella and her little empire at the Blue Warehouse. It was no longer enough.

There had been a play that Wendy had taken him to see at the Everyman. 'We should try it', she'd said. 'Broaden our experience. You might even enjoy it.'

It had been a new experience, for sure, but the only part of it that he had truly enjoyed had been the interval, spent hastily swallowing drinks in the bar. Macbeth. He hadn't really warmed to it.

That one line, though, remember? About life being nothing more than a tale told by an idiot, full of sound and fury, signifying nothing? That one line, at least, had made sense.

And life still signified nothing, and since Bearsden, the sound and fury were noticeable only by their absence. He was bored. Even worse, he was beginning to feel redundant.

He had no interest in art. No interest in public relations. No interest in shuttling illegal funds around the place. No interest in working shifts in the powder room alongside Fat George. No interest in any of that.

"I've been thinking, Freddy, now that everything's going so well, maybe we should take the opportunity to expand."

"You don't think we're making enough?"

"We're doing okay. But the kind of business we're in? There are predators everywhere. You know that."

"So we keep our heads down."

"We keep our heads down, and someone big and bad is likely to come along and bite them off. Predators. Everywhere."

"And your answer is to bring us up against even more predators?"

"The solution is to grow. Become bigger than the competition before they squeeze us out or take us over. You saw what happened with Tug. And there are even bigger boys operating locally."

Freddy had a further sip of his flat white as he took a long, thoughtful look at Jack. He glanced around, checking there was no one within hearing distance.

"That's so not the way I see this going. We're already making more than enough money. If we simply carry on as is and keep our collective nose clean, then I don't think anyone will trouble us."

"And if they do?"

"If they do, then we deal with it. Like we did with Tug. You seem to be good at that kind of thing. But I think Tug was a one-off. If you recall, it was John D got us into all that. And he's out of it."

"I just feel that we should try to be a bit more proactive."

"But we are being proactive, as you so quaintly put it. I've been very busy blending the public face of our business into the local social structure."

"You've swanned about at the Art Shop opening night, chatting to d-list celebs and whatnot. I grant you that."

"Don't forget our exhibitions and our prize money. People notice these things."

"Gordon Donnelley certainly noticed, didn't he? He was about to write up the whole operation."

"Donnelley is a no-mark art critic. You and Horse put him in his place pretty easily. And we can field enough guns when we need to. Our group, right now, is a good size. Maybe an extra pair of hands to help out in the powder room? But that's about it."

"A good size for what?"

"A good size to manage. Too big, and you risk losing cohesion. People start to get ideas of how they could do things better."

Jack could see that the conversation wasn't exactly going his way. He tried a different tack.

"So, are you planning to go over to Fuerteventura anytime soon?"

"You know what? I never thought I'd settle over here again. But I've been thinking that this might be a good place to spend my declining years. I've managed to sell one or two paintings, and I'm beginning to develop a bit of a following around the city."

"So who's looking after things at the finca while you're here? You haven't been back there in a while. Fran?"

Freddy looked shocked. "Fran? God no. Don't want Fran getting involved in things up there. I keep Fran and the finca strictly separate."

I bet you do. Now you've got your nice, new housekeeper installed.

"Miguel and Ana will both still be there. Not that there'll be a whole lot for them to do while I'm away."

"I was thinking of going over there for a few weeks myself. We need to sort Hamish's villa for one thing."

"What do we do about his place, anyway?" asked Freddy. "We should think about terminating the rental."

"Maybe, but I can deal with that after I've had a look through his stuff. I want to think about how to handle this."

"Not quite with you. Handle what?"

"Hamish's dosh. He must have pots in that offshore account Giuseppe set up for him. I'm thinking that money should go to Stella."

"Whatever. I'm not sure I mind either way."

22

Stella knew all about the gun Jack had hidden in his odds and ends drawer in the bedroom they now shared. She had found out quite a lot about the latest man in her life from the contents of that drawer.

It was careless of him, she felt, to leave evidence of his 'business' trips in there. Evidence he could easily have got rid of. But he hadn't. He kept all his recent payment slips in a couple of A5 envelopes. A habit she imagined he might have developed during his time as a jobbing PI when it would have been important to collect the paperwork for his expenses.

And so Stella had been able to find out, amongst much else, about a bar bill he had paid on a ferry out of Hull and petrol he had bought at a filling station at someplace in the Netherlands. Jack's paperwork was useful that way.

Equally helpful was his phone. He had the thing on fingerprint recognition, making it a simple matter to open it while he was sleeping, especially on those not-infrequent occasions when he'd had a few too many whiskies.

All in all, she found it easy to keep tabs on her new partner. Did he realise, she wondered, that he had an app on his phone that recorded his movements? Probably not.

It wasn't that she didn't trust him with other women. She wasn't even sure whether the occasional act of unfaithfulness would trouble her greatly. Not that there had been any indication that anything like that had taken place. He seemed to be very much a one-woman kind of man.

One thing she was sure of was that she was not in love with Jack. She was fond of him, just as she had been fond of Gus. And she did enjoy their more intimate moments - and she saw to it that there were enough of them to ensure he felt no compulsion to stray.

The only man she had ever truly loved had been her first husband, Claude. But even though it had been less than a year since his tragic fall into the cellar, that relationship already seemed like it belonged to a different lifetime, a time when she had never needed to worry about much more than her weight and the smooth operation of her nightclub.

Not that Claude hadn't had an edge to him. She had been well aware of his gangland connections. But Claude had been more of a gentleman gangster who had left all the dangerous stuff to brother Gus. And anything that was in the least dangerous had happened off the premises. No hint of trouble had ever intruded within the walls of the Warehouse.

All that had begun to unravel after Claude's death. Gus had been no kind of gentleman, and without Claude to direct his actions, the risks had escalated rapidly, resulting in disaster and an untimely end for her new husband.

Since then, she had come to rely on Jack to keep the wolves at bay, and so far, that strategy seemed to be working. But Jack was something of an unknown quantity, with his rundown semi up on the Point and his mysterious trips away from home.

And his connection with the character they called 'Horse' was a puzzle. He and Jack were polar opposites in lifestyle and appearance. And no one got to be as rich as Horse obviously was simply by renting out a few shipping containers, did they?

And Jack had no visible means of support, as far as she could see, apart from the Art Shop thing he was running with Freddy. But that had come about too recently to explain much.

All this meant that he might need to be watched. So she watched him. Carefully.

"Did you give any more thought to my suggestion of selling up and moving away from here?" he had asked one quiet afternoon. "You did say you always intended to retire somewhere warm."

"I did, but I don't think I'm quite ready to retire just yet. And I feel warm enough here for now. Ask me again in a few years."

If you're still around a few years from now, was what she thought. But she didn't say it.

"I'm going over to Lanzarote on business in a day or so if you want to come along. Give you a break."

He felt safe inviting her. He knew she wouldn't feel able to leave the Warehouse, even if she wanted to.

"Can't arrange a relief at such short notice. You know that. And I'll have the decorators in soon to refurb the function room. I'm just too busy."

"Fair enough. I shouldn't be gone all that long."

And he'd booked himself a seat on the plane out.

Why was it, she wondered, that men were such tricky creatures? You'd be thinking they were going along happily, behaving themselves, and then they'd go off and do something totally unexpected. They could be secretive, too, when they felt like it. Up until Gus's time, she hadn't minded that. She hadn't wanted to know what Claude, or Gus for that matter, was getting up to. But after what had happened with Gus bringing trouble in so close, she realised that her trusting attitude had been a mistake.

"So what's this business on Lanzarote then? Something interesting? You never want to tell me anything about what it is you do."

"Oh, you know, artwork. That kind of thing. Tracking down bits and pieces for the gallery. Talking to artists."

She knew that was a lie. Since when did dealing in art mean you needed a gun? It wasn't even as though the stuff the Art Shop sold was particularly valuable.

Freddy was the one who was clued up about art. And maybe Hamish knew a little. But Jack? Never. She had long ago worked out that the artwork rigmarole was just a front. But for what? Gangsterism had run alongside and through her life like a hidden seam of lead through rock. It had held Claude and Gus on their course and had now, it seemed, pulled in Jack as well.

She had known Jack in her youth and had lost touch with him. And then, last year, he had come back into her world as a down-at-heel private investigator in a crumpled blue suit. As for his involvement with the Art Shop, it was Hamish, she knew, who had been the driving force behind all that. It would have been Hamish who would have drawn him into whatever was really going on down there.

*

Freddy Davidson was surprised to find he was enjoying himself. He had intended his trip to his home turf to be nothing more than a short visit to touch base with his grandson, Junior, and his fruitful new partner, Hamish.

Getting involved in the artwork down at Hamish's new project, he had regarded as little more than a side issue, a kind of hobby.

Except that it hadn't turned out that way. It had turned out to be a cover for the lucrative drug dealership that Hamish had been building in company with Jack Charnley. Too good an opportunity to pass up.

The last two years, spent in painterly reflection in his remote finca, were beginning to feel dull in comparison to the life he was living at present. Back at the finca, he had for a long time been nothing more than an unrecognised painter and a lonely expat eking out an existence on the modest allowance he took each month from Junior's Limo Hire.

But now, almost magically, everything had changed. He had a substantial stash of funds, growing from his recently established money laundering activities and his even more recent drug wholesaling. He had somewhere to display and sell his artwork. And he had a seemingly legitimate and respected role in society. If he got bored, he could call on the services of the attractive young 'housekeeper' he'd recently been able to afford to install back at the finca. These were valuable assets.

But life, he knew, could throw up the odd problem once you stopped hiding away from it, and at the moment, his problem seemed to be with Jack Charnley. The man, who used to know his place, now wanted to run things his way. Charnley didn't have the good sense to leave well alone.

It was eight p.m. when he arrived at the Blue Warehouse. He was due to meet Jack upstairs in the apartment to touch base and clear up any operational details before Jack flew out to Lanzarote.

Being so early in the evening there weren't many people in the bar. But Stella was there, sitting in her usual spot at the end of the counter. The glass by her side, he noticed, was empty.

"Evening, Stella," he said, strolling across to where she sat, perched on her barstool. "Have a drink with me?"

"If you want to pay for it, Freddy. A Prosecco might be nice."

He signalled to the bargirl.

"Prosecco for the boss here, and I'll have a glass of lager," he said, handing the girl a note.

The girl served their drinks and put the change on the bar top.

"I must say, I'm surprised to see you're still in town. I would've thought you'd be missing all that sun too much by now."

"The sun, I do miss," he said, taking an exploratory sip of his drink. "But not a great deal else, if I'm honest."

Not entirely true since he did miss Fran and Ana. He missed them each in different ways. With Fran, it was the friendly companionship and the sex. With Ana, it was the sex.

"And, to be fair, it isn't always cold and damp over here, is it? We do enjoy the odd fine day."

"So you're thinking of staying for a while?"

"Hard to say. A few weeks, perhaps. I'm interested in helping to get the Art Shop off to a good start."

"Well, that seems to be going okay. Jack certainly spends a lot of time on it. Not that I have any idea what it is he does over there. He's not exactly clued up on paintings, is he?"

"He's mainly on the financial side. And the admin. I tend to help out with the artistic stuff. And the PR."

"Speaking of artistic stuff," said Stella, "I was thinking it might be good to have a painting or two in here. Maybe even a half dozen or so. Dotted around the place. What do you think?"

Stella had a nice line in winning smiles. She tried one now.

"That can only be a good thing," he said, returning the smile. "You can never have too many paintings, in my humble opinion. Why not drop in at the Art Shop sometime? I'm certain we'll find something to interest you. If you let me know when you'd like to call, I'll be sure to be there."

"I might just take you up on that, Freddy," she said, finishing her wine. "Want to give me your number?"

23

Jack was surprised to find just how much he was looking forward to being amongst the colourful warmth of Honda again.

Standing in line for a taxi outside the airport, he watched the changing colours in the evening sky. A few scattered clouds were glowing purple in the sunset, bleeding into scarlet at the edges.

The queue shrank quickly enough until there was only one person ahead of him, a man around his own age, carrying a small, old-fashioned suitcase. The man turned to scan the approach road before glancing at Jack. He was wearing a dark grey suit and shirt and a clerical collar.

"Looks as though we're out of luck at the minute," he said.

"They shouldn't be too long getting back. They're usually pretty quick."

"On holiday?"

"Sort of. Bit of business to attend to, but nothing much. I'm here for a break mainly. You?"

"To do the Lord's work," said the man, smiling. "If you're staying anywhere near me, we could share a taxi. Save you waiting."

Jack had booked himself in at the Hotel Diamanté for his first night. He had stayed there before, and he liked the place. He liked the beach view, the unfussy serve-yourself dining area and the down-to-earth bar with its vinyl-topped tables. The villa would feel too abruptly lonely at this darkening hour, and he wanted the noise and company of town.

"I'm hoping to stay in Arrecife, at the Diamanté, if that's good for you."

"I can drop you at the doorstep. I have a room at my church not far from you."

The taxi arrived within five minutes, and on the drive into town, the man with the suitcase introduced himself as the Reverend Neil Jones. He was, he explained, returning from a visit to a sister church in Liverpool, and he wondered whether his new acquaintance would care to share a meal and a glass or two with a fellow Liverpudlian the following evening, if he wasn't otherwise engaged.

"I would," said Jack, surprising himself. "Come down to the Diamanté around seven if you like. I'll probably be in the bar."

Fifteen minutes later, as he climbed out of the taxi outside his hotel, the Reverend Jones pressed a card into his hand.

"Contact details," he said. "Should you find yourself in need."

He had eaten on the plane and had no immediate need of another meal; a stiff drink or two was what he craved.

He could have made his way downstairs to the bar and drunk his fill. Or he could have gone to the little twenty-four-seven down the road and bought himself as much booze as he wanted. But he was too tired. He needed to sleep. He kicked off his shoes and lay down on the bed. He closed his eyes. Fifteen minutes would do it. Then he could go in search of a drink.

His slumbers were far from peaceful. Vlad sat taped onto his chair, lit by the flashing and flickering of fireworks, his throat a gaping, bloody wound. Hamish clawed his way up through the floor of the basement, his jaw hanging, his expression dark. His quick nap became ten hours of nightmare-riddled sleep.

It was later the next morning, after breakfast at the hotel buffet, that he found the time to examine the card that the Reverend had given him. It said:

Reverend Neil Jones BTheol (Hons)
Church of Miraculous Salvation
Arrecife

Amongst the usual contact details on the reverse was an address. He thought he might check it out on his way to find a comfortable bar for a lunchtime glass of beer.

He took a stroll up to the address on the Calle de la Plantation. An unremarkable street, narrow and quiet, leading away from the road by the beach. There was a mixture of retail and commercial properties on the first block, tailing off into residential terraces. He found the church wedged into a gap between two terraced blocks. It was located in an old stone building fronted by equally elderly iron railings. Three stone steps led up to the double front doors in what looked like Spanish oak painted over with deep green paint, now badly faded. One of the doors stood open.

A notice board informed anyone who might be interested when the next service would be held. All were welcome, it said, to use the church for private prayer and meditation. It was not yet noon, but the heat was already beginning to build, and Jack felt drawn to the cool darkness of the interior.

There was no one else inside. As his eyes adjusted to the gloom, he could make out a lectern and a raised pulpit. Possibly there was a kind of altar farther back. There were rows of wooden chairs and bare plaster walls. It was small, nothing like the size of most of the church buildings he remembered from his sparse attendances at various weddings and funerals down the years.

Acting on impulse, he made his way along the aisle between the two blocks of chairs and took a seat somewhere in the middle. It was much cooler than the street, and the place had a distinctly restful atmosphere. His lunchtime drink could wait for a few minutes.

Maybe it would be good to sit quietly for a while and try to clear his mind. He focused on the unlit space inside his skull and gently wafted away any thoughts vying to make their presence felt there.

Wasn't that what people did when they meditated? It was supposed to help somehow. It was supposed to help...

"It was supposed to help," he heard someone say as he was jolted suddenly back into wakefulness, "people to clear their minds of anxiety and worry. Of guilt."

He had been asleep, and now others were here, behind him somewhere, speaking quietly in the stillness.

"Of demons," said another. "You could speak of it that way. Yes, clear one's mind of demons. Los demonios."

He got clumsily to his feet, feeling groggy, pushing his chair over the stone floor. It made a scraping sound, which seemed unduly loud in the quietness. He went back along the aisle towards the sunlit street framed in the doorway. As he passed the two figures sitting farther back, one glanced up at him. Reverend Neil.

"Catch you later then, Jack. Don't forget. Your place at seven."

Too groggy and confused to make a more coherent response, he merely grunted and half raised his hand as he walked on and out, down the stone steps into the murmur of the street. How had the Reverend Jones known his name? He had no recollection of telling him.

It didn't take him very long after that to find a suitable bar, not too upmarket.

Three glasses of powerful lager went some way to restoring his sense of equilibrium. He ordered a steak sandwich with fries.

His plan that afternoon had been to pay an initial visit to Hamish's villa along the coast in Honda. But with each fresh glass of beer, that seemed less and less likely. It wasn't a problem. There was no hurry, and towards the end of his fourth lager and the start of his fifth, things were starting to look decidedly unproblematic. He stopped drinking then and ambled amiably back down Plantation Street and by the beachfront to the hotel.

When he reached his room, he found the place newly cleaned, his bed made, and the balcony door open slightly. He could smell the sea, mixed with the slightest hint of fried steak from the restaurant a few doors down. A pleasing combination.

He went out onto the balcony and slumped on the lounger, prepared to doze away the afternoon.

He slept fitfully, waking now and again to listen to the sounds drifting up from the road below and the gentler sound of waves coming to shore on the sandy beach. By four o'clock, he was feeling unaccountably guilty about wasting time. He would take the walk up to Honda after all.

Before leaving the hotel, he took a bottle of vodka from the bag he had checked onto his flight out from John Lennon and put it into his backpack.

Once outside, he called into the convenience store, where he bought three small bottles of vodka and dropped these into his pack as well.

He recalled how he had walked this same route with Hamish on more than one occasion.

The heat of the afternoon tired him, and he was glad when he could leave the broad walkway and turn onto the side street to reach the villa, partway up the gentle slope from the oceanside. He punched the code he remembered into the box on the gatepost, and the gate swung back to admit him.

An English garden at home on the Point would have been overgrown had it suffered the same lack of attention as the one he now walked through. But this collection of rocks, gravel and semi-tropical plants presented no such problem. A few modest piles of dried leaves were the most of it. He could deal with that another day. He pulled out the door key he'd brought from Hamish's room at the Warehouse and let himself inside.

This was his first visit since Hamish's death, and memories of his dead companion lurked in every corner. He made an effort to ignore them as he set about doing what he had come here to do.

He took the vodka bottle from his backpack and stood it on the worktop in the kitchen. Before leaving home, he had emptied the contents into a mixing bowl and mixed in a half kilo of powdered cocaine. He was testing out the practicalities of smuggling coke dissolved in liquid.

The bottle had come successfully through the check-in and the flight. The issue now was to divide the liquid it contained into the smaller ones he had bought at the start of his walk. He opened each of these and poured them into a large glass jug he'd found in one of the cupboards. Next, he stood each of the empties, in turn, in the sink and filled them carefully with the vodka and coke mixture.

Not much later, he locked the place up again and walked back into Arrecife.

He was resting in his room when the front desk rang to say that his dinner guest had arrived.

It was ten minutes after seven when he got down to the buffet area to find the Reverend Jones, complete with clerical collar and dark grey suit, examining the selection of starters laid out in the dining area.

"Jack. You're here, after all. I'd begun to think you'd forgotten all about our little dinner."

"Sorry if I'm a bit late. I'd dozed off, that's all. Glad to see you could make it. Is it okay if I call you Neil? Or would you prefer reverend?"

"You call me whatever seems most appropriate, and I'll carry on calling you Jack if that's alright?"

Maybe this was a mistake. It's not what I do. Dinner with strangers. Is it? And a fucking Rev to boot.

"So let's get started, shall we? You're hungry, I hope?"

"Very. Doing the Lord's work gives one an almighty appetite."

They selected a starter apiece and strolled into the spacious dining area to find themselves a table. It was a little early for most, and the place was practically empty.

"So, Jack, it's good to be breaking bread with you, but before we eat, would you mind if I offered a few words of thanks to our Creator?"

"Can't see why I would object to that, Neil. Go ahead."

"Would you care to join me?"

"I'll pass if that's okay," he said, putting down the fork he'd just picked up. "Not really my thing."

The Reverend Jones put his hands together and bowed his head. "For what we are about to receive, may the Lord make us truly thankful," he murmured. "Amen."

They ate their way steadily through three courses, fitting in a bottle of wine en route. Their conversation was mostly inconsequential chit-chat about life in the Canaries and a potted history, from the Reverend

Jones, of the development of his church and what he referred to as his 'ministry'.

"And do you find that there's much call for your sort of business hereabouts? I get the impression that the market for what you offer is shrinking, year on year."

"The need for God's word is infinite, Jack. The world contains an ever-increasing number of troubled souls, and the only answer to all that trouble comes from the Lord."

"Through you?"

"It's one route of many. I provide a conduit for the divine if you like. Why not come to a service and see for yourself? Tomorrow's Sunday, and we have a service every Sunday morning at ten-thirty. It's mainly for British expats, so it's nearly all in English."

He felt himself beginning to panic. He usually gave any unnecessary attendance at any church activity a wide berth and sensed he was in danger of being boxed in by his new acquaintance.

"Sorry," he said at once. "Busy, I'm afraid. Business to attend to."

The Reverend Jones let his disappointment show for an instant before recovering enough to suggest that they moved into the hotel bar for another drink. Jack took the opportunity to order a second bottle.

"No point in trailing back and forth to collect the drinks," he said. "This should keep us going for a while."

"Not sure I should have too much more," said Neil. "A half bottle is usually my limit. Maybe just a couple."

Not wanting to put any pressure on his dinner guest, Jack drank most of the wine himself.

*

He woke in his room the following morning, feeling decidedly hungover. He had a hazy memory of Neil wishing him goodnight and leaving as the second bottle came to an end and then further memories, increasingly blurry, of at least two glasses of scotch.

All he could manage for breakfast in the hotel bar was a double espresso. He was intending to call in at the convenience store and buy a few essentials to take with him up to Honda. He felt sure the walk would help to clear his head.

For once, the morning was cloudy. Even so, he was damp with perspiration when he sat down at the kitchen table in the villa with another coffee. Maybe it would be simpler and easier to move in here and save all the trudging about. Not that he wanted to be cooped up on his own. He'd grown so used to life with Stella and the Art Shop gang that the prospect of being completely alone again was unappealing. So perhaps a better plan would be to base himself at the Diamanté, where he could be alone in busy Arrecife. He had never been prone to feeling lonely in a crowd.

He retrieved the three vodka bottles from the worktop and stowed them in his backpack. Carefully opening one of the bottles, he took a sniff and registered the familiar mixture of flowers and chemicals. Then he dripped a little of the liquid onto a fingertip and rubbed it along his gum until he experienced the slight numbing sensation he was expecting.

Breakfast at the villa became lunch, slices from a crusty baguette spread generously with butter. If he was certain of anything, it was that his diet needed urgent attention. But then, he reasoned, many things needed urgent attention and never received it, so what did one more matter?

In the afternoon, he took a taxi down to Playa Blanca and stood in line with the tourists waiting to board the ferry for the half-hour boat ride over to Corralejo. From there, a second taxi took him to La Oliva and Davidson's finca.

A couple of hundred yards from the finca and well out of sight of the place, he paid the taxi driver and asked him to park up and wait for half an hour or so. Then he walked on up to Freddy's volcano-side residence and in through the gate.

The building sat in the centre of a large patch of rock-strewn ground, marked out by low walls constructed from slabs of lava. Here and there, someone had worked to arrange piles of coloured volcanic rock amongst the cacti growing at random around the place to create the effect of a cactus garden.

It did not take long for Jack to locate a suitable pile of stones to conceal the first vodka bottle. He wiped it free of fingerprints with a tea towel he'd brought along for the purpose and hid it where no one would be likely to find it by accident. Not even the ground squirrels, which roamed the area in large numbers, would be able to mess with it, secured as it was beneath the heavy rocks.

Then, as quietly as he could, he tried the front door. It was unlocked. Way up here, in the sparsely populated lava fields, few would expect an uninvited guest or a sneak thief to walk into the house in the middle of the afternoon. But he wasn't looking to steal anything.

A quick look around showed him that Freddy's Mercedes wasn't on the premises, so it was unlikely that Miguel would present a problem.

Gently, he opened the door and went into the small, dark hallway he remembered from his last visit. The room he wanted was to his right, and the door stood open. He walked quietly through. The same large, gloomy space with the same barred windows at the rear, overlooking the sunlit, rocky area at the back of the house. Through one of the windows, he could see Ana stretched out on a sun lounger, working on her tan. She was lying face down with her head over the edge of her lounger, reading a book resting on the ground in front of her. She was a beautiful woman. She was naked. For a moment, he was rooted to the spot, unable to take his eyes off her.

He crossed to where a large grandfather clock stood against a side wall, ticking reassuringly into the gloom, and took a second vodka bottle from his backpack and wiped it clean. Reaching up, he managed to push it over the ornately carved and gilded woodwork around the top of the structure. The bottle landed with a dull thud inside the crown. It was unlikely that such a heavy item would be moved about much if it ever was. Unlikely, too, that Ana would trouble to climb up there with a vacuum hose or a duster on cleaning day. Nobody was going to find that bottle anytime soon.

The third bottle he placed on top of a wall unit in the kitchen, pushing it to the back, out of sight.

Had anyone found him in the house, he would have said that no one seemed to have heard his knock and that he was there to collect Freddy's mail. But there would be no need now for such a clumsy excuse.

He took out his phone and crept up to the window from where, aiming neatly between the bars, he snapped a clear image of the sunbathing Ana. He stepped back to take a second shot, this time including the bars and a small beer stein holding an assortment of pens and pencils, sitting on its own at the end of the sill. Only then did he allow himself to leave.

Satisfied that there was nothing more he could achieve at the finca, he walked quickly down the slope to the taxi for the drive to the ferry.

A little over four hours after leaving the villa in Honda at lunchtime, he was climbing out of a different taxi in front of the Diamanté.

24

"You can, of course, just look at a painting, or any artwork for that matter, and decide more or less at once whether or not you like it. But often, a more considered approach will pay dividends."

Freddy was standing in front of the gallery wall at the Art Shop, explaining to Stella how, exactly, one should view art.

"That sounds like me," she said, taking a sip of the Prosecco Freddy had poured for her. "Snap decisions, I mean. If I bother to look at all. But it isn't my thing as a rule. Looking at paintings."

Better shut up, she thought. Stop babbling. Let the man talk.

"Well, they're there to be looked at," said Freddy, slightly puzzled. "That's the whole point, really. It's the way you look at them, though.

"For instance," he waved his arm towards the large abstract they were standing in front of, "this particular piece is not interesting in the conventional sense. There is no recognisable image."

"It's just lines and splodges mainly, as far as I can see," said Stella. She was actually thinking that the 'piece', as Freddy seemed to want to call it, was more like the mess you had to clean off the floor if you'd been particularly careless when painting a ceiling.

"Splodges, yes," agreed Freddy. "It's an abstract. Obviously. There's no familiar iconography you can relate to."

"And it's all done in grey, isn't it? Various shades of grey. Even the background."

"There is a tiny smudge of red in there," said Freddy. "It's down there, look. Bottom right. A red smudge. See?"

"I see it. Is that good, then? The red smudge?"

"It's there to help the viewer to relate to the rest of the thing. To the absence of colour. See?"

"And...?"

"So what one could infer from the absence of any recognisable form, the absence of symbols, the almost total absence of colour is that the artist is trying to convey a sense of freedom, expressed through his rejection of the normal artistic conventions. You see?"

Stella tried to feel the painting's sense of freedom, and she did feel, for a moment, that she might have come close. She wanted to please Freddy by responding positively to the art lesson he seemed so keen to provide. But she soon had to face the fact that all she could manage to glean from this particular artistic experience was a set of grey splodges on a grey canvas. She was about to admit as much when she noticed the signature on the thing, an inconspicuous 'FD' painted in black on the light grey of the background.

"Yes," she said. "I do think I can see what you mean."

She wanted to be positive. She realised just how fragile a man's ego could be. Especially when the man was trying hard to impress an elegant and sophisticated woman. And she was aiming to establish a good relationship with Freddy Davidson.

Precisely why this should be important was unclear to her, except that being on good terms with Freddy might provide her with options that could prove useful in the future.

So she smiled at him and asked, "So who's it by then this...?" She leaned forward to check the notes on the white card fixed to the right of the canvas, "Liberation?" The notes were printed in a tiny font, which she found hard to read. She squinted and read a little more.

"Ah," she said. "It's one of yours, isn't it? How clever you are."

A bit too much, she thought, that 'how clever you are'. What's that word? Patronising? Now he's going to think I'm mocking him.

But he didn't.

"That's kind of you," he said. "Glad you like it. Another Prosecco?"

Encouraged by Stella's response, Freddy spent a further ninety minutes talking her through the rest of the collection. By the end of this ordeal, she had exceeded her intended Prosecco allowance for the day by two glasses.

On the plus side, she was feeling nicely tipsy. And she hadn't needed to say much beyond making the occasional encouraging comment. It was time, she felt, to look for a way out of this particular afternoon.

"Well, this is all very nice, isn't it? I've enjoyed it. But I think I'd better be getting back to the Warehouse. Get everything ready to open up."

"And the paintings?"

"Hmm?"

"For your nightclub. You were choosing five or six to hang around the place?"

"Ah," she said, suddenly remembering. "Yes, well, I mean, I liked them all, really. And yours, of course. Can I leave it to you? It's not so easy to choose."

"Certainly," he said, smiling broadly. "And I'll put a discreet notice next to each of them with a price and a number for the Art Shop. So it'll all be for free, and you won't need to handle any sales yourself. That okay?"

Freddy was at the Blue Warehouse quite often after that. He would turn up when the place was closed, bringing one painting at a time, and make a great show of wandering around, stroking his chin and peering intently at empty wall space. Before hanging a piece, he would insist that Stella came to approve his choice.

"We'll give each one a month or so, and then I'll switch it out for a different piece. Keep it all fresh."

So, she thought, the man is intent on becoming a regular feature in my life. What exactly is he after? Is it simply more sales for his artwork?

Around three, most afternoons, Stella would make herself a snack and a cappuccino in the little kitchen behind the downstairs bar while she cashed up the tills and checked the stock levels, ready for the evening. Freddy would often arrive at that point to do his thing with the paintings, and long before the end of his first week, he had a standing invitation to join her for a coffee.

"You've been so hospitable," he said one afternoon after hanging a landscape just inside the main entrance. "I'd like to repay your generosity. Why not let me take you out to dinner sometime? Somewhere nice."

She'd expected it, but his move made her feel off-balance. He wasn't the kind of man she'd been used to dealing with. It wasn't that he was pretentious. There was plenty of pretension on offer amongst her regular clientele. It wasn't even that he went on and on about art and couldn't seem to find a subject they had in common. The thing that unsettled her most was that he didn't drink. At least, not more than one or two small measures at a time. Socially and professionally, this was beyond Stella's normal range of everyday experience.

Well, she thought, I could give the man a try. What can it hurt?

And the couple of visits she had made with Freddy to the Art Shop had confirmed her suspicion that there was something more than involvement with artwork going on down there. Why else would that man they called 'Fat George' be working in the basement most of the time? And Junior Davidson, too. When she had asked Freddy if there was anything interesting to see on the lower levels, he'd put her off by saying the staircase was dangerous, the basement too dirty and that there was nothing much to see down there beyond the packing and storing of stock.

When she had gone over to the stairs anyway and hovered there briefly, as if she might be about to climb down, he hadn't been able to move her back into the gallery quickly enough. He had taken hold of her arm and all but pulled her away.

25

Jack had solved the problem of his daily trudge to and from the villa by hiring an electric bike from the hire shop at the end of the block. He simply collected the fully charged machine each morning and then dropped it off again each day when he was done.

After three nights at the Diamanté, he decided to move into the villa after all and hired the bike for the week.

By this time, he had managed to look through most of Hamish's paperwork and found nothing significant. He began a forensic search of the place to see if anything of interest had been hidden there.

He started in the bedroom, where he drew a blank until he got to the small painting hanging on the wall. It was an original, in oils, set in a deep frame. The artwork depicted what appeared to be Jesus, kneeling in prayer and illuminated by a light shining down from Heaven.

Not the most likely item for Hamish to have on his wall, thought Jack, as he reached up to take the painting from its hanger.

It was heavy, too heavy for a simple painting. Even before he removed the hardboard cover from the back of the thing, he knew what would be hidden inside. A handgun. It was a compact semi-automatic, a 9mm Sig Sauer.

God knows where he got that. Maybe he smuggled the little bugger in somehow?

There was a box of ammunition wedged in next to the Sig. He checked the clip. Ten rounds. And a round already in the chamber. It looked as though Hamish had been expecting trouble. He put the gun and the ammunition back inside the frame and carefully replaced the cover before rehanging the whole thing on the wall.

Let's hope I never have a need for you.

Once his search was completed, there was nothing more he could usefully do in Honda. But he'd grown to like the place and felt no compulsion to make a hurried return to the cold of the encroaching English winter.

His days now fell into a regular pattern. Each morning, he would wake late, shower, and do his best to shrug off the effects of the previous night's drinking over an espresso in the kitchen. He would eat a simple brunch of scrambled eggs and smoked salmon. This he would wash down with a half bottle of something white. After these exertions, he would stretch out on the lounger under the patio awning and fall asleep again. One thirty or so would find him on the sandy beach of a little bay a short walk away. He would wade about in the gentle swell and maybe even swim a few metres. Then, he would lie on the sand and doze in the sun.

Later in the afternoon, he would take the bike and zip along the oceanfront to buy groceries and wine. Later still, after a second shower, he would don his cleanest and smartest jeans and tee-shirt and ride into Arrecife, or south by the beach, to a suitable eatery for his evening meal. He would supplement the meal with a half bottle of something red.

Once back at the villa, he would sit out under the stars and listen out for the sound of the waves hitting the beach while the cicadas tuned up, ready for their nightly concert. Invariably, this procedure was accompanied by yet more wine.

Somehow, he always managed to make his inebriated way to his bed, where he sank into unconsciousness until the rays from the morning sun had edged across the bedroom and hit him in the face. Then, the whole happy performance would begin all over again.

Days passed, and he lost all track of time, along with his ability to care about it. Up until this trip out to Honda, he hadn't realised just how tense and how tired he had become. He'd grown addicted to risk - a kind of slow-burn adrenaline junkie. And now, here on this sunny coast and freed, however temporarily from all responsibility, he could relax. Pretty soon, he told himself, he would feel good enough to begin a daily exercise routine.

There was a loud knocking at the gate.
"Señor!"
Someone was shouting. He hauled himself upright from the lounger.
"Por favor! Señor!"
He padded over to the gate and opened the little door covering the grill. A man and a boy were standing there. The man seemed only vaguely familiar until he recognised the manager of the bike rental.
"You pay only for a week," explained his visitor in halting English. "Now ten days, si?"
Jack pulled back the gate and waved his visitor inside. It would be okay. He'd had time to sleep off his lunch. He jammed his wallet into his pocket and unplugged the machine from the socket where he had left it to charge before locking up the house and wheeling the bike out into the street. The man and his boy had arrived on an electric bike of their own, a tandem.
He rode alongside his visitors into Arrecife, and at the bike shop, he settled his bill and surprised himself by making a sudden and unplanned purchase of a brand-new electric bike. Then, in a surge of happy

enthusiasm, he added a small trailer, perfect for moving supplies to the villa.

As bikes went, his new purchase was far from being inexpensive. It felt odd to be buying something on a whim after all those years of penny-pinching. He still hadn't got used to having money to spend. But he did have money. He had pots of the stuff, accumulating faster than he could ever hope to spend it.

Riding his new machine along the oceanfront, he realised that as much as he was enjoying his change of lifestyle, it couldn't last. Eventually, all the drinking would wear him down, and he'd begin to feel bad. And then he would have to stop cold to get himself back together again. Just as he always had to. He was used to it.

Later that day he called Freddy.

"Okay there, Jack. Getting a nice rest?"

"I am, for sure. I'm still at Hamish's place. Haven't found anything here to worry about, so I'm enjoying the break. Everything good your end? Stella? The Art Shop?"

"No probs. You should take a few weeks and relax. Everything's fine here. Why wouldn't it be?"

"No reason."

"So, you phoned me because...?"

"Just checking. You know how I fret. And to say that I'm having such a pleasant break here that I might take on the villa for myself. Hamish had the place on a long-term rental, and I can't see it would be any problem switching me in as the tenant."

"Good idea. On a related topic, I've already spoken to Giuseppe about stopping the payments into Hamish's offshore account. We can split his share between the three of us."

"He must have loads of cash in there by now. What do we do about that?"

"I'll talk to Giuseppe, but I don't think there's any way we can access it. Not given how it's been set up. Maybe we'll leave it be and wait until it's all been drip-fed into H's regular account. That'd be the easiest way to empty the offshore. We can't let the bank know he's dead just yet."

"Especially since, as far as everyone else is concerned, he isn't."

"Quite. I'm not too sure what'll happen to his regular account. Once they twig he's disappeared, they'll likely freeze the cash until he can be declared deceased. In the end, it could all go into Stella's retirement fund."

"I don't think we can affect things either way," said Jack. "So that's it, then. Let me know if you need me for anything, but I'm planning to stay over here for a while."

He rang off and then realised he hadn't spoken to Stella since he'd left the UK. A mistake he needed to correct at once.

"Hello?"

"Stell. S'me."

"Who's this?"

"Very funny. It's not been that long."

"Almost two weeks. I was thinking you'd gone on walkabout, like Hamish. I still haven't heard from him either."

"I'm sure Hamish is okay," he lied. "You know how he is. But if you're feeling lonely and neglected, I can get the next flight back. There's been no trouble, has there?"

"No. Everything's fine. And you needn't worry about me feeling neglected. I'm quite capable of looking after myself when I need to. And, anyway, Freddy's been keeping an eye on things. He comes around most days, so I'm certainly not lonely. Far from it."

"Right. So that's okay then."

This was suddenly sounding ominous.

No wonder Freddy was happy for me to stay over here. The bastard's making moves on Stella.

He couldn't think of anything sensible to say.
"So, that's all good then."
"I'll phone again soon."
"If you like. See you when I see you."

Something in Stella's tone had disturbed him, and he certainly didn't feel comfortable with the idea of Freddy being constantly on the scene. Freddy was a womaniser. That was obvious. He had two women over here. And why wasn't he hurrying back to be with the lovely Ana? Why had he not taken her along on his trip to Liverpool?

So much for peace and tranquillity. That's always the way of it. Turn your back for a minute, relax, and stuff happens. He was confused. To go running home now would seem wrong. To stay away would be taking a risk. Did he really feel so strongly about Stella? He opened a fresh bottle and settled down to think things through.

26

Freddy was feeling good about the way things were going. Charnley had gone swanning off to Lanzarote and left him with a clear pitch. He had already established a foothold at the Blue Warehouse and got himself on friendly terms with Stella. And tonight, he was taking her out to dinner. It was true, he had to admit, that he'd been hankering, just lately, to get back to the beautiful Ana. She was at least twenty years younger than Stella Beard and an altogether more alluring specimen.

But then, Stella did have the Warehouse, which, if things worked out that way, would be a great UK base. He would have less need to rely on Charnley and could work more closely with Junior over at the Limo Hire.

Maybe, everything considered, it was time for Charnley to go.

But how?

Freddy was no killer. At no point during his life of crime had he had the slightest inclination toward violence. His involvement in the raid on Tug's place had been as peripheral as he could make it, and even that had felt like way too much.

On the other hand, whilst he himself had little capacity for violence, he had no objection to enlisting the help of others to carry out any violent acts his objectives might necessitate. It was all a question of distance. So if Charnley was to disappear, there was the problem of just how he was going to make that happen. He needed to consult.

"I don't know," said Junior. "It would feel odd to be topping someone I've worked with. Personally, the worst I think I can say about the guy is that he's a bit of a pisshead."

He was in the office above Junior's Limo Hire.

"I was making an effort to get along with Charnley, but it feels like every move I want to make, he's got some different idea about what we should be doing."

He could hardly believe he was doing this. Sitting, more or less calmly, discussing Charnley's murder with his grandson. It was, of course, all Charnley's fault. The idiot was forcing his hand.

As for Junior, it didn't feel as though he should be trying to involve the boy in this at all. But who else to turn to, to trust? And, in the end, everything he was doing would ultimately be to Junior's benefit. He was only doing what was best for his grandson after he himself was long gone.

And people died all the time. From all kinds of causes. What did one more matter? Nobody was going to miss Jack Charnley.

"I'm not necessarily suggesting you should kill the bugger yourself. Not if you don't want to. But maybe you know somebody who might? A professional. I'll pay whatever it takes."

"Let me think about it, Grandad. I'll see what I can come up with."

*

It wasn't long before Jack decided that he needed to cut short his trip and get back home to deal with his Freddy problem. There were just a couple of items he wanted to attend to before he went.

He needed to get himself officially recognised as the tenant of the villa. He liked the place too much to risk losing it. So he went into Arrecife with whatever paperwork he could find, along with a letter of authorisation bearing a neatly forged signature, and sorted things with the estate agent in charge of the arrangements.

Señor Beard, he explained, had been involved in a serious traffic accident and would not be able to leave the UK, or even his hospital bed, for some considerable time. And as Señor Beard might never be well enough to visit the villa again, he was spending time on the island to sort out the poor man's affairs.

He explained that the place had taken his fancy.

In response, the agent was happy to do what it took to make the switch and forward any necessary documentation to Jack.

The tenancy of the villa attended to, he phoned Fran.

"Hello, Jack." She sounded pleased to get his call. "Are you back in Arrecife?"

"As good as. I'm in Honda. I'm staying in Hamish's villa, just taking a break. You free for lunch? We could do Star City again if you like?"

He was waiting in the busy cafe when she arrived. He pulled out a chair for her and got her settled at the table.

"I've taken the liberty of getting us a bottle of something white and dry," he said, smiling and tapping the side of the wine chiller as he sat down opposite.

"We needn't finish the whole bottle if you feel it's too much."

*

If Freddy had been unhappy before about the way it was going with Jack, then he was even more unhappy now. What business did he have taking Fran out to lunch and parading up and down the town with that stupid little dog?

Fran had told him all about it.

He might have found the situation easier to accept if things had gone better with his dinner date with Stella.

Why on earth had she accepted his invitation and drunk all that Prosecco, and invited him in for coffee, if she hadn't intended to sleep with him? It didn't make sense. And the stupid woman had made matters even worse by claiming that she hadn't actually invited him back at all. He'd invited himself, she'd said, despite her making it clear that she was tired and wanted to get to bed. Well, there was 'going to bed', and there was 'going to bed', wasn't there? What was he supposed to make of her behaviour? He wasn't a fucking mind reader.

And now Charnley was here, strolling about the place, grinning. Like he knows something I don't. Takes over the fucking villa. Takes Fran 'out for lunch' what the fuck ever that means. And now he's back in the apartment.

They were sitting at their usual secluded table in Maggie May's. Jack was fiddling with his phone as the waitress came over and placed a double espresso in front of him and a flat white in front of Freddy. They were regulars. She knew which of them had which drink.

"So everything was okay, then, was it? While I was away?"

"Of course. What were you expecting?"

"Nothing less. Just checking. I would never have gone breezing off to the villa if I hadn't felt I was leaving everything here in good hands."

The cheeky little bastard. He was really pushing it.

"Oh, and Fran sends her regards. Before I forget to mention it. We had a nice lunch."

"She told me all about it. Said she was a bit worried about the amount you seemed to be drinking. Said you looked to have had a few by the time she arrived, and then you drank most of a bottle with the meal."

"I may have had one or two over the odds, but I was still compos mentis. I had a lot on my mind."

They both heard the dinging sound coming from the phone in the pocket of Freddy's expensive tweed jacket. He made no move to check it out.

Jack pushed his chair back and stood up.

"Gotta go for a pee. Won't be long. Don't let her clear my cup away. I haven't finished."

There was a dead fly lying on the seat next to Freddy. He considered dropping it into Jack's espresso. Then he thought it might be safer to look at his phone instead. It was an image sent from an unknown number. He opened it up. It was a shot of one of the barred windows in his finca. He would have recognised the window even without the beer stein. Through it, he could see a naked woman, face down on a sun lounger. Ana?

Then another ding. Another image. Clearer this time. Free of the bars. Ana, for sure.

"Nice."

Charnley. The sneaky little bastard was peering over his shoulder.

"Looks like someone I should know. Friend of yours?"

"It's Ana. My housekeeper."

"Well recognised, Freddy. And you can't even see her face."

He pushed his chair back sharply, causing Jack to have to dodge quickly to one side. Then he was striding towards the door on his way out.

"I'll get these then, shall I?" He heard Jack call after him. "You know, you've hardly touched yours?"

*

"What's the matter with Freddy these days?" asked Stella. "He's changed."

"As in?"

"As in, he seems preoccupied. He's usually so lively. Outgoing."

"He's probably focused on getting things sorted before he jets off back to that hidey-hole of his in Fuerteventura. Loose ends at the Art Shop. That kind of thing."

Puzzled and confused, more like, was what he actually thought. Freddy would have suspected him of sending the images, of course, even though he had taken care to use a burner phone to do it, using a number Freddy wouldn't have known. Just in case. It would follow that he would have to suspect that Jack had been up there in his finca, getting up to who knew what.

And he would have to be wondering about the loyalty of his staff. Why had Miguel allowed some intruder into his house? What else had this person been doing there? What was Ana's role in all of this?

There would be all kinds of interesting questions for him to ask once he got home, and he'd already booked his flight for the next day.

Jack was in the basement, working on a bottle of scotch and checking the stock. Fat George and Leggy had said goodbye and gone after a long day. Junior had left earlier.

The experiment with the vodka had been encouraging, and after he was done downstairs, he aimed to do some online research about exporting to various destinations abroad.

"Drinking again? You know how alcohol can damage your health."

It was Junior's voice. What was he doing back here?

"Works both ways, Junior. Booze has given me such a lot down all these years. I have to give the stuff its due."

"Well, at least it isn't going to kill you."

Something in Junior's tone signalled danger, and he turned, already fearing the worst. Junior Davidson was standing in the doorway with a handgun pointed in Jack's direction.

"Because you are the one who's aiming to do that? That what you mean? And there's me thinking we were colleagues, buddies even."

"It would all have been okay if you hadn't stepped on the Old Man's toes so much. I'm sorry to have to do this."

He said nothing. He felt sure Junior would be ready to pull the trigger if he'd set his mind to it. But he wouldn't want to do it in here and leave himself with a mess to clear up and a body to move.

"We'll go down to the lower basement. Then you can dig yourself a grave next to Hamish. He'll be company for you."

"And why would I be inclined to do that, exactly? You haven't explained that bit."

He was surprised at his own tone of voice. He sounded self-assured and confident when he felt anything but. The Davidsons had made their play sooner than expected. Still, he was prepared. The Davidsons were always going to be way too late. He just needed to be careful.

"I don't want you to have to suffer unnecessarily. I really don't. And if you co-operate, I'll make sure of it. Otherwise, this could be much more painful than it needs to be."

"It needn't be painful for anyone. Once you realise that my death will result in Freddy receiving a visit from the local cops over in Fuerteventura."

"That's so unfucking likely. You'll be just like our friend Hamish - off the radar. No one will have a clue where you are. I shouldn't think anyone will even care. Maybe your Mrs Beard will worry a bit, but given your gangster lifestyle, it'll be a long time, if ever, before she'll risk talking to the authorities."

"You think?"

"You're going to become just another missing person. That's all."

"If you kill me, there'll be nobody to stop the email that I've scheduled to fire off to the police."

"What email?"

"The one that I've set up on an account I opened for the specific purpose of telling the bizzies where they can find evidence to link Freddy baby with serious drug dealing. He'll get a long enough sentence to ensure he dies inside."

"I don't believe you."

"There's a second email pointing the finger at your good self. Kill me, and you'll have no way to stop both of them from being sent. You need me to be around so I can keep moving the scheduled send date along. Insurance, see?"

Junior lowered his gun a little. "I'm not too sure about any of this," he said. "I'm going to have to consult."

"Be sure to tell Fredders 'hi' from me. And don't waste your time trying to call from down here. You'll get a much better signal up in the Art Shop."

"Don't try to leave. I'll be right at the top of the stairs. Where's your gun?"

"And why would I tell you that?"

Junior left to make his call. He could hear him muttering into his phone on the staircase. Then Junior shouted down to him.

"Come up here. Grandad wants to speak to you."

He climbed the stairs, taking his time. Junior handed him his phone. He had it on speaker.

"Freddy? Nice to hear from you. How are things?"

"What's all this fucking nonsense you've been telling my boy? This could all go very badly for you."

"As opposed to digging my own grave down in the basement here and getting a bullet in the head? Very badly in comparison to that? You aren't at your persuasive best today, are you, good buddy?"

"You're a dead man, Charnley."

"I doubt it. As I told your boy here, I've seeded your life with so much evidence the police will have no problem ensuring that you rot in jail. There's more than one email in more than one special account, scheduled to go off to the cops if I'm not around to reschedule them when they're due. They'll tell them exactly what you are and where to find the proof. And there are more to do the same for your grandson."

"Very clever, Charnley, but I don't believe you."

"I plan ahead, Freddy. I suspected that things might come to this at some point. Not this quickly, perhaps, but that doesn't matter. From now on, you and Junior will be answering to me. Get used to it."

There was a pause. Obviously, he thought, the idiot's considering whether or not to go for broke.

"Would you like some proof? Help you make up your mind?"

"Such as?"

"You know I was inside your finca while you were away. I sent you those shots of your lovely housekeeper."

"All that proves is that you're a sneaky bastard, Charnley. And I already knew that."

"One thing I did was plant bottles of cocaine solution in places you would find difficult to explain. Along with other things which I'm not going to tell you about."

Another pause. He was beginning to enjoy himself. He was in no kind of hurry.

"I can't see how you'd get your hands on enough of the stuff to do that. It's not like you even know anyone over here. A few wraps bought from some nightclub dealer aren't going to impress the cops too much."

"Oh, I think they would, Freddy. But don't worry. I've planted more than that. Much more. There's no way you could find it all. But the cops would because I'd make sure they knew where to search. Take a look on top of the wall units in your kitchen. I'll wait."

There was a pause in the conversation. He could hear Freddy muttering to someone. Maybe Miguel or Ana. He heard what sounded like the scraping of a chair along the floor. A few grunts. Then, another pause.

He handed the phone to Junior.

"You won't be needing that now," he said, indicating the gun Junior still had pointed at him.

"I'm going back downstairs. I'm busy. And don't be late for your shift tomorrow. There's a lot to do."

Down in the basement, he waited, listening. Then he heard Junior as he walked across the office floor above his head and the bang of the door as he closed it behind him.

27

"So you're off to the villa again, are you?" asked Stella. "You haven't been back long."

"I'm aiming to split my time between there and here from now on. Get someone you can trust to run this place, and you could join me. I've asked you before. Why not think about it?"

His flight wasn't until the following day, and it had been a while since he had checked on things at his house, so he drove out there that afternoon.

Just an average-looking semi. On an average estate. In an average suburb. Average at his end, at least, whatever it might be at Horse's end of town.

It was a gloomy day in mid-November, with grey clouds hanging low over the rooftops. It wasn't raining yet, but he could smell the rain in the air as he climbed out of the Qashqai onto the drive.

There was something about the moist, dullness of the light that made it feel, somehow, as if he were stepping back into a different life, a life long since left behind. Like a ghost, returning to check on what had once been all too familiar surroundings. It was not a cold day, but he couldn't suppress a shiver as he searched his pockets for his door key.

And then Tooth appeared. Like magic. The man must have some kind of psychic radar. He was looking much older, Jack noticed. That had happened suddenly.

Why isn't he speaking to me? Usually, he's here to interrogate me or put me straight on something.

"Hello there, Alan. Long time, no speak. Everything good? Missus okay?"

Tooth looked as though he was about to cry.
"Alan?"
"She's dead."
"Marj is dead?"
Tooth nodded, obviously holding back tears.
"Oh, God. Alan, I'm so sorry. When? What happened?"
"Yesterday. She just collapsed, coming down the stairs. Phoned the ambulance. Dead. Don't know why yet."

Jesus. Poor old fucker. What do I do?

He looked at Tooth, standing there on his drive in the gloom. He looked grey, haggard, desolate, like a man who hadn't had much sleep.
"Want to come in for a coffee? I'm aiming to have a Pot Noodle. Want one?"
He nodded. Jack found his key, unlocked his front door and ushered him inside, pushing the pile of mail out of his way with his foot. He turned up the heating and took Tooth into the lounge.
"Sit yourself down, buddy. I'll get your nosh."
He went into the kitchen to boil the kettle, leaving Tooth slumped on the sofa. When he came back with the coffee and the noodles and a couple of forks on a tray, Tooth's face was wet, and he was dabbing at his eyes with a crumpled piece of paper towel.
He knew he wasn't going to be good at this.
"Well, Alan. You've had a shock there. I didn't see too much of Marj on the whole, but she always seemed a nice person. To talk to."
Perhaps she had been, but he couldn't recall a single conversation he'd had with Marjory beyond 'Good morning' or 'Looks like rain'.
"Lovely woman."
"You can't imagine."

"I can, actually, old buddy. That accident in Paris. Remember?"

Tooth nodded.

"Yes. Course."

"And you've been married for much longer than I was, I know. How long has it been?"

"Fifty-four years. Our anniversary is next month."

It sounded about right. He knew Tooth was edging into his eighties.

"Is there anyone you should call? Anybody taking care of you?"

He shook his head.

"No family. No friends, really, not now. Everyone's gone. Dead, most of 'em."

They sat in Jack's lounge, listening to the breaking rainstorm begin to drive heavy drops against the windowpanes, and ate their meal. It didn't look to him like Tooth intended to go home to his empty house any time soon. He felt sad. He'd spent years avoiding Alan Tooth. Dodging what he now began to realise must have been his increasingly desperate attempts at conversation.

You're a heartless bastard, Charnley. Do something helpful.

"Would you like to stay here tonight, Alan? You can have the spare room. Give you a bit of distance."

Tooth nodded.

"Thanks, Jack. I appreciate it. Thanks."

"Just sit there and rest. I'll go round to yours and make sure everything's switched off, and I'll lock up, shall I? I've got a spare toothbrush and a nightshirt you can use. Shower?"

Tooth shook his head. "Thanks."

He went out and ran across the two adjoining driveways, through the rain, to Tooth's open front door.

It was his first time in years inside Tooth's house. For the second time that afternoon, it felt like he was stepping back through time, all the way back to the seventies. Judging by the look of the place, very little had changed in Tooth's place since then. The patterned wallpaper, the curtains, the carpets and all of the furniture and appliances seemed ancient, apart from a large modern tv set fixed to the wall in an alcove by the tiled fireplace.

No kids. Few visitors. His and hers carpet slippers. Little in the way of wear and tear. A very neat time warp. And clean. Impeccable housekeeping.

He found the kittens in the kitchen, topped up their food and water, and replenished their litter tray.

Tooth, he realised, didn't have enough years left on the planet to get over the loss of his Marj. He couldn't bear to think of him living alone in this house of memories until his own end came to claim him. It would be ages before he would even be able to bring himself to move Marj's slippers from their resting place in the hall.

Fuck it. This is too much. Get a grip.

He switched off the lights and took the key hanging by the front door. He pulled the door closed behind him and heard it lock with a loud click as he hurried off again across the driveways.

Tooth alternated all that evening between reminiscing about his life with Marjory and periods of morose, deeply focused silence. Jack responded instinctively. He gave him several stiff whiskies, which Tooth, non-drinker that he was, obediently downed.

He'd sipped cautiously at the stuff to begin with. But partway through his fourth glass he developed an enthusiasm for single malt, which Jack found at first heartening and then unnerving.

"Maybe we'd best ease off on the whisky now, Alan. You should get to bed. I'm pretty sure you'll sleep tonight. I need to go through this mail and do some other boring stuff."

He was careful to stand close behind his guest as he made his way upstairs, just in case. Then he left him alone to sleep it off.

"See you tomorrow, then," he said, closing the door. "Earlyish. Got a flight to catch."

Tooth was snoring gently before he had even got himself back downstairs.

You'll have to sleep fully dressed. I draw the line at that.

The following morning, to Jack's amazement, Tooth was up first. He could hear him in the bathroom as he dressed.

He found sliced bread and a slab of butter in the freezer. He had to use a hammer from his tool kit to force the kitchen knife through the butter and remove a chunk to put in the microwave. Eventually, he managed to produce buttered toast and some instant coffee for the two of them.

"Sorry it's not much, but I wasn't expecting to be here overnight. And I'll have to leave soon. Need to go into town to collect my stuff before I have to get myself to the airport. You know how it is."

"Can't say I do. Never actually been in an airport. Flying about the place just wasn't a thing back in the day. And after Marj's agoraphobia forced her to give up work, there wasn't really the money. In the end, we couldn't go anywhere much. It was all I could do to get her to come to the supermarket with me in the car."

"I'm going to have to leave you on your own. You sure there's no one I can call? One of the other neighbours?"

"No. Thanks, but there's no one. You're the only neighbour I ever speak to. There's nobody else."

"I'll look online for some numbers you might want to call if things get tough. I'll write them down for you. You already have my number. Okay?"

"If you think that's best."

He spent a hurried ten minutes with one eye on the clock, noting down phone numbers for Social Services, Age UK and a couple of other helpful-looking outfits. He handed Tooth the list before walking him over to his own house and getting him settled into an armchair.

"Keep these handy. I'm going to be out of the country for a while. I'll call in on you when I get back. You're welcome to use my place whenever you feel in need of a change. I've left a spare key on your sideboard."

Sitting in the departure lounge at John Lennon later that day, he found his thoughts returning to Tooth over and over again. Tooth's situation, his loneliness, his apparent lack of funds and seeming absence of any sort of purpose over the past years was the kind of situation, he supposed, that so many fell into without even being aware it was happening - until it was too late. The kind of future he himself might have been heading for had he not happened to fall in with Hamish Beard and Freddy and their little band of criminals.

But there was a price. 'The price of freedom is eternal vigilance.' Some American president from way back had said that, right? Jefferson? He could google all that later, but he knew he wouldn't.

Constant vigilance was a difficult call. He could see that. And along with the need for vigilance went the need to be able to take action when necessary. It was okay for now while he was still reasonably capable. But that capability would gradually, inevitably, diminish, and he would become like the Ageing Moose.

The Ageing Moose, as he had once been horrified to witness in a nature film on tv, had steadily become unable to do what it had always been good at in all those years since it had left its mother's side and grown up to be a giant of the wild forest. Unable to outdistance the predatory and hungry wolf pack. Unable to turn and face down any predator which attempted to corner it.

He had watched as the doomed creature had been found and trailed all day, back and forth along the banks of a forest stream by the pack snapping at its heels until, exhausted, it had been dragged down and torn to pieces.

Unhappy with the direction his thoughts were taking, he bought a copy of the Daily Mail and settled down to read and wait, one eye on the boards, watching for his gate number to show.

His phone rang. Freddy.

"Yeah?"

"So you managed to hide a bottle of funny-smelling booze in my kitchen. So what?"

"Don't dick about. You know as well as I do what that smell means. And that bottle's only a small sample. There's a lot more of the stuff dotted around your property. Along with other bits and pieces of evidence I can point the cops at if I need to. So try to behave."

"So you're safe. Maybe. For the moment. Just tell me what the fuck it is you want."

"Simple. I want you to come to terms with the fact that what I say goes. I'm in the airport now. We'll talk when I get over there. Not on the phone.

He cut the call. He knew that Freddy would cooperate with his new strategy. He had no better choice.

Back again at the villa, he considered having an early night. Then he found the jug of vodka he had left standing in the fridge on his last trip. Vodka wasn't something he would normally drink, but the thought of flushing the stuff away went against the grain. It was, after all, alcohol.

By the very early hours, he had managed to drink half of it. It had been something of an heroic experiment and a challenge, but, in the end, he had to admit defeat. Vodka was never going to be his thing. On the plus side, he slept soundly.

The following morning he was well into his second coffee before getting busy with his phone. His first call was to the Reverend Neil.

"Jack." The Reverend's tone was friendly, sounding pleased to hear from his new acquaintance. "What can I do for you?"

"Oh, nothing in particular, Rev. Just letting you know I'm back on the island and wondering who I might be able to spend a little drinking time with later on?"

"Could be you called the right number. I'd be happy to split a bottle or two with you this very evening if you like. The bar in the Diamanté around eightish?

"I'll be there."

He supposed that this was how you did these things - turned acquaintances into friends. The now-dead Hamish aside, it had been a long time since he had gone out of his way to arrange to spend leisure time with another man. Not often since his army days. But that had been different. Going out on the town with your buddies from the camp was what you did. Women friends were different again. That was only natural. But this? This felt odd. You read all sorts about clerics.

Still, there wasn't time to mess about. It might take forever to get to know somebody on the island if he didn't push it, and he needed to create a credible front for the lifestyle he had in mind.

His next call was to Freddy, who sounded not at all pleased to hear from him and far from friendly.

"What?"

"We need to talk. I'll come to you. Be there around lunchtime. Get that nice new housekeeper of yours to set an extra place."

The taxi dropped him at the gate outside Freddy's finca at one o'clock. Miguel was there, in the shade of the carport, hosing the dust from the Mercedes.

"Miguel," Jack greeted him as he strode up to the door. There was little point saying much more than this. The man wasn't one of the world's great conversationalists.

"Dias." That was all he heard in return. Par for the course. So far, so good.

He pushed the door open and went into the gloom of the lounge. Freddy was sitting on a sofa, flanked on each side by the bright sunlight of the barred windows.

"Buenos tardes, Fredders. Everything okay?"

"Fuck off, Charnley."

"Now, now. No need to be so tetchy. How would it be if we were all like that when events weren't quite moving our way?"

"Get one thing straight, Charnley. I have no intention of doing anything on your say so. If you think you're going to run things back in the Baltic, then that's up to you. But I'm out. Clear?"

"Very clear," said Jack, settling into an armchair opposite Freddy.

"And don't think there's any way for you to stay safe if you set the cops on me like you've threatened. I'll make sure they get you too."

"Of course you will. That's exactly what I'd expect you to say. You're nothing if not predictable."

"So you've had a bit of a wasted trip, then. See yourself out, can you? And don't bother coming back."

He sat on in silence for a few long moments, considering what tone to take in making his response.

"And how do you intend to continue to cultivate your luxurious new lifestyle when I cut off your cash flow? These apartments you're planning to buy. And the yacht?"

"I'll get by. I still have the money laundering to fall back on."

"Not without Junior, you don't. Not so easily, at least. And he works for me now. And if you don't change your attitude, you won't be getting any more cash to launder from my end. We can manage all that well enough without you."

"But I'm not without Junior, am I?"

"You will be if I decide to put a bullet in his head. He seemed pretty relaxed about the prospect of doing that to me, so why wouldn't I?"

It's all so simple, really, he thought. All this gangster stuff. A bit like when you were a kid, surviving the schoolyard. It's all a question of being willing to respond to a threat by escalating things to the next level. Of course, you'd need to be capable of following through or at least be convincing enough about it. And Freddy wasn't one for taking too many risks. So he was going to lose.

Freddy seemed, suddenly, to collapse in on himself.

"I...," he began. "I..., I'll..."

"You'll what? You'll do exactly what I tell you. And you'll do it nicely and with a cooperative attitude. It's important for people who work together to get on well. You're an intelligent man. You can see that.

"So, where's that lunch?"

"There isn't any. Ana's not here this afternoon. I expected you to be gone by now."

"No matter. Miguel can drive me to Corralejo later for the ferry. I'll get something there. I'm hungry. And as for all this. I suggest we just consider it a bit of a reset, and everything'll be fine. But we have business to discuss first."

"Like?"

"Like expanding our operations into new areas."

"I told you I wasn't happy about that, didn't I?"

"You'll get used to the idea. Why don't we have a beer while we discuss things?"

There was no response.

"A beer?" said Jack.

There was still no response, so he got to his feet and headed off to the kitchen.

"Save your legs," he said, grinning. "I can see you've had a bit of a shock."

He ambled off and came back with two cold cans of lager. He tossed one to Freddy and sat down.

"So, there's a few things I have in mind," he began, pulling the opener from his can and taking a long swig.

"I'm thinking of operating further afield. Here would be a good place to start, don't you think? What with you being so well established here already."

Still no response.

"How about we move some of our product out here, to the islands? We could base our operations here, in your finca."

"You're kidding me."

"We might dissolve some of our stuff in some suitable liquid. Just like I did with the vodka I planted on your property. Get it up to your place here and then recover it for distribution to dealers on each of the main islands. Could be big, eventually."

No response.

"This could be a great place to start our growth programme. Holiday destination, lots of youngsters spending money. Perfect."

"As I thought I'd made clear when you raised the possibility of expansion last time, I see no need for it. We already make enough money, and we're doing it relatively safely. Why take the risk?"

Good. The old man's talking to me again. Progress.

"It's not just about the money. It's about building an enterprise. Having something to get out of bed for every morning. To me, any extra cash I make is a way of keeping score, as much as anything. Life can get to be totally pointless if you don't work at it. I think that's obvious."

"If that's what you think."

"I'll leave all that with you to mull over for a while, then we'll talk again. Next week, maybe."

There was a knock on the door leading in from the kitchen, and Miguel stepped into the room.

"Terminado."

"Okay. Tienes que llevar al Señor Charnley a Corralejo. Entonces puedes recoger a Ana."

"Bueno," said Miguel. He left, closing the door behind him.

"He's going to collect Ana to drive her back here later, so I've asked him to drop you in Corralejo en route. You'll need to go now."

"It's been a pleasure," said Jack, getting up. "Please don't disturb yourself. I can see myself out."

He got back to the villa, feeling pleased with the progress he'd made. As though he was well on the way to becoming the person he had always been fated to become.

Waiting for the ferry in Corralejo, he had munched through a tuna sandwich, but the day had been a full and demanding one, and he was already hungry again. He searched hopefully through the fridge and the cupboards but found nothing of much use. Tomorrow would be soon enough to lay in some groceries. He would eat at the Diamanté while he waited for the Reverend Jones to show up.

He phoned Fran.

"Jack?"

"Guess what? I'm back here in Honda for a while. You busy?"

She wasn't, she never seemed to be busy, and they arranged to meet for a walk and a coffee.

"It'll be exercise for the wee doggie and give you the chance to admire my new wheels. I have my own transport now, so I can be over there in fifteen minutes, tops."

She was waiting outside with Keith when he arrived.

"When you said 'new wheels', I thought you meant a car," she said, laughing, as he parked and locked his bike. "I never saw you as a cyclist."

"And I'm not really," he said, bending down to pet Keith, who was barking loudly in greeting and pawing enthusiastically at his leg. "Not the sort who uses bicycle clips, at least. It's electric. No pedalling. Fancy a go?"

"Some other time, maybe. Right now, this dog needs his walk."

They walked at an easy pace up to the little lagoon, the Charco, and found a vacant spot at one of the pavement cafes, packed, as always, with tourists.

They sat, sipping their coffees and chatting, while Keith sought out the patch of shade beneath their table. It was, as usual, a warm day, with the heat rising back up out of the paving, and Jack was glad of the rest.

Suddenly, unexpectedly, Fran reached across and took his hand in hers.

"It's good to see you again, Jack. I've missed you."

"Oh," he said, struggling to find an appropriate response. "Have you not been seeing a great deal of Freddy lately?"

"I see Freddy hardly at all," she said, keeping her hand firmly in place. "He spent all that time over in Liverpool, and now he's home, and there's been nothing. Whenever I phone him, he doesn't seem to want to talk much. Hasn't been over to see me once since he got back."

"Ah," he said, unsure what exactly was expected of him. "It's like that, is it?"

"It's that Ana. I know what it is."

"If you think so, Fran. Not my place to comment, really. You see that."

"You don't need to say anything. It's very clear to me that I'm in the process of being dumped."

"If that's true, then I'd have to say the man's an idiot."

She squeezed his hand.

"That's kind of you. We needn't discuss it. I just thought you should be aware of the situation, that's all."

The stroll back to Fran's apartment block across from Star City was slow and thoughtful. Their conversation was mainly about Keith and how well he had settled in with Fran. They filled in any awkward gaps with some talk about property prices in Arrecife.

And then, as they arrived at the apartments, he explained that he had been to the finca to see Freddy that very day.

"Just business. I wasn't there long."

"Was she there?"

"Ana? No. She was out somewhere."

She invited him up to her apartment. He must be hungry, she said. She would make him a meal. They could, maybe, open some wine.

"That would have been really nice," he said, realising that it would sound like a hastily improvised excuse, "but I can't. There's someone I've arranged to meet. Too late to cancel. It wouldn't be polite."

She smiled, but he saw the disappointment flicker briefly in her eyes before she made the effort to conceal it.

So. Now there's that. Careful now. Don't just rush in.

He rode his bike down the oceanfront to the Diamanté and arrived in time to catch the seven o'clock opening of the dinner buffet. Then there was a good half hour to spare after his meal before the Reverend Jones was due to show up to share a bottle or two.

He had to hope the man could separate business from pleasure, that he wouldn't feel compelled to try to recruit him into the faith. Start down that road, he told himself, and there's no telling where you might end up. Maybe on your knees in some draughty church, muttering your deepest yearnings into empty space.

He would let the Reverend have his say, which needn't take long, and then they could both relax and enjoy the evening. The Reverend Jones, he suspected, was going to prove to be a companion drinker of some stature, a feature missing from his life ever since the death of Hamish. He might not choose to become a member of Neil's congregation, but he felt sure that Neil was already a member of his.

It would be good to begin the proceedings on a relatively level playing field, so he decided to wait until Neil arrived to join him before adding to the two glasses of wine he had drunk with his dinner. Maybe a short stroll would be best.

Daylight lingered on the western hilltops when he strode off along the oceanside in the still-warm air. He felt relaxed. He thought of his earlier walk with Fran. Obviously, her time with Freddy was coming rapidly to a close, if it hadn't already, and she seemed to have identified him as a suitable replacement.

Would he welcome that? Apart from his recently developed situation with Stella Beard, he'd not had a significant relationship with a woman in years. He'd tried more than once, it hadn't worked out, and he had retreated into his safe place and stayed there. Stella was the first one in all that time to draw him out. And while their relationship had its intimate side, it was rooted as much in the practicalities of running a city-centre nightclub as anything else.

When he got back to the bar at the Diamanté, the Reverend Jones was already waiting at a table with a bottle of Rioja and two empty glasses. Jack almost didn't recognise his new drinking companion. He'd been looking out for the man's neat grey suit and his clerical collar, but this time he was dressed in the standard-issue tourist garb of jeans, tee-shirt and baseball cap, a casual jacket hanging from his chair back.

"Evening, Rev," he said, sitting down. "Dumped the official outfit tonight, have we?"

"We have indeed. I'm hoping to get a little merrier than the uniform allows. It's considered bad form to be spotted giggling over a couple of empty wine bottles wearing one's clerical threads."

He poured them each a generous measure of Rioja.

"But isn't there something in the Good Book about your man Jesus turning water into vino? There's a seal of approval there, right?"

"It's true. The wedding in Cana. A famous story, but the emphasis there was more on a demonstration of miraculous power than an actual piss-up."

"Well, I'm hoping it's going to be more the other way around tonight. Not that I have anything against the occasional miracle," said Jack, pausing to take a long drink of his wine. "So, how was your day? Been doing the Lord's work?"

"As always. Spent the afternoon at the bedside of a terminally ill member of my little flock. An elderly expat who left it too late to get herself back home. It happens. Sad, really."

"Ah," said Jack. "Hence the need for a bit of a piss-up. No worries there, buddy. I'm your man."

"And your good self? How'd your day go? Busy?"

He topped up Jack's glass.

"Somewhat. Been over to a place called La Oliva, on Fuerteventura. Business to attend to with someone over there. Curious type. Lives halfway up a volcano in an old farmhouse."

"Anyone I might know?"

"Freddy Davidson? I doubt it. He isn't exactly a churchy sort of bloke."

It was almost ten by the time they left the bar. Jack had intended to ride home on his new bike, but Neil talked him out of the idea.

"You're much too far gone. It wouldn't be a good plan. Use a taxi. In fact, I'll get one for you. I have the number."

He made the call and said he would wait with Jack until it arrived.

"It's a kind of car hire thing really," he confided. "Not actually a taxi. Not strictly regulation, I suppose. But the guy's safe and reliable. I use him a lot."

He couldn't help but notice that, as well-oiled as he himself seemed to be, the Reverend appeared sober by comparison. Odd. But, almost at once, the car arrived, and Neil was helping the now very drunk Jack into the rear seat. To his surprise, Neil climbed in beside him.

"I think it's best I see you get back home safely. You're in a worse state than I thought. We don't want you falling over in the street."

Surely he wasn't all that far gone? Perhaps he should argue the point? He fell asleep.

Ten minutes later, on the footpath outside his villa, he realised that someone was holding him upright, propping him against the garden wall.

"The number, Jack. Try to concentrate. We need to open your gate. What's the combination?"

"Easy," he said, his speech heavily slurred. "Battle of whatever. One, zero, six, six."

Someone else, over in the shadows, punched in the number, and the gate swung open. The someone else came over to help Neil manoeuvre him in through the garden and up to the front door.

"Key?"

He felt the pockets of his jacket being searched. Then they were inside, and he fell asleep again.

Most likely, he would have slept the sleep of the overwhelmingly drunk until way past dawn, but the pain argued against that. It was sharp, excruciating and made him cry out despite his stupor. And then he was wide awake, realising that something very intense had happened to the toes on his left foot. He was blinking back tears.

He was slumped on the sofa in the villa, the pain pulsing through him in waves. He was panting. Across from him, the Reverend Neil was now swimming into focus, sitting on a chair. He was holding something. Next to Neil, immobile on a second chair, a young man in a dark suit was staring at him.

He switched his glance back to the Reverend, who was also staring at him. Like the younger man, he was expressionless. He was holding a hammer.

"Sorry about that. Nothing personal, okay? Just business. We need to make sure that you understand your position in all this and that you take us seriously."

"You broke my toes," he gasped. "With a fucking hammer?"

"Calm down now. I doubt they're actually broken. Painful, yes. Bruised soon, too. But let's hope they aren't broken."

"You bastard!"

"I've told you once to calm down. I can do the other foot, too. If you like."

He said nothing. How bad was this? Pretty fucking bad was how bad it was.

"We want this to end well. We brought you home, didn't we? So you wouldn't have to come all the way back from town on a dangerously drunken bike ride. We want to help you through this."

"Yes. I get that. I see that now."

The pain was beginning, slowly, to subside into a dull throb. He fought down the urge to vomit.

"Okay, so now that you're awake again and we have your full attention, we can get down to business. That's what this is. A business meeting. Try to think of it that way."

"Already on it. Business meeting. Right. You're here to make me an offer. That it?"

"Excellent. You've got it in one."

He considered making an excuse, needing to visit the bathroom, so he could go by the bedroom door where there'd be just a chance he could make it inside and grab the gun from behind the praying Madonna before they could stop him. But there were two of them, and it was likely that one of them, at least, would be armed with something more than a hammer. And how could he be sure they hadn't already found and removed the Sig?

Park it. Find out what they want.

Neil hunched forward on his chair, looking at Jack more intently now. He was tapping the hammerhead into the palm of his left hand as he spoke.

"Okay. So we have a proposition we'd like you to consider. We've been watching you for some time. You and your buddy Davidson. And we feel you would fit nicely into our operation."

"Oh, goody."

Neil paused and said nothing for a few moments as if he might be considering the pros and cons of going to work on Jack's other foot.

"Right," he said hurriedly. "Didn't mean to sound flippant. Sometimes I simply can't help myself. Nerves, see? So, you were saying?"

Neil pursed his lips for a moment before continuing.

"Our organisation is in the drug business, just like yourself. Unlike you, we have an international reach and a business plan to extend that. We aim to be everywhere and to be the first place buyers think of going when they want any one of a whole range of products. Wholesale."

He was dizzy. Forget the thing about grabbing the gun. He really did need the bathroom.

"Gonna vomit," he grunted, pulling himself up. "Bathroom."

He made the mistake of putting all his weight onto his injured foot as he stood. He felt the increase in pain at once and settled for limping hastily across the room. The younger man followed him and waited in the doorway, watching as he retched over the lavatory bowl. He wiped his mouth on a hand towel and limped back with it to the sofa.

Neil handed him a glass of water as they sat down again.

Sipping at the water, he quickly considered his options. There were no good ones. He chose the least problematic and sat back to listen to what the Reverend Jones had to say. For now, he would cooperate.

"We've already made one approach. Unfortunately, when an organisation is expanding as rapidly as ours is, there's a need to be pulling in new people at some speed. This can occasionally lead to misjudgements. To the wrong sorts of operatives being recruited. You understand?"

"I think I get your drift."

"You and your little mob over there in the Baltic were slated to be brought on board some time ago. Sadly, the person we had handling that project was not up to the task, and he failed us."

"I think you have your wires crossed there, Jonesy. No one from your side approached us. Unless they were dealing with Hamish or Freddy, and I never got to know about it."

"Hamish Beard was too hard to pin down. We know all about him - how he can simply disappear from time to time. And Freddy was mainly spending his time in the Canaries. Junior Davidson, we decided, was too young and inexperienced. We needed someone down to earth. Someone local and dependable. We chose you."

Despite his situation, Jack was intrigued.

"The only approach, as you put it, that I was aware of was the cack-handed performance turned in by that crazy, Scottish bastard. Tug. Surely you don't mean him?"

"I can only apologise for the way he did things. He didn't handle it well."

"Are you telling me I have to deal with Tug? I was hoping I'd done for the idiot."

"Not at all. You didn't kill him if that's what you thought, but let's just say that Tug is no longer on our team. He messed up. We don't hold on to people who mess up like he did."

"And now you're trying to repeat the same mad performance. That it?"

"Not even close. I'm senior management. I don't normally work at this level, but we're stretched. And we want you. We think you're worth the effort."

"You hit me with a hammer."

"If it helps, I can tell you that I wouldn't lower myself to wielding a hammer, as a rule. I'd leave it to my man here, but I wanted to be sure you suffered no permanent damage. It's just a bit of bruising. That's all. To get your attention and to make a point."

"Thanks for explaining that. It makes me feel much better."

"So, going forward, you belong to us. We'll give you leeway on running your end of things, but we will always have overall control.

"You'll continue to develop your Baltic operation, and we'll take a cut of your expected profit.

"You'll take an increasing amount of product from our importer in Glasgow. We set the price.

"Clear so far?"

"Crystal."

"And that would've been it. If you'd gone along with Tug."

"But not now."

"Not now. Now, we've become so impressed by how you've handled your business and brushed Tug and his boys aside that we've decided to give you more responsibility."

"No, thanks. I'll pass."

Neil chuckled. "It's not a choice. You do what we say, and your cut should more than make up for what we take out of your coke operation. And there'll be other benefits, like access to information and resources. Maybe even protection if the situation demands it."

He reflected on the advantages such benefits had given Tug. What was Tug's role now? Being dead somewhere seemed the most likely.

Okay. So play along, and we'll see. Not a great deal of choice.

"And this new responsibility is...?"

"You're going to oversee the setting up of our operation here in the Canaries. That's good, right? You'll make money. We all will."

"Let's hope so."

"We will. We'll give you all the help you'll need. Like I said. Right now, though, I think you aren't looking too sharp. Slurred speech too. Get some sleep and be at the church tomorrow at midday. We'll talk some more."

28

It was cool inside the church, the street noise a muffled drone. He could see Neil up at the front, standing at the little table that served as an altar. If he had brought the Sig along, he could have shot the fucker dead right where he stood. But the other guy, the younger one, would know at once it was him, and they'd come looking - to punish him. If he played it smart, he should still be in with a chance.

There was no one else in the church. He walked quietly up to where Neil was standing and cleared his throat.

The Reverend turned to face him.

"Sorry to interrupt your communion with your boss there, Reverend, but we have a meeting, right?"

"Yes, we do, Jack. Glad to see you're so punctual. And you've cleaned up. Good. I do like my people to be clean, even if they can't be smart. Hungry?"

"You're reading my mind."

Neil led him through a side door into a small, simply furnished office. On the desk were sandwiches and a jug of fruit juice.

"Sit down, please. Eat. There's ham, or there's tuna. You okay with juice, or would you prefer something stronger?"

"Juice is fine. And in the interests of clarity, I'm not a full-time alky. I just like to binge occasionally."

"We wouldn't be having this conversation if you couldn't control your intake when necessary. I know you're not a complete alcoholic. I know a lot about you. How's the foot today?"

Jack sat down at the desk and picked up a sandwich.

"I'll live," he said. "I appreciate your concern."

"I suggest we put all that behind us now," said Neil, smiling and sitting down opposite, "and look towards a brighter future. A mutually rewarding and enriching one."

Jack took a bite out of his sandwich. Tuna. He'd been hoping for the tuna, a good omen.

Neil poured them each a glass of fruit juice. He could smell the pineapple at once. He liked pineapple. Another good omen.

"So," said Neil, sitting back in his chair. "Here's the thing. We're setting up a new hub here in Lanzarote. We've found a site, and we have a couple of hands already lined up. We need you to help. To take charge of the next stage. So finish your lunch, then Alejandro, the man you saw last night, will drive us both over there to have a look around."

What, in this life, he asked himself, is ever what it seems? The situation with the Reverend Jones, which had looked nothing but threatening hours earlier, was beginning to present opportunities.

Jack and Neil sat in the back of the Reverend's elderly black Mondeo as Alejandro drove them north on the LZ14 toward Costa Teguise. The road ran next to an industrialised stretch of coastline and through an area largely devoid of habitation. They had driven only a kilometre or so beyond Arrecife when Alejandro pulled off to the left onto a patch of rock and low scrub. From there, the Mondeo moved slowly along a rough track up to an ancient, stone-built barn. Beside the barn stood pens and shelters, housing goats with kids.

"Okay," said Neil. "Time to get out."

Neil and Jack climbed out of the car, leaving Alejandro waiting behind the wheel.

Shooing aside a pair of curious goats, Neil led the way into the building. They were met by a man who Jack guessed was in his early thirties. Neil introduced the man as Matias.

"I'm glad you could make it, Neil. Let me show you both around our little operation here."

It took the best part of an hour, by the end of which he knew much more about rearing goats and turning their milk into cheese than he had ever wanted to find out. And he had made the acquaintance of Matias's two middle-aged, white-coated and white-hatted employees, Nicolas and his wife Paula.

He had also been presented with a complimentary cheese in a box to take home. Sitting again in the car with Neil, he risked a quick sniff inside the box. It smelled, unsurprisingly, and very strongly, of goat.

On the drive back to the villa, Neil outlined the role he had in mind for his new recruit.

"It's just like your Liverpool operation, except with Matias's cheese products in place of art. The coke will be brought in, in bulk, through Puerto Los Mármoles and driven up to the barn. Your job is to set up and oversee an operation there to split up the batches and fill orders coming in from dealers around the islands. And eventually, we hope, from dealers abroad."

"We're going to hide the stuff inside the cheeses?"

"Of course we are. The cheeses can be all sizes, and they all stink of goat. Perfect, really. And you start tomorrow."

"I don't believe my bike will make it up the track."

"We'll drop you at the car hire. Put it on your expenses. You'll find all this is worth your while. Just do what we all know you're good at, and be nice, and everything will be fine."

"And how do I run the thing in the Baltic if you've got me stuck out here?"

"You delegate. Soon as you've got things running smoothly at this end, you can go home for a spell. You'll see. It'll all work out."

"Where's my passport?"

"It's safe. Don't worry about it."

29

Freddy was feeling anxious. His last meeting with Charnley had not been to his liking. The crumpled little bastard had him over a barrel, and he knew it. That threat to kill his grandson? Would the treacherous fucker actually do that? But then he'd shot Tug, hadn't he? And Craig, too. So why doubt it?

His phone rang. Charnley.

"What?"

"I'm on a tight schedule right now, Freddy, so listen carefully. There's no time for pointless arguments."

"And?"

"Remember we talked about expanding our operations? Well, an opportunity's come up, and I'm following up on it. And you're lucky because I'm doing it all somewhere else and not up at your finca."

No response.

"So you need to get your arse back to Liverpool and take charge of our Art Shop business, right? Asap."

No response.

"And you need to know that I've done a side deal with a third party, so expect deliveries from there. Should be relatively small scale at first while things bed in, but it'll grow. George is okay with keeping the books, and he'll share them online with me, so I'll still be dealing with the receipts and payments. You're going to be there to front the thing and sort out any urgent issues. Got all that?"

No response.

"I don't have time to fuck about. And neither do you. Just say yes, and then you can book your flight. Okay?"

There was a short silence from Davidson's end, and then, "Yes."

Jack terminated the call.

Freddy tried to forget how much he had come to despise Jack Charnley. He needed to put aside his anger and think clearly. Something unexpected must have happened to make the man change the script so suddenly. Only yesterday, he'd been here, throwing his weight about, and now, all at once, he didn't have time to do what he had always done and take care of the Baltic end of things. He sensed disarray. And disarray for Charnley meant opportunity for Freddy Davidson.

He booked a flight to John Lennon for early the next day.

*

It was a busy evening in the bar, and Stella was trying her level best to do her thing by perching on her barstool, sipping occasionally at her tall glass of fizzy white, and looking elegant. But this particular evening, she found it hard to get her head together. It was confusing.

All she had ever wanted was the Warehouse, regular shopping in town, a steadily growing pension pot and a dependable man at her back to ensure her security and provide a bit of company. The one area she couldn't seem to get quite right was the dependable man side of things. At first, she'd thought Jack would be a good fit for the role. That he'd stick around and behave. But he'd turned out to be into something dodgy down at that Art Shop thing he was running with Hamish. And now, he was prone to whizzing off to the Canaries for days or weeks on end. Doing what?

And where, come to that, had Hamish got to? He'd gone missing again. Not that he'd ever been particularly reliable either.

And, to add to the confusion, Freddy was coming back to Liverpool for a spell. He'd phoned to tell her and said he just needed to pop in to rotate the paintings he'd hung around the place. The last time he'd been here, he'd been all over her, and she'd gone and drunk too much on that dinner date and almost let him stay the night. Which would have spoiled things with Jack. There was no way it wouldn't have.

One thing she was sure of. She was getting to be too old for all this. But still, she would try her level best to leave her options open and keep the pair of them in play until she could identify the safest way to go.

So she'd been more than a little surprised, or even shocked when Freddy breezed into the bar with his much younger, very beautiful and nicely tanned companion.

The beautiful companion was carrying a large cardboard box of the type used for transporting paintings.

"Hi, Stella," he said. "This is Ana. My housekeeper at the finca. She's helping me with the artwork."

"Oh," she said. "Right."

"We're going to swap this for one of the other paintings," said Ana. "It's one of Freddy's new abstracts. Very colourful. Just what the place needs to cheer things up a bit."

Cheeky bitch, she thought. Housekeeper? Really?

"Get you something to drink?"

Ana looked at Freddy.

"No," he said. "Thanks anyway, but we want to stash the other painting down at the Art Shop and get back to our hotel for dinner. Okay if we do the swap now?"

"Go ahead," she said. "That's fine."

So, she reflected, as Freddy made his way over to a painting hanging at the far side of the room, Ana trailing after him with her cardboard box - that's that, then. There'll be no getting Freddy interested now, even if I wanted to.

As it stands at the moment, she thought, motioning to the bargirl to give her a refill, it looks like it's make things work with Jack, or start over with somebody new. And I really don't think I have the energy for that.

*

It didn't take long for Freddy and Ana to get back to the Art Shop with the painting they'd replaced. The place was closed to customers and locked, and Freddy had to punch in the code for Jack's newly installed security system to get them inside. But the lights were on, and there was the sound of movement coming from the basement.

Fat George appeared at the top of the staircase.

"All done down there, Boss," he said. "Ready for tomorrow."

"Good," said Freddy. He took hold of Ana's elbow and steered her back toward the exit. "We only wanted to stash this painting, so we'll leave you to close up. See you in the morning."

"Your people work late, don't they?" asked Ana as they left. "It's going on eight-thirty."

"It's just FG crating up tomorrow's deliveries. That's all."

"You must be selling a lot of paintings. I'm impressed. Didn't you say artwork was slow to sell? How do you do it?"

If there was one thing Freddy disliked about Ana, it was her inquisitiveness. The woman wanted to know about everything and everyone. Sometimes, he thought, it might have been best to have stuck with his weekends with Fran in Arrecife and stayed hidden away with his paintings up at the finca. Or maybe just tried harder with Stella Beard. He felt sure he could have won her round in the end, and at least Stella knew when to keep her nose out of things. But then again, he wondered whether it wouldn't be simpler to tell Ana everything and try to bring her into the business. She was young, enthusiastic and efficient. She could be an asset. It was a risk, though. And if she chose not to play ball and turned awkward? Then they would have to remove her, and he didn't even want to have to think about that.

"How's about we forget about dinner at the hotel and get a Chinese? I know a good place on Whitechapel. We could walk if you feel like some exercise. It's not far."

30

He arranged to have a hire car delivered to the villa later that day and took a taxi to the Diamanté to retrieve his bike from its parking spot. It was proving difficult to come to terms with his new situation. Ever since he'd decided to give up being a nobody and got himself into the drug business, there had been a succession of people only too keen to tell him what to do. First Hamish, then Freddy, and now this Reverend Jones snake in the grass.

It was self-evident that the guy was yet another psycho. And a sadist. A man who used violence as an opening gambit rather than a last resort. Still, he had to admit that as a management tool, it was effective. He was certainly paying attention to everything his new boss said and did.

Normally he would have combated the stress he was under by drinking himself to sleep. But he needed to be mentally alert from the get-go tomorrow, so bingeing on scotch, he decided, probably wasn't the best idea.

He searched out his pack of Sleep Nites. The dosage was strictly one or two pills only, with no alcohol. He took two and washed them down with a large whisky ten minutes before climbing into bed.

A little over eight hours of dreamless slumber later, he woke feeling rested and well.

By nine o'clock, he was back at the goat barn. Neil and Alejandro were already there, standing outside in the midst of a group of curious goats, discussing something with Matias. Matias was smiling.

Neil left the others in conversation and came over to greet him as he climbed out of his newly hired Hyundai.

"Good to see you're making an effort, Jack. Come with me and meet your boys."

They walked around the side of the building and into the yard at the rear. The yard was empty, except for a caravan parked at one end of it. And two young men. They reminded him of some of the illegals he'd seen around the island and on the tv news, risking everything to drift across from the African coast in flimsy boats in a desperate search for something better.

Would they consider this to be something better? He couldn't begin to guess.

The two men were sitting on a low bench in the shade by the caravan, a line of washing strung out behind them. They got to their feet as Neil and Jack approached. Both looked apprehensive.

They came to a halt opposite the pair.

"Guys, this here is Señor Charnley. He's your boss. You do whatever he tells you."

He turned to Jack.

"They're yours to command, Jack. They won't give you any trouble. The taller one is Omar. Shorty's called Hasan. They claim to be Moroccans, but who would know? They speak English well enough. And Spanish too. Talented guys."

"Morning, fellas. Nice to meet you both. You call me 'Jack', okay?"

There was a murmur in response from Hasan, but neither was keen to look him in the eye. They seemed far too subdued for a pair of youngsters.

"They live in the caravan. In rent-free luxury. Matias and his wife keep them supplied with food."

Let's hope the poor bastards like goat cheese.

He took a few seconds to assess his new workforce. They looked healthy, well-fed and decently clothed. Jeans and tee shirts, like almost everyone below management level out here. But they looked scared. He wondered whether Neil had been busy with his hammer. That would be enough to scare anyone.

"Come and take a look inside at where you'll be setting up."

Neil was already walking towards a doorway at the back of the barn. Jack followed.

They went through into a large, high-ceilinged room, windowless save for a small window over the door. The room was in good condition, with a sealed concrete floor and walls finished in smooth white plaster. In the far wall was another doorway.

"This is it," said Neil. "The door across from you connects with the cheese-making effort up front. You'll want to get your two boys to work and set this up like the operation in your Art Shop."

"We're going to want tools and materials. Where am I supposed to get it all? And what do I use to pay for it?"

"Not your problem. Unlock your phone and give it to me."

He handed over his phone and watched as Neil keyed in a number.

"You have Alejandro's number in there now. Call him for anything you need. He'll have it delivered to you. Pronto. Anybody gets nosey - just tell them you're extending the cheese-making and storage facilities. Simple."

He looked around. The only other things in the room were a fridge, a bench, a table and two chairs by one of the walls. On the bench, he saw a stack of paper, along with a container holding sharpened pencils, pens and markers.

"Paula will feed you and keep the fridge stocked. You can use that to sort out any extra drinks and snacks you might want."

Is this good or bad? Trapped up here with two strange Moroccans and a barn full of goats? But what can I say? Nothing that might upset the psycho, for sure. Go with the flow. Learn.

The first morning, there wasn't much for the Moroccans to do but sit on their bench while Jack punched lists of tools and equipment and some basic materials into his phone. These he sent off to Alejandro.

At midday, Paula came through with coffee and sandwiches for Jack and his workforce. He ate while he worked. Not long after lunch was finished, the deliveries began to arrive, and he was able to get Hasan and Omar busy with unloading and moving the stuff inside.

That afternoon, he sketched out the diagrams for the timber partitions, benches and storage racks they were going to need to handle the coke. It was simple enough, and his small workforce seemed to have no trouble understanding what was required. Any attempt at conversation with the pair beyond what was necessary for progressing the task in hand quickly degenerated into a series of monosyllabic responses.

Over the following days, the work went smoothly, with Jack returning each evening to his villa and the Moroccans retiring to their caravan in the yard. In under a week, they had the place ready to open for business.

The Reverend Neil came to inspect their progress and give the arrangements his approval, and the day after that, the first consignment of white powder arrived. It was vacuum-packed inside a luggage bag in the back of a small white van emblazoned with the logo used by Matias for his goat cheese enterprise.

Jack showed Hasan and Omar how he wanted them to cut, weigh out and divide up the powder to fill the orders emailed in by Alejandro each morning and how to pack and seal them into the hollowed-out cheeses supplied by Matias. The cheeses were shipped out in the van.

There was a shower in the yard and laundry facilities for their work clothes, which, in the case of Hasan and Omar, amounted to a pair of briefs each.

It was a simple system, and it worked well. He got a phone for Omar and gave Alejandro the number. From then on, he left the day-to-day running of the place to the Moroccans.

"Time to get yourself back to Liverpool and check up on our operation there," said Neil. "Make your presence felt, go through the books, do a stock count. And don't let them forget who's in charge."

It was the Sunday of their second full week of operations, and Neil was sitting with him on the patio at the villa. The new coke room was closed on Sundays.

"From now on, you'll get a percentage from the take here, as well as from the Liverpool end, paid into your offshore account. Just keep things running smoothly and follow my instructions, and you'll do okay."

He felt relieved. He'd been waiting for this moment. A modest amount of freedom was being returned to him.

"I'll need my passport."

Neil reached into his pocket.

"Here," he said, throwing the passport onto the patio table. "I don't believe you'll try to run off. You have too much invested in your new life. But in case you're tempted, you should know that if you do, we'll find you, and we'll finish you. And not in a nice way."

He didn't doubt the Reverend's sincerity. An unsupervised trip home was as good as it was going to get for now. He would be patient.

"And you would expect me back here when?"

"I'm thinking maybe as long as three weeks at each end of things for now? But it's up to you. Your responsibility is to keep our operations, here and in Liverpool, running smoothly and trouble-free. Anything goes wrong, and it's on you. Clear?"

"And Freddy Davidson? He's on the books at the minute. And he's expensive."

"Your problem, Jack. If you want to keep him on the strength to help you, you pay the guy out of your cut. Or get rid of him. I don't mind which."

"You wouldn't care if I used him to supervise things at this end sometimes? As a stand-in?"

"If you can make it work, it might be a good idea. If he drops the ball, we'll be coming after you, not just him. Like I said, win or lose, it's all on you."

31

It was the first week in December, and the Point was cold and gloomy. By the time the taxi dropped him at the semi, the weather had deteriorated, and it was drizzling softly. His Qashqai was still in place on the drive, glistening wetly in the glow of the streetlights. The nightlight in the porch had already turned itself on, and the heating was on low. A small mountain of mail had built up behind the door. He flicked through it. Nothing important. He dumped the whole pile, unopened, into the bin in the kitchen.

Despite the gloom and the drizzle, it felt good to be back. The unfashionable and sparsely furnished sixties semi was, and always had been, his bolt hole and his refuge. Even Vlad's intrusion hadn't managed to dispel that sense of being home and safe. He doubted that anything could.

The place smelled of dust and ancient furniture and old floorboards, mixed in with long-forgotten late-night fry-ups, empty wine bottles and over-spiced takeaways. You couldn't buy that smell. It was priceless.

There was a full bottle of malt on the worktop by the sink and a clean glass. Thank God for that. He needed a drink. After two weeks under Neil's scrutiny, when he hadn't dared to indulge himself, he felt he needed to binge. He deserved to relax.

And he was hungry. He phoned for a pizza. Anchovies and malt whisky. It didn't get much better. He poured the first glass and savoured the taste. He stood the bottle beside him on the side table and slumped down into the armchair. He could worry about business tomorrow. He could deal with Freddy then.

He was into his second glass when the pizza boy began banging on the front door. Very soon now, he really would get that bell fixed.

He handed over a big, grateful tip and went back to his armchair, but just as he'd opened the box and the aroma of the anchovy-heavy topping had hit him full in the face, he heard more banging.

It was Tooth. He'd forgotten all about Tooth. The man was standing there, looking lost. He hadn't shaved in a couple of days, and on Tooth, that was far from a designer look.

"Alan."

"Yeah. Hi. Saw someone leaving your house. So I was checking everything was okay. Wasn't sure if you were back."

The drizzle was settling on Tooth, giving him a soft gleam in the porch light. He showed no sign of being about to go away.

"Want to come in for a bit?"

He couldn't believe he'd said that. One of his cardinal rules for life at the semi was to avoid inviting any of the neighbours inside. Invite someone in, and you've no way of knowing how long they might stay. And then you'd need to make conversation. But he had already broken that rule for Tooth. He'd been here before.

"Thanks, yeah."

And then he was in, brushing past Jack, through the porch and into the lounge. By the time Jack had followed him in, his elderly neighbour was settled into the other armchair.

He knew his pizza would be cooling off, there on the table, waiting. He looked across at his visitor.

"How've you been, Alan? Finding it tough, I imagine."

"A bit. The days are the worst. I've been taking a pill at night, but I think I should stop that soon."

An awkward silence.

"Want some pizza? Anchovies?"

"I don't want to take your meal."

"You'd be doing me a favour. Really. Didn't realise I'd ordered such a big bastard."

He got a plate and a knife from the kitchen and cut the pizza in half.

"You been eating properly?"

He put half on the plate and handed it to Tooth, who stared down at it like a man who had possibly never eaten a pizza before. Or certainly not one with double anchovy topping.

"I've never had one of these. Has a strange smell."

"Anchovies, Alan. Bit strong, that's all."

He wasn't surprised. In all the years he had lived next door, he had never known the Teeth to venture out much. And he couldn't recall when he'd last seen them have a visitor. They'd been left behind in a decades-old domestic landscape that simply hadn't taken any account of a changing world. Their idea of a snack would have been tinned spaghetti on toast, anchovies a foreign land.

"Whisky?"

"Don't drink as a rule. Marjorie didn't really approve."

"I seem to remember you putting away a fair few the last time you were here. Try one anyway. Might help you cut the sleeping pill. Single malt. Full of nutrients."

He fetched a second glass and poured Tooth a large measure.

After the pizza and two more whiskies, Tooth was beginning to nod off. There'd been a tearful interlude when he'd told Jack his life story, which, despite his being almost eighty, didn't take long. What to do with him now? He'd planned to drink, and he was pretty sure his guest had reached his limit.

"Want to stay here again tonight? A night away might help, even if it is only next door."

Tooth muttered something incomprehensible.

"Spare bed's like you left it. Let's get you upstairs."

He managed to haul Tooth up onto his feet and guide his unsteady progress up the stairs and into the guest room. Getting him to lie down on the bed was easy enough. He pulled off his shoes and dropped them onto the floorboards at the bottom of the bed.

That's it, buddy. That's as far as I go with the personal care. Sleep well.

Feeling an urgent need to get back to his drink and his comfortable armchair, he had to all but force himself out into the drizzle to lock up Tooth's place for the night.

*

Gloomy daylight. Backache and a raging thirst. A rising sense of panic that he might be very late for his shift at the goat farm. And then relief as he realised where he was. His semi. Sanctuary. He'd slept fully dressed in the armchair again.

Fuck it - Tooth! Maybe just leave the old guy where he is. What's the harm?

Ninety minutes later, he was back at the Art Shop. It felt like he had never been away. Freddy was there.

"Let's get a coffee somewhere," he said. "Need to talk."

These days 'a coffee somewhere' always meant Maggie May's. They found a table in their usual shadowy alcove beneath the staircase. It was secluded enough. No one would hear them there.

"So the thing is, Freddy, everything's changed."

"That's good. Because it fucking well needed to."

"Just shut up and listen. It's important, and it affects you. It affects you big time."

"Go on, then," said Freddy, leaning back on the bentwood chair. "Surprise me."

"You can forget whatever you might have believed about who's in charge of our business activities. All your ideas are yesterday's news. It appears that we are now being run by A.N. Other. Totally."

"Can't say I'd noticed."

"Even so, you need to come to terms with this very quickly."

"Maybe you've had a bang on the head or something, but I'll give you a chance to explain what the fuck ever it is you think you're talking about. Who is this A.N. Other?"

"An outfit called the Church of Miraculous Salvation. The bit of it that affects us, in particular, is fronted by one Reverend Neil Jones."

"A church? And in what sense do they now run things?"

"In the sense that they control the money and that we do what they say. Or else."

As patiently as he could, he explained to Freddy his recent experiences on Lanzarote, but, even as he was doing so, he began to see the lack of credibility in his account. And well before his tale was finished, he had begun to wonder whether he had allowed himself to be taken in, intimidated and made a fool of.

"So, some guy who calls himself a reverend has hit you on the toes with a hammer, and now he controls us. Is that it? That what you're telling me?"

"There was this other guy, too. This Alejandro."

But Freddy had stopped listening. He was consulting his phone.

"Okay, I've just googled the church. On the face of it, the results appear to lend your claims some substance."

"As in?"

"As in, this Miraculous Salvation outfit of yours has several branches. Liverpool, Arrecife, Valencia, Civitavecchia and, wait for it, Santa Marta."

"Civitavecchia? Santa Marta?"

"Rome and Colombia, it seems. They're all seaports in western Europe and Colombia. You haven't even bothered to search on all this, have you?"

"I've been busy."

"Well, your story's looking like it could be credible, at least. I tried to warn you, but it looks as though you've managed to land us in the shit. Congratulations. And thanks for nothing, arsehole."

"You could try to bear in mind that I hadn't really done anything beyond having a nice time at the villa. Nothing dangerous. Zilch. Nada. Fuck all."

"Really?"

"Yes, really. And I might point out that I was the one who tried hard to tell you that if we didn't grow quickly enough, we'd get swallowed up. And guess what? We have."

But he had to admit he was surprised at Freddy's response to all this. He'd been expecting a tremendous hissy fit of some sort, and being called an arsehole didn't even come close. Just went to show you never could tell how people were going to react. He looked Freddy in the face. He was ignoring him, frowning.

"We should check out the local branch of the Miraculous. Not us, I mean, not me. You. You look more the type, and they already know who you are."

Promising, he thought. It looks as though Freddy might come on board.

"I will. I'll get over there right after this. Where exactly is it?"

"Somewhere off Leeds Street. You'll have driven past it. An old church hall on the edge of some clearance."

Freddy showed him an image of the place on his phone.

"I think I know the building. Used to be a carpet warehouse, if I'm not mistaken."

"Want another?"

He signalled the waitress for two fresh coffees. He intended to walk over to Leeds Street. He needed the exercise, and a further shot of caffeine could only help.

"So, under the new regime, things are going to have to change."

"Like how?"

"Like I now have to split my time between overseeing the goings-on at the Art Shop and doing the same back in Arrecife. I can't be in two places at once, so I'll either have to rely on running things over the phone or get someone to alternate with me. Want the job?"

"What's the pay?"

"I'll give you half my cut, whatever that turns out to be."

"The alternative?"

"There isn't one. You'll be out on your ear."

"You can count me in for now while we check these guys out and get a better fix on all this. Then we'll see."

It was less than a mile across town to the Leeds Street branch of the Church of Miraculous Salvation. The church was open, but the morning service was long over, and the place was empty. He went inside and found lines of chairs arranged in rows on either side of a central aisle, in front of a long, low table supporting a modestly dimensioned cross in gleaming brass. The whole arrangement was very similar to the church he'd seen in Arrecife.

He took a seat at the back and waited. After a few minutes, a door at the head of the room opened to admit a man, a priest, in his fifties, in a grey suit and a clerical collar.

Without looking directly at him, the Reverend Jones walked slowly over to the table and bowed his head for a long moment in front of the cross. Then he walked the short distance down the aisle to stand close to where Jack was sitting.

"I'm afraid you're too late for the service. Would you like me to pray with you?"

"Not today, thanks, Neil."

There was a thoughtful pause. Then Neil sat down next to him.

"Then how can I be of help to you today?"

"Just a social call, kind of. I wanted to check out your place. See who I might be dealing with over here. Us all being on the same team, as it were."

"You're checking out the lie of the land around your new situation. Due diligence. I like that. So now you know where we are, should you have need. But you do, in any case, have my number. So, if there really isn't anything I can help you with?"

Jack got to his feet, and Neil did likewise.

"Right now, I have business to attend to, Neil. Be seeing you soon, I'm sure."

The Reverend Jones said nothing as Jack walked out of the church and back into the cool December greyness of the Liverpool lunchtime.

32

"I'm going to pop over to the Art Shop for a couple of hours," said Jack, pulling on his jacket. "Freddy and Ana are due to fly back tonight, and I want to make sure everything's okay."

They were in the apartment, and Stella was busy with her makeup in front of the bedroom mirror.

"See you later, then, shall I? I'm just making myself look beautiful."

"You couldn't be more beautiful than you are already, Stell, believe me. I won't be home late."

The compliment was well-intended, but he suspected it might have come across as glib, and that was bad because he'd noticed that Stella seemed to have developed a need for compliments lately. Was it simply her age?

He tried again.

"You look gorgeous, as always." His parting shot as he left.

When he arrived at the Art Shop, it was almost lunchtime, and Leggy was finishing his morning shift, changing some of the artwork on display in the gallery. Fat George was working in the basement with Junior, making up packages, as usual, for delivery the following day. The whole operation ran smoothly enough these days, whether he was there or not. Even the new deliveries beginning to arrive from Glasgow had been absorbed into the workflow without a hitch. At some point in the not-too-distant future, he realised, there would be a problem with Horse when the Church would have to decide whether to squeeze him out or incorporate him into their operation. But for now, all he really needed to do was to show the flag occasionally and keep on top of the accounts. Two sets of accounts. One for the legitimate business of retailing paintings and another for keeping track of the strictly illegitimate side of things going on downstairs.

Everything was as normal, apart from the luggage parked in the corner of the office, waiting for Freddy and Ana to collect on their way to the airport.

"I'm going out to find myself some lunch," he told Leggy, who was busily dusting a large, garishly coloured landscape painting. "You can go whenever you like. Just lock the door and leave those two downstairs to do their thing."

He'd noticed that Leggy was becoming more and more arty these days. Maybe it was the day release to art school and the people he was mixing with, but that strange hairstyle with the centre parting and the speckled bow tie he was wearing seemed to add something to the atmosphere of the place. Something weird.

Maggie May's, he thought. Steak pie and chips.

When he got back to the Art Shop, the door was unlocked, and there was no sign of Leggy or of anyone else until he stepped through the doorway into the office, and Ana appeared at the top of the basement stairs.

She looked startled to find him there, although she did her best to hide it.

"Here on your own, Ana? Where's Freddy?"

"Oh, he won't be long. He's gone to buy some euros for later. We're completely out."

"You were downstairs," he said, not making it sound like a question or an accusation - just a statement. To see what she would do with it.

"I was looking for the loo." She was bending down over her luggage, her back to him, fiddling with something.

"Through there," he said, pointing across to the corner of the gallery. "It says 'Toilet' on the door. You'll see it. You walk past it on your way in."

"Oh," said Ana. "Right."

What the fuck has she seen down there?

He went down to the basement. The light was on in the anteroom, but the door to the powder room was securely locked, and the small red light above it, which indicated when the room was occupied and in use, was unlit.

So, Leggy, Fat George and Junior had all gone off on a lunch break, leaving Freddy and Ana in charge of the shop. And that would have been fine until Freddy had gone, leaving Ana on her own.

And there was that, wasn't there? The puzzle as to what Ana was doing with Freddy. She was an attractive, vivacious young woman, and Freddy was very far from being an appropriate partner, even if he was paying her way over the odds. Stuck in that gloomy old finca for weeks on end, with Freddy painting his days away, and she doing what exactly? Cleaning, tidying? Ironing Freddy's shirts?

A girl like Ana could easily have got herself a much better deal. A younger man, an interesting place to live, a social life. Either she was a very unusual young woman, or there was something more, something he'd missed.

And there was another issue that was bothering him. Something Freddy had said about Ana having postponed a trip she had only recently booked to Madrid to visit her mum, who was, suddenly, seriously ill. He hadn't given it any thought at the time, but now he had to wonder why she was fitting in this trip to Liverpool rather than going straight to her mother's bedside.

But then Freddy came back, shouting to tell Ana that he had the euros and asking if there was any coffee going.

"Ana's using the loo right now," he said. "Help yourself to coffee. You can get me one too, if you wouldn't mind."

*

Freddy hadn't even had time to finish his drink before the airport taxi arrived, and they were gone. Leggy, Fat George and Junior straggled in from their lunch break, and Jack worked on, pouring over paperwork and the office laptop all afternoon. Then Leggy went off to get the train back to his mum's in Old Swan, and Junior came up from the basement with Fat George, and they both left for the day.

He went downstairs, put on a lab coat against the white dust, and checked the stock levels, adding in the packages for tomorrow's deliveries. After that, he returned the lab coat to its hook and went back to work on the laptop. He produced a full statement to hand over to Neil when required. Nothing traceable, no emails, just a printed sheet without a name. It would be meaningless to someone who didn't know exactly what it was. And everything meaningful on the laptop was encrypted.

He checked his watch. Eight o'clock. Time for another coffee while he waited. He'd had a text that morning telling him to be ready for a visit at eight-thirty.

The Reverend Jones seemed pleased with the statement. He seemed pleased also with the way the basement was organised when he went down to put on a lab coat and check the stock for himself.

Back in the office, he sat down at the desk with Jack.

"Individuals like yourself are a rarity in this business, Jack. You have good organisational skills and an ability to work successfully with all sorts of people. And you know how to keep your head down and not draw attention to yourself."

"You're making me blush."

"There's really no need to be so self-effacing, even if you are inclined to make a joke of it."

He leaned forward, spreading his hands on the desktop.

"I'm at liberty to tell you that my superior, the Bishop, has you in mind for promotion. If you're interested, you can have a career with us. A real career."

The Bishop? Jesus.

"I'm flattered, but I simply can't see myself conducting church services. I'm not particularly religious."

"We don't need you for that. It's more for the business side. The world market for salvation is growing exponentially. You must be aware that conventional religion and politics have long been failing to provide the answers everyone wants. Old-style consumerism is driving itself onto the environmental rocks. People are turning more and more readily to drug-based solutions."

"And you guys aim to be at the forefront in providing them. I get that."

"Take it from me that for us, the future can be golden. But we have a problem. We're in a race for this market, and we don't have much time to establish ourselves on the kind of global scale we're going to need very soon now if we're to succeed. We need individuals like you to help us grow."

It was true, he felt, that the small-scale operators were doomed. Anyone should be able to see that. And maybe the only sensible way forward was to accept affiliation with, and subservience to, some bigger outfit.

And if that was the case, then how much simpler and safer to join the bigger outfit just as soon as the chance presented itself.

"What would I need to do?"

"You'd need to distance yourself from any day-to-day operations on the ground. Like this one. Put someone else in charge. Is there anyone you could trust?"

"There's Freddy Davidson or his grandson Junior. Either of those. Probably Junior at this end. Keep Freddy over in the Canaries."

"And it might be an idea to not spend all of your free time over at that nightclub place. Visit, by all means, and stay the night when you want to. Nobody expects you to become a monk. But maybe you should hold on to that house of yours up on the Point as your main domicile. It's all about front. It just looks better."

"Let's say I'm in. What's up next?"

"This." He reached down into the briefcase standing by his chair and pulled out a plastic bag, which he placed on the desk.

"In there, you'll find a small, leather-bound bible, a couple of clerical shirts and collars and a plane ticket. You'll also find details of an offshore account in your name. Accept our offer, and there'll be five thousand a month paid in, whatever."

"Doesn't sound like much, all things considered."

"That's only expenses. There'll be more, a lot more, in bonuses per job. The amounts will be generous, depending on the take and the profits at the time. And there'll be two thousand per month going into your regular account when you give me the details. That'll be your stipend from the Church. Your cover. Okay?"

"Maybe."

"Do well, and there's promotion down the line. Big money to come. You'll soon see how it works."

"The plane ticket?"

"Manchester to JFK return. I fly out there before you, and you go early next week. You fly back two weeks later."

"And I go out there to do what?"

"What you're good at. We're opening a branch of the Church over in Queens. You'll be there to advise on setting up a coke room a couple of blocks away. An operation like the one you have here and the one you set up for us on Lanzarote."

"Okay, sounds like the sort of thing I can do."

"And another thing. It should go without saying, but I'll say it anyway. Don't talk to anyone about any of this. No one knows you're going to New York. We should keep it like that."

*

Stella was nonplussed. It was so typical of the way things seemed to be going with her, she thought, ever since she'd lost Claude. She didn't ask much for pity's sake. And she had a lot to offer in return. But just when it looked as though she had Jack nicely in place for the duration, or at least for the foreseeable, he'd decided he needed to spend more time back at his semi.

But that hadn't been all.

"You're what?"

"A deacon. In the Church. It's my new thing."

It might have been a joke, please God, but it plainly wasn't. He had that expensive-looking bible and that funny collar like the ones priests wear.

"You can't be serious!"

"Watch me," he'd said.

"But she knew it was just a front. He was too much of a boozer, too interested in sex and food and the ways of the flesh. And there was that business he had going on down at the Art Shop. Whatever that was. Something dodgy, for sure.

"And how will you keep tabs on your gallery thing from your semi? Freddy's not here to do it. You'll be spending time trailing in and out of town. What's the point?"

"I won't need to be there such a lot in future. Junior's going to look after things. It's sorted."

She quickly ran out of arguments. And she drew the line at pleading. She'd never done that with any man. She had too much class for that. It wouldn't have been so bad if Hamish had been here, but he'd been gone for ages now. Was he ever coming back?

"Suit yourself, then. But don't expect to come waltzing in and out of here whenever you feel the need."

And whatever else, she certainly wasn't going to sulk. Not at her age.

She sulked. It made no difference.

"Look," he said, trying to be conciliatory. "We're okay, aren't we? We're an item. And it's not like I'm leaving, is it? But I have to spend time away from here for reasons not unconnected with business. See?"

"Just fuck off."

*

He hadn't wanted things to go that way with Stella. She'd been there for him when he needed someone, and they made a good couple. But maybe this deacon thing wouldn't be for long, and he didn't feel he had the option of explaining everything. He didn't want to involve her in his activities. It was far too dangerous. She deserved better than that.

When he got back to the semi late that same afternoon, it was already beginning to go dark, and he could see from some distance away that his house lights were on. He let himself in quietly through the front door and went as silently as he could into the lounge. Police? Predators?

It was Tooth. Slumped in an armchair and snoring. Thank God he was snoring. He might have been dead. Still moving as quietly as he could, he went through to the kitchen and closed the door.

He unzipped the travel bag he'd brought in with him and changed into his clerical shirt and collar. Then he made himself a coffee, got his phone and made a call. It took a while to get a response.

"Hello, Jack. Where are you?"

The man sounded groggy. His sleep must have been a deep one.

"I'm closer than you think, Alan. How are things?"

"Okay, I suppose. Considering. You coming home soon?"

"I'm here already, Al. I'm phoning because you were asleep. And I didn't want to scare you. I'm in the kitchen having a coffee."

He heard Tooth getting up and making his way across the lounge. This would be a good opportunity to test out his new persona. Tooth's head appeared around the door.

"Greetings, brother Tooth. May the peace of God be upon you."

"Jack? Why are you wearing that collar?"

"I'm a deacon now. A trainee deacon. I've joined the Church."

"My God."

"Not quite. Just a deacon for the moment. Like a hot beverage? Have you been here since I left? It's been weeks."

"Sorry, Jack. I know I should have asked, but I didn't expect to be here all this time. Can't relax at mine.

Can't sleep. Marjory's there, wandering around. Her ghost. I come round here to rest sometimes. I'm sorry."

"It's all right. Really. Sit down here, and I'll get you a coffee. Did the funeral go okay?"

"It went well enough. Mrs McCourt from over the road came with me. She's taken the kittens. It was just us and the funeral director's people. I slept here a couple of times. I'm sorry."

"It's fine. Don't worry." He put a coffee in front of Tooth and sat down opposite him at the ancient kitchen table, the same one he and Wendy had bought when they were busy setting up home together. It was chipped and stained, and its hard vinyl top had a few cigarette burns from the old days. The table was here to stay. He would never get rid of it.

"Do you find it difficult? Staying at yours?"

"It's Marjory. Her spirit's too strong yet. I think she must be waiting for me. She's everywhere in the house. And in a way that's good. But she doesn't ease off. I just can't relax."

"Maybe she'll be gone soon. It's been a while."

"Are you really a deacon?"

"A trainee. Like I said."

"Could you come round and say a few words? It might help. With your bible?"

"I'm not trained for that kind of thing, Al. You're thinking more of an exorcism, and my understanding is that that's more for mischievous types of spirit. Not Marj."

Typical, he thought. My first day as a cleric, and I'm in danger of being pushed in at the deep end.

He remembered Beat's funeral. His mother-in-law. Another sparsely attended affair. He took a long look at Tooth, now staring morosely into his coffee cup. In all the decades he'd known him, the man had done virtually nothing worth mentioning. Nothing at all. But at least he'd had Marjory to sit with and to talk to. And now even that was gone. It was pathetic. There was no way he was going to spend his remaining years as Tooth had. Just waste them. His lifestyle might well be largely illegal, but it was purposeful, eventful and often exciting.

"So what exactly have you trained for then, Jack? In the deacon area?"

"Oh, you know, mainly bookkeeping, accounts. That sort of thing. You kind of start off with that and work your way up."

"Right. I think I'll go home now and go to bed. Thanks for the coffee."

33

Apart from a little turbulence just past the halfway point, the flight out to JFK was uneventful, and he dozed through most of it, slumped in his seat with his head against the window. He'd been up late thinking about nothing much and working his way as far down a bottle of single malt as it was safe to go if you didn't want to get to be too drunk to function. Then he had snored away a couple of hours in the armchair, fully dressed and wearing his dark shirt with its clerical collar, his bag packed and ready, waiting for the three a.m. airport transfer to collect him for the drive out along the Sixty-Two to Manchester.

Flying against the clock meant it was still midmorning when he dragged his luggage out of the arrivals hall and got himself a taxi to the address in Queens. In less than twenty-five minutes, he was standing on the sidewalk on Jackson Avenue, staring up at the Thirties-style frontage of a long-unused cinema. It had a 'SOLD' sticker over the weathered 'FOR SALE' board nailed to the brickwork.

All it took then was a text to get the Reverend Jones to appear from the alley at the side of the building.

"Glad to see you made it, Reverend," said Neil, smiling. "Grab your bag and follow me. There's a side door down here. I have coffee waiting."

Inside, Jack followed as Neil led the way through an interior that had been left largely untouched since the cinema had closed.

"We haven't done a great deal in here so far. We're considering leaving the place mostly as it is. There's not much difference between a film show and a sermon, so why not?"

They reached the storage area behind the screen.

"Get your coffee and leave your bag here, and I'll take you over to the place we've got earmarked for the coke room so you can check it over."

"Is it far?"

"No. Two blocks, that's all. It's an industrial unit we own on Forty-Fifth. We can walk."

"You have people ready to do the work?"

"A couple of illegals, like in Arrecife. They make the best workers for this sort of job. Absolutely zero interest in going anywhere near the authorities and nowhere to run to if they get it into their heads to leave. And they work for peanuts. Perfect."

"And they don't ever get tired of the long hours?"

"We pay slightly over the odds so they can send money home. That tends to do it. If it doesn't, no one's going to miss them if they disappear. No one who counts, at least. Mostly, they stay in line."

They walked over to the industrial unit, situated at the end of a short track running beside a mini-market. There wasn't much to look at, just an empty storage area that looked as though it had once been used as a workshop of some kind. A couple of rusty chain hoists and a metal bench had been left in place. There was a big drive-in doorway, which Jack could see would have to be screened off. Apart from that, setting up the coke room would be reasonably straightforward.

"You could have done this yourself, Neil. You saw what we did in Arrecife."

"I don't have time. I'm due in Rome in three days. As I told you, we're growing fast, and four weeks from now, I'll have another job lined up for you. I hope you like to travel."

"Doesn't give me a problem. I can take it or leave it. So what next?"

"Next, we collect your bag and get a cab over to the Church's apartment in Manhattan. You'll love it. You'll be staying there while you're in New York. You can unpack and rest up there today. Catch up on your sleep."

"Sounds good."

"Tomorrow, I'm going to New Jersey to pick up your workforce. We'll billet them in the cinema for now. I'll leave you with the keys for the apartment and the church and for this place. When I get back, I'll introduce you to the guys who'll be working for you, and you can start asap."

"Tools, equipment, materials? I can't call Alejandro."

"Just go online and order whatever you need."

He handed Jack a credit card. "You're in charge."

*

The apartment was like nowhere he had ever been. Seven floors up, overlooking Central Park, and 'luxuriously appointed' - as the jargon sometimes goes.

He seriously doubted that he would have been able to afford anything even remotely similar if he'd stayed on as his own boss. A luxury apartment in Liverpool, maybe, with views of the river. But here in Manhattan? It could be that choosing to throw in his lot with Jones's outfit had been the right decision after all. Not that it felt as though he'd had much choice.

The Reverend Jones walked over to a chest of drawers and opened one. It seemed to be full of napkins. From underneath the napkins, he pulled out a pistol in a leather shoulder holster and handed it to Jack.

"A little something to help keep you safe. Wear it whenever you're out of the apartment. And that's not optional. We do have enemies."

He sat by the large window in his room for a while, gazing out over the park. It was a sunny day and unseasonably warm for early December. And it was colourful. People were strolling, jogging, roller skating, cycling, walking their dogs. Kids were running about.

Sipping steadily at a glass of the bourbon he'd found in the drinks cabinet, he imagined that he might make a habit of getting down there himself each morning before breakfast and maybe break into a slow jog. He'd rest up a little first, though. Best to take these things slowly.

He'd been up since three a.m. UK time, and he wondered if he could be suffering from jet lag. Or was that when you flew in the other direction? He was too tired to work it out. After the bourbon, he lay down on the kingsize bed and fell asleep.

When he woke suddenly, wondering where he was, the afternoon had begun to shade into evening. Through the window, over the park, he could see the Manhattan skyline lit up in the darkening sky. He no longer felt tired and wandered through the apartment, admiring the furnishings and looking at the enormous paintings on the walls. There was no sign of Neil.

He had a quick shower and put on his clerical garb.

He made sure the keys that Neil had given him were in his pocket, put on the shoulder holster with the pistol and got the lift down to the ground floor. There was no doorman or receptionist, no one in the hallway as he let himself out onto the street. It was pleasantly warm, and the evening breeze blowing gently over from the park smelled fresh. He walked down onto Fifth Avenue and strolled down past Trump Tower and the MoMA, enjoying the buzz of the place and the lights. He was in Manhattan, and he felt as though he was walking through some kind of energy field.

He decided to go back to the industrial unit in Queens. He wanted to get a better idea of the dimensions of the place he was dealing with and sketch out a couple of possible layouts in his head. That way, he could avoid feeling guilty about getting slightly hammered on the bourbon later. And if he didn't hit the booze, at least a little, he knew he'd just end up being too hyper and wouldn't sleep.

He thought it would be more interesting to use the subway than a cab. It would help him acclimatise and get the feel of the place.

He walked down to the stop at Fifty-Third and bought a ticket. The train came almost immediately, and five minutes later, he was back on the street at Court Square. From there, he used his phone to find an easy route of two or three minutes to the unit.

The mini-market was closed and shuttered, and the track alongside was in darkness. There was a car parked halfway down. He checked it out as he walked past. No one. He was fumbling in his pocket for the key when he noticed that the door to the unit was open, leaking a flickering sliver of light from inside. Jones? His relaxed mood dissipated rapidly as he sensed the possibility of danger. Should he play safe and walk away? Maybe not the best choice. Right now, he would have the advantage of surprise. If he let things hang until tomorrow, he might not have. At least he should check it out.

He considered pulling out the gun from his shoulder holster. Not yet. It might just encourage the other party to fire first. This was, after all, the USA, and he wasn't too sure of the local gun etiquette.

Cautiously, quietly, he pushed open the door and slipped inside. There was someone at the far end of the unit, standing on the bench with a flashlight, doing something high up on the wall. He found the switch and flicked on the lights. The figure spun around and stared right across at him.

"Jesus. Ana? What in the name of all that's...?"

She had a screwdriver in her right hand and something small and black in the left. She kept hold of the screwdriver. The other item she pushed into the pocket of her dark grey jeans as she hopped down from the bench.

"Hello, Jack. Nothing personal, but I was hoping not to bump into you out here."

The ailing mother, the trip to Madrid? She'd been coming to New York all along.

"You were planting a bug?"

She was edging towards him. Slowly.

"What can I say? It's what I do. You caught me."

Suddenly, he realised the danger. The screwdriver was long, with a thin blade. She hadn't left it on the bench. He was heavier than she was, but he knew that would be his only advantage. Ana was young and fit. She was armed with that screwdriver. She had to view him as an adversary, and he was well out of condition. A rival gang? Who else would she be working for?

"I'm a cop, if you're wondering. And I won't tell you who I work for. That's classified."

She stopped edging towards him. She was close enough now.

"You'd better drop it, Ana. I'm armed, but I don't want to have to kill you."

The threat didn't seem to worry her, and she didn't drop the screwdriver.

"From your point of view, killing me would look to be one of your options, but I can assure you that it isn't. I'm very well-trained and in great shape. Before you could even draw your gun, which that little bulge in your jacket tells me you have in a shoulder holster, I can have this blade pushed down into your neck. Or your eye. Or the back of your mouth."

He didn't rate his chances at anything better than evens, if that.

"So...?"

"Even if you succeed in killing me, which you won't, there'll be someone else to replace me. And next time, you probably won't be so lucky. You're a marked man, Jack. We know all about you. Think about it for a minute. I'm in no rush."

"I could just disappear."

"Think so? Catch a flight or cross a border, and my people will know about it almost instantly. You could try somehow making your way down south and sneaking across into Mexico, but I doubt you'd stand much of a chance. It's so not your thing."

"You have a very low opinion of my capabilities."

"Being realistic, that's all. You should be, too. Think about it. Even if you made it over the border, you'd be up against it. I doubt you speak fluent Spanish, and the gangsters and police they have down there are pretty fierce. You'd be in way over your head."

He briefly considered the idea of simply turning and running hell for leather for the street, but he knew she'd be onto him before he reached the door.

"Live or die," she said. "Your choice. And I can offer you a safe path through all this."

Zip it. Just listen.

"Work for us. Feed us information. Nothing else in your life would need to change. Absolutely nothing. This is a big operation. It's huge. We aren't interested in you or anyone at your level. We're making our way up the drug networks globally. Big-time gangsters. Bent politicians. Russian oligarchs."

"You'd leave me alone?"

"You'll take your chances with the local cops, as always, but we will try to help you if you get caught.

And we won't touch you as long as you feed us good info. Simple."

It didn't take much working out - his best option.

"Okay," he said. "I'm in."

"I'm parked outside. Come and sit in the car, and I'll fix you up with contact details. You need to give me your gun for now. Standard procedure. You can have it back when I have you safely in the system. Shoot me then, and my people will know right away it was you. Use your left hand and take it out slowly. Go near the trigger, and I'll kill you."

Give her his gun? Or make like he was going to? At least it meant he could get the thing into his hand, albeit the wrong one. One step at a time. He reached inside his jacket and pulled the pistol from its holster. The warm metal and the weight instantly reassuring. He'd made sure it was ready to fire before leaving the apartment - so his next step should be what, exactly?

He glanced at Ana. Did she want his gun so she could kill him with it? Possibly. As he looked at her face, trying to read her intention, he saw her eyes move quickly to look at something over by the door. There was a noise behind him and then the sound of gunshots - two in quick succession. He heard at least one of the bullets zip under his right ear.

The second shot caught Ana in her left shoulder, throwing her backwards, twisting from the waist as she fell.

He pivoted toward the door and dropped to one knee as he switched hands and brought his weapon up to a firing position. Neil was standing just inside the doorway, looking past him at the stricken Ana lying on the floor behind. It was a moment needing a decision - a fork in the road. He aimed the pistol at Jones's chest and pulled the trigger.

The weapon that the Reverend Jones had himself provided for Jack to use was a Glock seventeen, nine millimetre - a neat handgun. He had never fired one before, but the range was short, and the Reverend presented a big enough target.

The sharp recoil jerked his arm, and he had to adjust his aim quickly before he took his next two shots. The Reverend Jones fell to the floor.

He walked purposefully across to the Reverend's prostrate form, keeping the Glock on target. He kicked the gun from Jones's outstretched hand before reaching down to pick it up. The man looked dead. He ran back to where Ana was struggling into a sitting position and held out Jones's weapon, grip first. Offering it to her. She dropped the screwdriver and took it. Then he grabbed hold of her collar and pulled her to her feet.

"We have to get out of here right now. There could be more of them."

"Get his phone," she said, speaking between gasps of pain. "Give it to me. I'm going to need it."

He found the phone easily enough and pushed it into the pocket of her jeans. Then he grabbed her gun hand, holding it behind her back as he marched her to the door and through it, with the Glock held against her head.

Out on the driveway, he spotted two shadowy figures crouching on either side of the car.

"Neil's hit," he called out. "I've got this one. Go help the Reverend."

The two figures stood up, hesitated briefly as he pushed Ana steadily toward them, and then ran toward the unit. Each of them held a gun.

He rushed Ana to the passenger door.

"Your keys!"

"It's remote. Use the button."

He bundled Ana into the car and ran around to climb into the driver's seat. He started the engine just as Jones's two gunmen came out of the unit at a run. He reversed at speed, back up to the road, and swung out onto the highway on squealing tyres with the angry blare of a horn from behind. Out of the corner of his eye, he caught sight of a flash of gunfire from the darkness of the track.

"Turn right two blocks along," said Ana. "There's a diner. Drop me there and then dump the car further off."

"You need attention. You're bleeding."

But she was already texting someone.

"Just do it. Then you'd better get back to wherever you're supposed to be tonight and act dumb. There's every chance those two goons won't be able to identify you. It's dark enough."

They were outside the diner, where a brightly lit panel above the window said 'Big Burger'.

"This the right place?"

"Yeah. Hand me the jacket in the back."

There was an old leather jacket lying on the rear seat. He passed it to Ana and helped her as she struggled into it.

"I'm going in to get a coffee and wait. Someone will be here to collect me in ten minutes or so. Leave the car around the corner. They'll take that too."

"You're looking pale, Ana. Let me help you."

"I'm fine. You need to go. Move this car."

With that, she stepped out onto the sidewalk and walked across to the entrance of the Big Burger diner.

He watched as she pushed open the door and went inside, to be hidden at once behind the steamed-up windows.

He took off his shirtfront and clerical collar and stuffed them into his jacket pocket. It was all he could do by way of disguise, and he just had to trust it would be enough. His main hope had to be that the gunmen had fled the scene. But even if they were out searching for Ana and himself, he reckoned the odds were against his being spotted and recognised before he made the short distance to the station at Court Square.

No one saw him, and his subway ride deposited him at a stop on Seventh, from where he walked briskly back to the apartment building and let himself into the lobby using the code someone had written on the apartment's key fob. The apartment was just as he had left it, not all that long before, empty and luxurious.

Did anyone other than the Reverend Jones even know he was staying here? He had to assume that the Church's two gunmen might well know, along with whoever it was that Neil had reported to.

Against that, he remembered Neil telling him that no one had been told about his visit to New York. He'd simply have to risk it.

He cleaned the Glock and sprayed it with some cologne he found in the bathroom to take care of any telltale smell of having been recently fired. Then he took a shower, making sure to use the same cologne on himself. He dressed in the jeans and polo shirt he'd brought in his travel bag.

A quick search through the drawer from which Neil had taken the gun turned up a box of nine-millimetre cartridges from which a few rounds had been removed. He took out three more and reloaded, giving him a full clip.

All that done, he poured himself a large bourbon and sat down in the comfortable chair in his room to think.

There was a good chance that no one but Neil had even known he was here in New York. It might all come down in the end to what the Reverend had told his two gunmen. It was possible that he wouldn't have bothered telling them anything much. In that case, he should follow Ana's advice and play dumb.

He had no contact details for anyone else in the New York branch of the Church. In fact, beyond a disused nineteen-thirties cinema building, there was no New York branch.

Playing dumb would entail spending the night in the apartment and then hanging around as if he were waiting for Neil to show up in the morning. And when he failed to appear, there would be no point in making a pretence of trying to get in touch with the man by phone. Ana had taken that.

Or he could leave now. He could put the handgun back in its drawer, tidy his room, pack his bag and go.

But that would look bad if someone else did happen to know of his whereabouts. They would have to wonder why he had left so suddenly. And they would come looking.

In the end, he decided that if no one had arrived to search him out by lunchtime the next day, they most likely wouldn't be coming to find him at all. And at that point, he would get to the airport hotel and take things from there.

After that, there was nothing to do but make his usual standby of scrambled eggs in the well-stocked kitchen before settling down again in his comfortable chair with the bottle of bourbon. He was getting to like bourbon.

The following day, he woke up late with a noticeable hangover. It'd be fine. He'd had worse. He got through his morning routine as quickly as he could and downed an espresso before checking around the apartment to ensure everything was in order. He put the handgun, in its holster, back in the drawer where it belonged. Then he opened the door and stepped out onto the landing.

Two men in dark suits followed him into the lift. He couldn't be certain they were the same two who had confronted him at the unit the previous evening, but he felt pretty sure they would be. They studiously avoided making eye contact as they rode with him down to the lobby. They were close behind as he made his way out onto the street. As he turned to walk down to Fifty-Ninth, where he intended to hail a cab, one came gliding to a halt at the kerb beside him, its driver leaning his head through the open window.

"You?"

"What?"

The two suits were right behind him. This wasn't looking good.

"This is for you. Get in."

The rear passenger door swung open. One of the suits was at his back now, his arm reaching around him to grab the door. His companion stepped off the kerb, waiting for a break in the traffic to allow him to walk around and get in the other side.

I don't think these guys are about to take me out for lunch. Time to run for it.

He dived into the cab, yanking the door closed behind him and hoping that the loud crack he heard was the sound of fingers breaking. The other man was already pulling at the far door. He drew up his legs and kicked hard against it. The door flew open wide, catching the man full in the chest and sending him reeling out into the roadway to bounce off the side of a passing car before thudding down onto the tarmac. The car came to a halt, stopping the traffic, as he slid out of the cab and took off along Central Park West. He ran until he saw an entrance to the park.

He'd intended to run through the park and out onto Fifth Avenue, but he'd only got as far as the fairground when his legs began to give out. He staggered to a nearby bench and sat down, gasping for air, his legs like jelly. People walking by gave him no more than a glance as they passed.

It was warm, unusually so for December, and he was thirsty. He found a cafe close by and bought himself a large cola to sip as he wandered down through the trees. It was hard to decide on his best way forward.

When he came to the Umpire Rock, rising up in front of him, he climbed up onto a ledge from where he had a good view of the approaches. He stretched out on the smooth surface to rest for a while in the unseasonal heat of the New York sun. From somewhere down by the trees drifted the sound of John Denver's Leaving On A Jet Plane.

That song again? I wish.

He allowed himself to close his eyes. He was too tired, too unfit, too hungover and confused to do anything else. And then, lying there in the open, in the middle of New York, he fell asleep. He dreamed he was far out on the ocean, alone aboard a leaking and sinking ship with no help at hand, no help possible.

34

It wasn't where he had envisaged spending Christmas. But he'd gone to a lot of trouble to cover his tracks in getting himself home and had no intention of blowing it. He'd risked a flight out of JFK to Madrid, and after a couple of days, he'd got a plane to Birmingham.

He took a train from Birmingham and arrived back at Lime Street Station, hooded, in the winter darkness. He scurried down to the rear door of the Art Shop, where Fat George waited to let him in.

He spent the daytime dozing on the camp bed up in FG's attic room, FG having been instructed to tell no one of his presence. At night, he mooched around the gallery and the office, watching the world through his laptop - a sad kind of existence but bearable for a short time.

He phoned Stella.

"It's not that I don't want to see you, Stell. It'd mean a lot to me right now, believe me. But for both our sakes, I can't take the risk."

"So, where are you hiding? Are you in the UK?"

"Really, Stell, it's better you don't know. I'll see you again when I can be sure it's safe."

The same day, he got a call from Ana, and everything changed.

"Jack?"

"You recovered?"

"I'm recovering. No problem." There was a short pause while she waited for him to say something more. When he didn't, she said, "My people have gone to some trouble on your behalf, Jack. We felt we owed you one."

"You do, for sure."

"So we've tidied up the New York end of things as far as we can. Those two hitmen have been dealt with, and the cab driver's been questioned pretty thoroughly. He was no more than a spare part. We think you're in the clear and good to go."

"Go? Where?"

"We want to use you more proactively. We'd like you to go back out to Arrecife and integrate yourself a bit more deeply into the Church. They're going to be more shorthanded than ever. They'll need you."

"So I'm safe now? You're sure?"

"We're as sure as we can be, but nothing's a hundred per cent guaranteed in this business, right? So stay cautious until you've sussed things out for yourself. You'll know soon enough."

"Comforting."

"Our best advice remains as it was. Play dumb. Just breeze back in there like nothing has happened. And keep us posted."

"Oh, God."

It was feeling more than a little dangerous. But then, didn't it always? And hadn't he got what he needed? Hamish was gone, and he could now wield the authority of the Church over Freddy and Junior. Even better, as long as he didn't push it and gave them what they wanted, he had Ana and her outfit watching his back. And if he really was in the clear, he was in a perfect position to begin his climb up the Church hierarchy. You just had to take a positive view of these things.

He decided to leave his bases and contacts in Liverpool and the Point out of the limelight until he could be sure that no one dangerous was waiting to come looking for him. For now, resurfacing on Lanzarote would be risky enough.

On the third day of January, with the first snow lying inches deep out in the yard, he booked himself onto the next available flight out to Arrecife.

He sent a text to Fran:

```
Hi - back over there the day after
      tomorrow. Dinner?
```

Before You Go

It looks as though you've reached the end of this book. If, as I hope, you've enjoyed it, would you consider leaving a review on Amazon? I would very much appreciate your input.

Thank you.

If you would like information about future books in this series, please 'follow' me on:

amazon.com

or

amazon.co.uk

Crime Fiction by this author:

Blue Warehouse Series:
Book 1: Deadly Money
Book 2: Gang Boss
Book 3: Damage
Book 4: The KnifeMan Murders
- the first Jack and Alice Thriller

Also by this author:

Humorous Sci-Fi:
Apocalypse Sundae

Printed in Great Britain
by Amazon